ULTRAVIOLET

EVERYTHING YOU BELIEVE IS WRONG

Sixteen-year-old Alison has been sectioned in a mental institute for teens, having murdered the most popular girl at school. But the case is a mystery: no body has been found, and Alison's condition is proving difficult to diagnose. Alison herself can't explain what happened: one minute she was fighting with Tori – the next Tori disintegrated. Into nothing. But that's impossible. *Right?*

When Alison meets Dr Faraday, a visiting psychologist, she feels an instant connection. More, he *believes* her story. But there's more to Faraday than Alison can possibly imagine…and the answers he will give her are…extraordinary…

Also by R J Anderson:

Knife
Rebel
Arrow

Find out more at:

www.rj-anderson.com
www.orchardbooks.co.uk

ULTRAVIOLET

R J ANDERSON

ORCHARD BOOKS

To Josh, who never stopped believing

ORCHARD BOOKS
338 Euston Road, London NW1 3BH
Orchard Books Australia
Level 17/207 Kent Street, Sydney, NSW 2000

First published in the UK in 2011 by Orchard Books

ISBN 978 1 40831 275 9

Text © R J Anderson 2011

A CIP catalogue record for this book is available from the British Library.

3 5 7 9 10 8 6 4

Printed in Great Britain

Orchard Books is a division of Hachette Children's Books,
an Hachette UK company.

www.hachette.co.uk

PART ONE:

SCENT OF YESTERDAY

ZERO (IS TRANSLUCENT)

Once upon a time there was a girl who was special. Her hair flowed like honey and her eyes were blue as music. She grew up bright and beautiful, with deft fingers, a quick mind and a charm that impressed everyone she met. Her parents adored her, her teachers praised her, and her schoolmates admired her many talents. Even the oddly shaped birthmark on her upper arm seemed like a sign of some great destiny.

This is not her story.

Unless you count the part where I killed her.

ONE (IS GREY)

The darkness behind my eyelids was thick and stank of chemicals, as though someone had poured black oil inside my head. My tongue lay like a dead slug in my mouth, and my limbs felt too heavy to lift.

Had I been sick? Was I injured? Or…

My stomach sloshed, rebelling against the thought. I couldn't be dying. I was only sixteen years old. Yet my skin itched with the coarseness of unfamiliar sheets, and the mattress beneath me felt rubbery. The air was stale and lukewarm. Where else could I be but in hospital?

As the oily slick across my senses thinned, colours and shapes crept into my awareness. Faint blue splashes of footsteps on tile, the dry buzz of air conditioning, a silken ribbon of murmurs outside my door. Muffled thumps from the end of the corridor felt like cotton puffs dropping onto my forehead, until they ended in a sandpaper rasp of, '*Nurse!*'

I winced, and opened my eyes.

I was lying alone in a room so stark that its blankness hit me like an assault. There were no IV stands or heart monitors, no bedside table covered in flowers and get-well cards. No windows, no cupboards, no shelves, not even a clipboard hanging on the wall. Nothing but the bed, and me in it.

My arms lay limp by my sides, skinny and white as ever. They looked whole enough, but the forearms were a mess of half-healed scratches and bite marks, as though I'd tried to shake hands with a wolverine. My wrists were chafed red, my fingernails were ragged stubs, and my grandmother's ring, a square-cut topaz I'd worn every day for the past five years, was missing.

I was staring at my bare finger when the door opened, and a woman in petal-pink scrubs came in. 'Good morning, Alison,' she said brightly. 'How are you feeling? Ready for some fresh air and a change of scenery?'

She talked like someone used to not getting an answer, the way people talk to babies or coma patients. Clipped to her pocket was a laminated tag that said *Rachael* – a shimmery purple-violet name with flecks of silver, one I'd always liked. But I couldn't recall ever seeing her before.

'What happened to my ring?' I tried to ask, but my whisper was so faint even I could barely taste it.

'*Nurse! Help me, nurse!*' screeched the voice in the

distance, punctuated by more thumping. But the aide didn't seem to hear it any more than she'd heard me.

'We're just bringing a wheelchair around for you,' she said. 'Can I help you sit up, Alison?'

'Where am I?' I asked, forcing out the words. 'Where are you taking me?'

The aide looked surprised, but it only took her an instant to recover. 'You're at St Luke's Hospital,' she said. 'But not for much longer. Your mom put in a transfer request for you, so we're going to take you to a place where you'll be with other patients your age, and where you can get the treatment you need.'

'What kind of treatment?' I didn't mean to sound hostile, but I was starting to get scared. 'What kind of place?'

'A good place,' she said soothingly. 'It's called Pine Hills. You'll like it there.'

I'd heard that name before, but right now I couldn't place it. My memories were all in a tangle. 'How long have I been here?'

Rachael's eyes flicked away from mine. 'Only a little while,' she said, but the words rang so sour in my ears, so unexpectedly foul, that bile rose in my throat. 'You were agitated, so we brought you here to calm down—'

'Not the room,' I gasped. 'The hospital. How long?'

'You were admitted on June 7th,' she said. 'It's the 22nd now.'

I sank back against the pillow, stunned. I'd been here for more than two weeks. Why couldn't I remember any of it?

'Let me help you get dressed,' Rachael coaxed. 'Then we'll talk.'

I struggled upright, a yellow-grey stink of sweat wafting around me. The clothes she held were my own, so clean and fragrant that I felt ashamed putting my filthy body into them. I wanted to ask for a shower, but Rachael had already tugged up my jeans and pulled the T-shirt over my head. Another aide appeared in the doorway with a wheelchair; she helped me over to it.

'It's been a hard couple of weeks for you,' Rachael said as she wheeled me down the corridor to a locked door, buzzed it open, and steered me through. 'So things will probably seem a little hazy for a while. But now your medication's really starting to work, you'll be feeling a lot better soon...'

She chattered on, but I wasn't listening any more. I was staring at the sign above the nurses' station. It said, in my hometown's two official languages:

My worst nightmare had become reality. I'd gone crazy, and my mother had locked me away.

I was six years old, watching my pregnant mother wash the dishes. Cutlery clinked, filling the air with sparkling bursts of colour.

'Do it again!' I begged her, bouncing in my seat.

My mother glanced back at me. 'Do what?'

'Make the stars.'

'Stars?'

It never occurred to me that she couldn't see what I was seeing. 'The gold ones,' I said.

'I don't know what you're talking about,' she replied, and with a child's impatience, I hopped down from my stool to show her.

'Like this,' I said, taking two spoons and clanging them together. Each clink produced another starburst, expanding luminous through the air between us.

'You mean,' said my mother slowly, 'the sound makes you think of stars?'

'No, it makes the stars. Why aren't you looking? You have to look,' I told her, and clashed the spoons again. 'See?'

My mother stood rigid, the bewilderment in her face

shading slowly into horror. Then she snatched the spoons from my hands and flung them into the sink. 'There. Are. No. Stars,' she hissed, her voice full of icy peaks and seething valleys. 'Do you hear me?'

'Yes, there are, they're right—'

My mother slapped me across the face. 'Don't argue with me!'

She'd smacked me once or twice in the past, but never like this. Tears sprang to my eyes. 'But...'

'No buts!' She backed away, one arm wrapped protectively around her belly. 'Just stop it. Stop pretending, or – whatever you're doing.'

'So you don't...see the stars?' I could hardly get the words out.

'No!' she shouted at me, her face a blotchy mask. 'Normal people do not see things like that!'

I felt like my insides were climbing up my throat. I wanted to burst into tears. But I could also see how scared my mother was – and worse, I knew she was scared of me.

So I swallowed. I forced my misery back, pushed it deep down inside myself, and I said in a small voice, 'I'm sorry.'

'Go to your room, Alison,' said my mother, breathing hard. 'Go and think about what I've told you. And I never, ever want to hear you talk about seeing stars or – or anything else like that again.'

I slunk out of the kitchen and was halfway up the stairs when a wavering moan floated up behind me, followed by another sound I had never before heard my mother make. It was a deep grey bubble, and it followed me all the way to my bedroom, where I flung myself down on the bed and sobbed until the air was full of them.

That day I'd learned that my mind didn't work the same as other people's – that perceptions I took for granted could seem incredible or even frightening to them. So I couldn't talk about the colour of three, or whether triangles tasted better than circles, or how playing Bach on my keyboard made fireworks go off in my head, because people would think I was crazy. And then they'd be scared of me, and wouldn't want to be around me any more.

So I hid those alien sensations inside myself, a secret I swore I'd never betray again. I made a few mistakes at first, because it wasn't always easy to know what was 'normal' and what wasn't, but by the time I was nine years old my transformation was complete. As far as the rest of the world was concerned, there was nothing extraordinary about me, nothing unpredictable, and *certainly nothing anyone needed to be afraid of.*

Until now.

'Alison, can I get you something to eat? Are you hungry?'

I shook my head distractedly, too shellshocked to speak. Rachael had parked my wheelchair in a little glass-walled office opposite the nurses' station, then excused herself to help another patient. The woman stooping over me was thickset and greying, a grandmotherly stranger.

'How are you feeling?' asked the older nurse as she pulled up a chair and sat down, pen and clipboard in hand. 'Any dizziness? Nausea? Headache?'

Ever since I saw that sign reading PSYCHIATRIC UNIT, I'd had all three. But I was afraid to admit it, because it would give these people another reason to believe that I was sick. I needed to convince them that I was better now, that I didn't need any more treatment, before they could find out about my colours and try to take them away.

'No,' I lied, and the gorge surged into my mouth so fast I nearly choked. I had to swallow three times to get it down again, and then fake a coughing fit before I could gasp, 'Could I – have some – water?'

The nurse filled a paper cup from the water cooler and handed it to me. 'How would you describe your mood right now?'

I suspected that *terrified* wouldn't be the best answer. 'I'm OK,' I said, and took another hasty sip as my stomach convulsed again.

The interview went on, the nurse asking questions and ticking off boxes on her clipboard while I gulped water and answered as briefly as I could. All the while my nausea came and went – I felt fine when I told the nurse that I couldn't hear any voices talking to me except for hers, but when she asked if I sometimes saw things that were invisible to other people and I said no, it came back again.

I had an uncomfortable sense that I wasn't fooling her, either. Her expression stayed bland, but her eyes seemed to pierce right into my head. Still, I must have done something right, because in the end the nurse thanked me, called Rachael back into the room, and went on her way.

'Your ride will be here in about twenty minutes,' said Rachael as she wheeled me out of the office. 'Would you like to call your mom and let her know you're going over to Pine Hills, so she can meet you there?'

Her words were peach with sincerity, and I could tell she really believed it was a good idea. Which showed how little she knew. I still couldn't remember much, but I was sure of one thing at least: my mother was the one who had sent me here. I'd worked so hard to convince her I wasn't dangerous…but in the end, it had meant nothing.

'No,' I said. 'I'll be fine.'

The sky above St Luke's was a rhapsody in blue, the northern Ontario sunlight so crystal-sharp that I could feel it even through the tinted glass of the lobby windows. And when Rachael wheeled me outside, the fresh air tasted so sweet it brought tears to my eyes.

'You're doing really well,' said Rachael, patting my shoulder. 'How are you feeling? Things getting any clearer?'

She didn't seem to think it unusual that I'd lost some of my memory. Maybe it would be safe to ask her a few questions. 'My arms,' I said. 'They're all messed up, and my ring's missing. But I don't remember how it happened.'

'I never saw you wearing a ring,' said Rachael. 'Maybe your mom has it. But your arms…well, Alison, you were in a very bad way. Sometimes, when people are in a lot of mental pain, they turn to physical pain as a distraction.'

My stomach turned to cold jelly. So all those bites and scratches…I'd done that to myself?

'You screamed and cried a lot, when you first came in,' said Rachael. 'You kept clawing at your arms and face, and banging your head against the wall. We did everything we could to calm you down, but…it took a while to find a medication that would help you.'

Was that why my mother had applied to have me transferred? Because the nurses at St Luke's hadn't been doing a good enough job of keeping me under control? 'This place,' I said, struggling to push the words past the tightness in my throat. 'Pine Hills. What kind of—'

Then the police van pulled up in front of the curb, and the words died on my tongue.

Rachael had told me in the elevator that a police officer would be escorting me to my destination. She'd assured me that this was routine, nothing to worry about. But as the officer stepped out to meet me, my pulse started to beat in 6/8 time.

His voice was gritty and rumbling, like boulders rolling down a slope. He was talking to my mother, asking her questions, but all I heard was a garbled roar...

'I'm Constable Deckard,' said the officer in a soft tenor, and the memory vanished as quickly as it had come. In his dark blue uniform and red-banded cap he looked serious but not hostile, and I tried to tell myself there was no reason to fear. *To Serve and Protect* – wasn't that the motto? Even if a policeman had come to my house two weeks ago, he was probably just helping my mother get me to hospital.

'Alison, the officer needs to put some handcuffs on you,' said Rachael. 'Would you hold your hands out for him, please?'

Instinctively I pulled my hands to my chest. 'But I...I haven't done anything wrong. I'm not—'

I didn't know how to finish the sentence. Not dangerous? Not a criminal? Could I be sure of either of those things any more?

'It's for your safety and protection,' said Constable Deckard. 'Standard procedure.' He jingled the cuffs at me. 'Hands, please.'

What would happen if I resisted? Would he grab me and force the cuffs on me anyway? I was afraid to find out. Especially since we were right by the front doors of the hospital, in full view of the lobby

20

windows, and I could already feel people staring. I held out my hands to the policeman, and he locked the cuffs around them.

Rachael helped me up the step into the van. 'Good luck, Alison,' she said, and shut the door.

Head down, eyes on my fettered wrists, I sat rigid while the van made its way out of the hospital grounds and onto the main road. Then I slumped against the window, gazing out listlessly as we passed the space-station architecture of Science North and the cerulean blue waters of Ramsey Lake. Rocky hillsides crowned with birch and poplar rose around us as we headed towards New Sudbury. If I hadn't known better, I'd have thought I was going home.

But we kept driving, past the city's outskirts to the highway beyond. As my apprehension grew, I tried to distract myself by counting inukshuks – human-shaped piles of stones set high on the rocks by passing travellers. But a few kilometres later we turned off onto a side road, and the sunlight dimmed as the trees closed in around us. Something pale flashed in the near distance, and I struggled upright for a better look.

It turned out to be a sign, with embossed letters that shifted into rainbow hues as I squinted at them: PINE HILLS PSYCHIATRIC TREATMENT CENTRE. A line of complacently looped script beneath read *Bringing Hope to Youth in Crisis.*

A good place, Rachael had said. *You'll like it there.*

Beyond the sign, a cluster of institutional buildings sidled into view. At first they looked separate, a peak-roofed longhouse surrounded by cabins; but as we drove closer I saw that they were all connected, like a hydra in the process of budding. In front of the hospital the trees surrendered to grass and asphalt; behind it, the forest shrank away from a courtyard enclosed in chain-link fence. As we drove by I glimpsed a girl pacing around the yard, all bony limbs and hair like a splatter of ink, talking and gesturing wildly with her cigarette.

There was no one with her.

A shudder rippled through me. I slid away from the window, flinching as my handcuffs clinked and gold starbursts filled my vision. This was all wrong. I didn't belong here. Even after what Rachael had told me – that the scratches and bites on my arms had been self-inflicted, and that I'd been brought to St Luke's screaming and struggling all the way – part of me still refused to believe that I could be anything like that girl.

With an effort I unclenched my fists and willed myself to breathe. *Calm, Alison. Whatever happens, you have to stay calm.*

The van slowed to a stop, and the door rumbled open. Humid, pine-flavoured air washed over me, to the tune of droning cicadas and the staccato call of a chickadee. I stepped out into the grip of my police escort, who marched me across the asphalt to a door at the side of the main building. It growled open at our approach and closed behind us with a steely click.

As Constable Deckard took out his key and fumbled with my handcuffs I stood meekly, shivering in the air-conditioned chill. At first glance the room looked like a dentist's office, with plaque-coloured walls and wintergreen furniture. But the sofa bled stuffing from a gash in its side, while the chairs and table looked like they'd been flung across the room at least once before anyone thought to bolt them to the floor. The wall beside the nurses' station had a hole in it the shape of a size-twelve running shoe. I hoped I wasn't about to meet that shoe's owner.

My handcuffs snapped open. The officer hooked them back onto his belt, then led me over to the admissions desk and introduced me to the two nurses on duty. They sized me up as though I were a time bomb, held a murmured conference, and finally told the two of us to sit down.

'It's going to be a while,' said my police escort. 'So make yourself comfortable.'

How I was supposed to do that with him sitting next to me, I couldn't imagine. According to Rachael, police helped transfer psych patients between hospitals all the time; it was a community service, she said, to make sure the ambulances stayed available for people who really needed them. But something in Deckard's manner, the watchful glances he kept giving me out of the corner of his eye, made me feel nervous and even a little guilty. As though I really had done something wrong, and he knew it.

But how could that be? I might have had a mental breakdown two weeks ago, but that wasn't a crime. And even if I had broken the law in some way...it couldn't be too serious, could it? I struggled to piece together the scraps of my memories, but they kept fluttering away from me.

'Want me to turn on the TV?' asked the officer, gesturing at the set bolted high in the corner.

I didn't watch much television; I found its fake, flat colours too irritating. But it would give the constable something to watch besides me, so I nodded. He flicked it on, and I listened half-heartedly to some American talk show until the clock's hands inched to noon and it was time for the local news.

I wasn't paying much attention by then. In fact,

I was almost asleep. But a few minutes into the broadcast, I woke abruptly at the taste of a familiar name.

'...*Tori Beaugrand, who disappeared on the afternoon of June 7th...*'

My blood ran hot, then icy, and my stomach clenched like a fist. Somewhere in the back of my mind a trapped memory fluttered, trying to get out.

'...*Ron and Gisele Beaugrand, parents of the missing teen, are offering a reward to anyone who comes forward with information leading to Tori's whereabouts. Meanwhile, police continue their investigation into the sixteen-year-old's disappearance, but so far no trace of her has been found...*'

'Alison.'

I blinked. Constable Deckard tapped my left arm, and slowly I turned it over to find four fresh, weeping scratches on the underside.

'Why'd you do that?' he asked.

'I – I don't know.' The scrapes were throbbing now, painting orange stripes across my inner vision. I closed my right hand around them, trying to press away the pain.

'Did you know that girl? Tori Beaugrand?'

Again that rustle of memory, like a pile of dead

leaves shifting in the breeze. But whatever was underneath stayed buried. 'I went to school with her,' I said. 'I didn't know she was missing.'

His brows went up. 'You don't remember hearing about her disappearance before?'

I shook my head.

'When was the last time you saw her?'

His voice had sharpened, taken on a new urgency. Like he thought I might actually know how, or why, she'd disappeared. But why would I? Tori and I didn't hang around together. We barely even talked. 'I'm… not really sure,' I said. 'In the cafeteria, I think? At school?'

'When?'

'At the end of lunch period,' I said. 'On Monday.'

Monday, June 7th. The day she'd disappeared. The same day I'd gone into hospital. But that was just coincidence…wasn't it?

'And what was she doing, when you saw her? Was she talking to anyone? Did she look frightened? Angry?'

I closed my eyes, straining at the memory. She'd stepped in front of me as I was heading out of the cafeteria door, demanding to know…something. But after that it was all a blank.

'I'm sorry,' I said. 'My memory's not very good right now.'

Deckard gave me a hard, searching look. But something in my face must have convinced him, because all he said was, 'All right. But there's something I want you to do. The minute you remember anything that might help us find Ms Beaugrand – any detail, no matter how small – you tell your psychiatrist, and have him call me. We'll all sit down in a nice comfortable place, and talk about it. All right?'

'OK,' I said.

'I can't emphasise strongly enough how important this is, Alison. Because if Tori's been abducted, if she's been hurt, and it turns out that you knew something that could have helped us find her but didn't say anything about it…that would be a very serious thing.'

My stomach twisted. Abducted? Hurt? I'd never been close to Tori, but I'd never wanted anything like that to happen to her, either.

'Do you understand me?' pressed Constable Deckard.

A thunderstorm was building between my temples, zigzags blurring the edges of my vision. In an hour or two, I was going to have a killer migraine.

'All right,' I said faintly.

'Alison Jeffries?'

By the time the nurse called me, the scintillating patterns behind my eyes had brightened from mango to tangerine, and my head felt as though it had been clamped in a vice. Gingerly I got up and walked over to the admissions desk.

'OK, Alison, I've got some questions to ask you...'

Over the next few minutes, they took my name, my history, and everything I owned, except, unfortunately, my headache. I was strip-searched with clinical thoroughness, and my clothing and shoes locked away. Then they made me shower and change into the shapeless pyjamas they'd given me.

Feeling like a damp scarecrow, I shuffled out of the bathroom to be met by the taller of the two nurses, who took my photograph and clamped an armband around my wrist before escorting me to an examination room. There a doctor with a drooping moustache looked me over from crown to soles and several humiliating places in between. He quizzed me about my medical history and looked grave when I told him I had a headache. He gave me two pills and a seat in a darkened corner, and I was still sitting there when the door opened and another white-coat came in. I looked up, into the muddy hazel eyes of the nicest man I would ever learn to hate.

'Hello, Alison,' he said. 'I'm Dr Minta.'

It turned out that this little, balding, square-spectacled man was the psychiatrist assigned to my case. And from the proud way he escorted me through the admissions wing and into the main building, chattering about programs and facilities all the while, you'd think he'd designed and built the whole place just for my benefit.

Unfortunately, I was in too much pain to appreciate it. The pills had muted my headache enough to keep me from fainting or throwing up, but I still felt as though someone had shoved a raw carrot into my eye socket. I wanted to beg Dr Minta to stop talking and let me lie down, but I was afraid of showing that much weakness. I wanted him to see me as healthy, normal, the kind of person who didn't belong in a place like this.

Everything inside the hospital was painted in tentative colours: eggshell, fog, rosewater. The hallways echoed silence, like the corridors of a high school during class. Nurses strode purposefully here and there, carrying files or clipboards; aides pushed trolleys, and a security guard followed us with his eyes. But I didn't see any patients. Maybe they were all in therapy or something.

'Let's sit down in my office,' said Dr Minta, ushering me through a door. The room beyond was as blandly soothing as the rest of Pine Hills, with dark leather furniture and walls the colour of milky coffee. I lowered myself onto the sofa, bracing myself for the interrogation.

'So, Alison. You're sixteen, isn't that right?'

I nodded.

'Just finishing up eleventh grade at Champlain Secondary?'

Another nod.

'You live with both parents? ... And one younger brother? ... How were you doing in school? Any difficulties there?'

I'd been afraid he was going to push me to talk about my feelings, but these questions I could answer easily. *Yes. Yes. Fine. Not really.*

'OK, Alison, let's do a little memory test. I'm going to read out a series of numbers, and you recite them back to me.'

I disliked numbers, and they didn't think much of me either. But even if they didn't always want to multiply or divide for me, I had no trouble remembering how they looked in a sequence. I rattled back the answers without hesitation until we got to the second test, where he asked me to count backwards from ninety-eight by sevens. At that point, the numbers flat-out rebelled, and after a few painful attempts at mental subtraction, I had to ask for a pencil and paper. To my relief, Dr Minta said that wouldn't be necessary. He made a few notes on his clipboard and laid it down again.

'So tell me. What do you think is your main problem?'

I blinked at him. Was this some kind of joke?

'All right,' said Dr Minta, 'let me put it another way. When was the last time you felt like your usual self?'

I was about to say, *I don't remember*, but then all at once I did. I'd been sitting in after-school detention, twisting a pen between my fingers, waiting for Mr Cartmel to finish marking history quizzes and tell me I could go. And all the while this high-pitched, maddening noise had been shrilling inside my head – because *she* was there, right beside me.

Tori.

My buried memories stirred again, pushing their way towards the surface. So close now…if I could just forget the throbbing in my head and the ache in my chest, if I could only concentrate—

'You seem distracted, Alison. Can you hear anyone talking to you right now? Any voices other than mine?'

The frustration of being interrupted, just when I was *almost* there, nearly snapped my composure. I wanted to tell him to shut up and leave me alone for a minute – didn't he realise how important this was? But I bit back the words. I needed this man to believe that I was in control of myself.

'No,' I said. 'I was just trying to think. Sorry, what was the question?'

Dr Minta kept talking to me for what must have been thirty minutes, asking me everything from my favourite part of the day to the name of our current prime minister. I did my best to stay focused, but the whole time my stomach kept heaving and the orange pulse in my head got brighter and brighter. By the time we were finished, I'd broken out in a sweat.

'Alison, you look pale. Are you feeling ill?'

I couldn't hold out any longer. I closed my burning eyes and nodded.

'Well, then, let's call it a day. You still need to meet with your rights adviser, but we can arrange that for tomorrow.' He picked up the phone on his desk. 'Marilyn, could you send someone to my office? Alison needs to go to her room.'

As we walked to the door, he said, 'I think we're off to a good start. Tomorrow we'll talk some more about how you're feeling and what we can do to make you more comfortable. In the meantime we're going to give you a room in our Red Maple ward, which is the most secure and private, but if you appear to be doing well, we can move you into Yellow Poplar and you can join some of our group activities.'

He made it sound like I was checking into a resort, not a psychiatric hospital. I had a vision of myself lounging by the pool in a bathrobe, sipping a fruity beverage while a nurse painted my toenails, and a little, hysterical giggle forced its way past my lips. Then I caught Dr Minta's eye, and all at once it wasn't funny any more. I toed the carpet and avoided his gaze until the aide arrived.

She was tall and athletic-looking, with dark hair sleeked back into a no-nonsense ponytail. Her name tag said *Jennifer*, which was a frilly sort of name; it didn't suit her. She led me past a conference room and a couple more offices, then down a short hallway to a set of putty-coloured doors. She swiped her keycard, and the lock opened with a *thunk* that weighed on my chest like a cinder block. I had to take three deep breaths before I felt light enough to move again.

Beyond lay a rose-tinted hallway lined with doors on both sides, most of them open. The walls were covered with scratches and greasy handprints, and the air smelled stale. Somewhere at the end of the corridor a hoarse alto voice was spitting out profanities. Another voice said firmly, 'Micheline, we don't use that kind of language here.'

The answering snarl crescendoed to a screech, and I stopped dead. I did not want to see whatever was going on down there. I did not want to meet Micheline, whoever she was.

'Here you go,' said Jennifer, opening a door. 'Dinner's at five o'clock, but you can stay in your room until then if you want. Or you could watch TV in the lobby and meet some of the other patients—'

'No,' I said quickly. 'I'll just lie down. Thanks.'

My new room was almost as plain as the one I'd woken

up in at St Luke's, with concrete walls and scuffed linoleum tile. The bed was narrow, the built-in desk dismally small, and in the bathroom I could sit on the toilet and touch the shower, the sink and the sliding door at the same time. But at least the room had a window, even if it was made of scratched plexiglass. And though I could still hear Micheline ranting in the distance, I was finally, mercifully, alone.

I crawled onto the mattress, pulling the blanket over my head. If I could just shut the world out, pretend that I was anywhere but here, maybe the pain in my head would go away…

'Alison, you have to get up. The police are here.'

My mother spoke in a whisper, but the taste of her fear was overpowering. Even through my cocoon of blankets I could feel her words searing my tongue, blazing behind my eyes, scalding my skin.

'Please, Alison. You can't keep hiding like this. You're sick, you're hurt, you need help—'

'Is there a problem, ma'am?'

There was a stranger in my room, beside my bed. The stench of his nearness was overpowering, like a slab of rancid meat, and I pressed my face into the mattress as another wave of nausea washed over me.

'She won't get up, officer. I've tried to talk to her, but I – I don't think she understands what I'm saying.'

He made a sceptical noise, and a scribble of brown wrote itself behind my eyes. From the back of the room came the shrill warble of a younger man: 'Ma'am, do you have any reason to suspect your daughter may be under the influence of alcohol or drugs?'

'Oh, no. Alison's not like that. She's never—'

'Is there any chance she could be concealing a weapon? Was she armed when she came in?'

'I didn't see anything in her hands. Only…' Her voice faltered.

'Yes?'

'There was some…blood.'

A ponderous pause. Then the officer said briskly: 'All right, Alison, I'm going to pull back these covers so we can look at you. On the count of three. One. Two.'

I clung desperately to the quilt, but the policeman was stronger. He ripped it out of my hands and tossed it aside. Hectic, relentless, the colours of my bedroom pounded at me, battering me with bruising force. I turned my face to the pillow and moaned.

'There's something on her fingers.' His blunt voice sharpened. He seized my hand—

My arms flew up, knocking him back with the

strength of raw panic. Blindly I grabbed the lamp off the night table, and flung it as hard as I could. Glass shattered in a cascade of electric-blue triangles, and then someone wrenched me off the bed and shoved me down on the floor—

I flung back the covers, gasping. My heart was beating so loudly I could see it, lime-green blotches pulsing too bright, too fast. Fighting the officers had been bad, but it wasn't the worst thing I'd done that day. Something had happened before that, something enormous, something terrible—

A wild swing. A sickening impact. Blood on my knuckles, hot and slick—

Tori stumbling back, hands clapped to her face—

A noise so loud, I thought my eardrums were exploding—

Her back arched in agony, mouth opening wide as she screamed—

The trickle of memories became a stream, a gush, a torrent. I gripped my head between my hands and rocked back and forth, inarticulate with horror. I hadn't meant to do it. I hadn't even known I could.

But I'd been so angry, and before I could stop myself…

I'd killed Tori Beaugrand. Torn her into a billion pieces, disintegrated her, with nothing but the power of my mind.

TWO (IS RED)

It couldn't have happened the way I remembered. It wasn't possible. People didn't just make other people disintegrate, except in superhero comics and sci-fi movies.

And yet the proof of what I'd done had been right there on the news: Tori Beaugrand, missing without trace. And implausible or not, I knew what I'd seen… what I'd done.

But how? How could I have done that to her? I'd never imagined anything to compare to the stark terror on Tori's face, the shriek that seemed torn from every atom in her body, as she began to dissolve. If I'd had even the tiniest suspicion that there was power like that inside me, that I could annihilate another human being with just a careless thought, I'd have run straight to the nearest hospital and begged them to do something, anything, to take that power away.

Even if it meant losing your colours? asked a sly voice in my mind. *Even if it meant never tasting a sound again?*

No, not that; the idea was unbearable. Surely it

wouldn't come to that. Why would my unusual senses have anything to do with this terrible new power inside me?

And yet when I remembered how I felt right after Tori disappeared, it seemed like the two things *had* to be connected, no matter how much I wanted to deny it. As Tori's last scream faded I'd collapsed to the pavement, smashed flat by a crippling weight of sensation. Suddenly I could sense *everything*, touch and taste and sight and sound and smell amplified beyond anything I'd ever felt before. Every millisecond had its own scent; every noise for kilometres rushed into my vision. It was too much, too fast, too intense – and between that and the shock of having killed Tori, I'd lost it completely.

Fifteen minutes later I'd stumbled up the driveway to my house, sobbing and clawing at my hypersensitive skin, my knuckles smeared with Tori's blood and my fingers sticky with my own. All I'd wanted was to crawl into my bed and hide from the world. But my mother had called the police, and they'd come and taken me to hospital, where I'd been strip-searched, sedated, and finally strapped to a bed in an isolation room. No wonder my conscious mind had finally decided that enough was enough, and shut down.

But now I remembered everything – and I had to force myself to keep remembering, no matter how painful it might be. I couldn't bring Tori back to life again, no matter how hard I wished for it; I couldn't even take responsibility for her murder, though God knew I'd tried. But somewhere in my past there must be an explanation for what I'd done to her, and I had to find it. If I couldn't fix what I'd done, I could at least try to make sure it never happened again...

'Welcome to seventh grade, class. As you can see on the board, I'm Ms Pocalujko – it's a hard name to spell, and I won't mind if you get it wrong at first.' My new teacher was young and pretty, with auburn curls and a quick, nervous smile. 'Most of you here probably know each other already...'

Most of us did, having gone to Diefenbaker Public since kindergarten. But as Ms Pocalujko rambled on, I glanced around and noticed a few twelve-year-olds I hadn't seen before. On my left, a baby-faced Asian boy who kept pushing his glasses up his nose. Behind him, a girl with a tight ponytail and a slack chin. And when I looked to my right—

I stared. I couldn't help it. I'd never seen hair that golden except in shampoo ads, and her eyes weren't blue, they were turquoise. She had flawless peach-tinted skin with just a hint of summer brown, and her clothes were stylish enough to have come from Toronto, or even New York. She caught me looking at her and gave a demure little smile, like an actress on the red carpet. Then she turned back to face the teacher.

I looked away, blood scalding my cheeks. My hair hung flat, the colour of cream of tomato soup made with too much milk, and my eyes were dull as rainwater. As for my skin – well, I might have spent the summer under a rock, if it weren't for all the freckles. And where the new girl had curves, I had only angles and despair. It was going to be an effort not to hate her.

At last Ms Pocalujko wrapped up her introduction and started handing out textbooks. I could sense the numbers glowering at me even before I opened the cover, and braced myself for another year of mathematical combat. But the new girl sat up eagerly, and when the problems went up on the board, she was one of the first to respond. Her hand rose in a smooth, confident motion, and as her loose sleeve fluttered back, I noticed a peculiar sun-shaped mark just above her elbow. It was only a half-shade darker than her tan, too subtle for a tattoo and too pink for henna. A birthmark?

She must have sensed my eyes on her, because when

she glanced back her expression was no longer friendly. Our eyes locked – and my head filled with a faint, high-pitched buzz, as though a mosquito were hovering just outside my ear. Rusty spots splattered my vision, and a bitter taste spread across my tongue. I blinked, swallowed, and shook my head, but the noise refused to go away.

For the next hour, my maths exercises sat untouched as I fidgeted and gnawed at my fingernails, unable to concentrate. My gaze kept sliding back to the girl with the mark on her arm, and every time the droning in my head got louder. And judging by the way she shifted her shoulders and edged around in her seat, my stare was unsettling her almost as much as the noise she made bothered me.

But no one else seemed to hear it. It was my own private torture. Even once we'd moved onto geography, I found it impossible to focus, and when the lunch bell finally rang I bolted up from my seat, half-wild with the urge to escape. But my classmates moved just as quickly, jostling and chattering and crowding the door, and before I knew it I was jammed up against the new girl, who looked at me with eyes cold as a glacier lake.

'Why do you keep staring at me?' she demanded.

'I'm not,' I said, but the words came out all prickly,

like baby porcupines. The shrilling in my ears was louder than ever. I backed away and bumped hard into one of the desks. Orange bloomed across my vision, but through it I could still see the angry puzzlement on the new girl's face. She whirled and stalked out.

'Is there a problem?' asked Ms Pocalujko from behind me.

The Noise was fading – no, it was gone. I let out my breath. 'No,' I said.

'You seemed very distracted this morning,' my teacher said. 'I hope you don't plan to make a habit of staring at your fellow students instead of doing your work.'

Humiliation washed over me. I'd always been a good student, or at least a hard-working one: it was one of the easier ways to keep my mother happy. But how was I going to pass any of my subjects this year, if I had to listen to that noise drilling through my head?

'Sorry,' I said. 'I'll try to do better.' Then as Ms Pocalujko's frown softened, I mustered the courage to ask, 'That new girl, the one I bumped into…what's her name?'

'Victoria Beaugrand,' said my teacher. 'But if you're curious about her, then maybe you should try talking to her. Outside of class.'

I forced a smile. 'Thanks. I'll do that.'

But I never did. Back in the present, I slid off the edge of the bed and leaned my head against the mattress, dizzy with the intensity of my recollection. I'd always had a good memory, but this...I hadn't been remembering that day so much as reliving it. I could still hear the Noise shrilling in the back of my brain, and it *hurt*.

But there'd been nothing in that memory to tell me why I'd disintegrated Tori. It was going to take time and persistence to figure out what had happened, and I could only hope that I wouldn't hurt anybody else in the meantime. Because if I lost control of myself again, with that much power inside...who was going to stop me?

I would have called Constable Deckard, if I'd thought it would help. I would have told him everything. But I had no evidence to back up my story, no way of convincing him to believe the unbelievable. In the first few delirious, pain-filled hours after Tori's death, I'd confessed to killing her any number of times. I'd told my mother, the police, the doctors at St Luke's. But they'd all thought I was out of my mind, and who could blame them?

Although…Constable Deckard seemed to think that I knew *something* about the Tori Beaugrand case. He probably knew I'd been the last person to see her before she disappeared; he might even suspect that I'd killed her. But with no body and no weapon, no reason yet to believe that Tori might not still be alive, he couldn't prove I'd been responsible for her death any more than I could.

Or at least I hoped he couldn't. I didn't want to go to jail; just the thought of it made goosebumps break out all over my skin. But once the police finished their investigation, I was afraid that I might end up there anyway. They'd swabbed my hands when they arrested me, and taken my grandmother's ring for testing – if they found the blood was Tori's, wouldn't that be enough to charge me with assault, at the very least?

If only I knew someone I could talk to. Someone who would not only listen to my story but believe it, and help me decide what to do. But that was too much to ask of anyone, even my father or my best friend Melissa. Unless they'd seen Tori disintegrate for themselves, they'd never be able to accept that I was telling the truth.

Her body contorted, her eyes wide with shock and horror—

'I'm sorry,' I whispered. 'I'm so sorry.'

But it didn't make me feel any better.

I spent the rest of the afternoon trying to sleep, without much success. The nurses kept looking in on me, and there were too many sounds from the corridor – bursts of high-pitched laughter, blue hisses and yellow mutters, the rubbery squeaks of shoes and wheels – for even my drug-fogged senses to ignore.

At suppertime, a burly aide named Ray tried to get me to eat in the kitchenette with the other Red Maple patients. I told him I had a migraine, and he took pity on me. He brought me a paper plate with a slab of battered fish, some soggy coleslaw, and a few withered-looking fries. The plastic cutlery was so flimsy I could barely eat with it. I forced down a few mouthfuls, then lay down and pulled the blankets over my head again.

'Hey, Alison, it's nine o'clock. Time for your meds.'

I didn't feel like I'd slept, but I must have. I turned over, wincing at the sudden trumpet flourish of light. Ray stood in the doorway, one hand on the switch.

'I'll show you where to go,' he said. 'You can get something to help you sleep better too, if you want.'

I worked my tongue around my dry mouth. My stomach still felt queasy, but my headache was gone.

'I...don't really want any more pills.'

'OK,' Ray said. 'But you still need to take your meds. Doctor's orders.'

You don't understand, I wanted to say. *I can't go out there with the other patients. What if I lose control, and end up doing to one of them what I did to Tori?*

But he wouldn't understand, and I didn't want to make him drag me out. So I took a slow, calming breath and followed Ray into the corridor, where a nurse was waiting with the medicine cart. About seven male and female patients – some barely more than children, others looking old enough to be shipped off to an adult facility any day now – had formed a ragged line, with a couple of watchful aides on either side. My heart stuttered at the sight of the girl with the inky spikes of hair, hunched at the end of the line. If I joined the group, I'd be right behind her.

'Don't be shy,' Ray rumbled, nudging me forward. Then he raised his voice and said, 'Hey, guys, this is Alison. Say hello.'

'Hi!' blurted one of the younger boys, but the others mostly ducked their heads and muttered, or gave no sign of noticing me at all. One by one they shuffled up to take their medication, then turned and headed back towards the TV's technicolour blare. The ink-haired girl snatched her cups from the nurse's hand and slammed them back like a double shot of whisky, then gave me a contemptuous glare before dropping them into the trash and stalking away.

'Never mind Micheline,' said Ray, taking my cups from the nurse and handing them to me. 'She acts tough, but she's a good kid really. Sure you don't want that sleeping pill?'

The corridor was clear now, the other patients safely gone. I looked at the pills in my cup. 'No, thanks,' I said, and swallowed them down.

'Good morning, Alison. My name is Shabnam. Please,' – the middle-aged woman extended an elegant hand – 'sit down.'

We were in a little office next to the nurses' station, with the door propped open for security's sake. Self-conscious in my hospital pyjamas, especially compared to Shabnam's silken headscarf and crisply pressed slacks, I took a seat.

'Now, this is the first time you've been able to meet with a rights adviser, isn't that so?'

Her lilting voice rippled like sunlight on water, making mesmerizing patterns in front of my eyes. It took me a few seconds to remember that we were supposed to be having a conversation. 'What? Oh. Yes. Sorry.'

'There is no need to apologise,' she said. 'I'm here to help you understand your situation, and what your rights are under the Mental Health Act. You see,' – she folded her hands and leaned across the table – 'you were admitted to St Luke's Hospital as an involuntary patient, which means that a doctor found you to be in danger of causing serious bodily harm to yourself or to others. You were also found incapable of consenting to treatment, so a substitute decision maker – in this case, your mother – gave permission for you to be treated with antipsychotic medication.'

None of that came as any surprise, but I wondered where my father had been during all of this. Had he ever questioned my mother's decision? Or had he just retreated into his shell, like he usually did when the two of them disagreed, and let my mother do whatever she thought best?

'After you had been in the hospital for seventy-two hours,' Shabnam continued, 'your involuntary status was renewed for another two weeks, since you were still deemed unable to understand your situation or make informed decisions about your care. During that time your mother applied to have you transferred to

Pine Hills, and it was agreed that this transfer would be in your best interests, so that is why you are here. Now, I have a form to give you.'

She slid a sheet of paper across the table. 'This is a notice to let you know that your new psychiatrist, Dr Minta, has completed a certificate of renewal, which will authorise him to keep you here as an involuntary patient for another four weeks.'

I stared down at the paper, willing the words to stop wriggling and let me read them. *I am of the opinion that the patient is suffering from mental disorder of a nature that likely will result in serious bodily harm to the patient, and/or serious bodily harm to another person, unless he or she remains in the custody of a psychiatric facility...*

'So this means,' I said slowly, 'that I'm stuck here until the end of July?'

'Possibly,' she said. 'However, you have the right to be informed of Dr Minta's reasons for his decision. And you also have the right to appeal, and ask that your involuntary status be revoked.'

My stomach turned over. I knew I was supposed to be here for my own safety and the protection of others, but I was far more likely to get into trouble at Pine Hills than I was at home. Here I was trapped and stressed out and surrounded by unpredictable people, with nowhere to escape if things got too much for me. But if I could get out of this place, and go somewhere safe and quiet where I could be alone…

'If I did appeal, how would that work?' I asked.

'Once they receive your application,' said my adviser, 'the Consent and Capacity Board will arrange a hearing here at the hospital within seven days. You can ask your lawyer to represent you, or I can help you apply for legal aid.'

That sounded good. I'd been hoping to talk to a lawyer anyway, if only to answer my questions about the police. 'And if I win my appeal?'

'Then your status would be changed to voluntary,' she said. 'You would be free to refuse treatment if you wish, and leave the hospital at your discretion. But if your appeal is denied, your next hearing would not be for another six months, or until you are on your fourth certificate.'

'My *fourth*?' My heart lurched. 'You mean my psychiatrist can just keep issuing these things?'

'If he thinks it necessary, yes,' said Shabnam. 'As I said, the current certificate authorises him to keep you here for one month. The second would last for two months, the third for three months, and so on.'

In my mind's eye I could see the calendar floating all around me, like a rainbow scarf. To be stuck here for months on end with no privacy and no freedom, forced to take drugs that fogged my mind and greyed my senses, unable to play my keyboard or do any of the other things I normally did to relax… How long would it be before the stress got too much for me, and I did to somebody else what I'd done to Tori?

I couldn't let that happen. I straightened up in my chair.

'All right,' I said. 'I want to appeal.'

I learned a few things, that first day on Red Maple. One was that the other patients didn't bother with the 'Maple' part; to them it was just Red Ward, the place where everything stopped. Being in Red Ward meant you'd been 'acting out' or were otherwise seriously unstable; you were an escape risk, or you were on suicide watch, or just too volatile to be trusted without close supervision. So once you'd had breakfast and taken your meds, you could play cards or board games in the lobby, and if you'd earned the privilege (which I hadn't) you might get ten or fifteen minutes in the courtyard before lunchtime. You'd have a short meeting with your psychiatrist or one of the nurses, and then at four pm an aide would turn on the TV. But that was pretty much all. No wonder the other patients seemed frustrated and depressed.

Another thing I learned was that being on antipsychotic medication makes you really, really tired. I thought that maybe they'd just given me an extra-strong sedative at St Luke's, but even after a night's rest, I didn't feel any less bleary. I borrowed some magazines from the lobby and tried to read, but the words swam away from me. Then I laid out a game of solitaire, but it took all my concentration just to get through one round. Finally I convinced the nurses to let me go back to bed, only to be reminded that being exhausted and being able to sleep are not always the same thing. So I ended up just lying there for most of the day.

I was still afraid to spend much time with my fellow inmates, in case something went wrong. So I asked if I could take my meals in my room, but the nurses refused. They only did that for patients who were sick or in isolation, they said. So at lunch and supper I had to join the others in the kitchenette. There were eight of us altogether, though the ward could hold as many as fourteen. The food was brought in from the cafeteria, and by the time it got to us it was lukewarm.

But we could also eat bagels (pre-cut, since none of us were allowed knives), or fruit, or yogurt. And there was plenty of milk and juice in the fridge. No tea or coffee, though – I guess caffeine would have been one drug too many.

I didn't talk to the others much. Some of them were manic or lonely enough to start up a conversation whether I encouraged them or not, and I soon learned more about their diagnoses, treatments and medical complaints than I'd ever wanted to know. But confronted with a patient like Micheline, whose face was set in a permanent scowl and was already carrying on a constant, muttered dialogue with the voices in her head, I didn't know where to begin. I knew I should try to be friendly, but what if I said something that upset her, and she freaked out? I couldn't risk getting into a fight, not after what had happened with Tori. So I mostly just kept to myself.

At last, the day shift ended and the night shift came on – including Ray, who ambled around the ward like a tame bear and smiled at me so sweetly that my eyes stung and I had to look away. The nurses called him 'Sunshine', and seeing him interact with the other patients, I could see why. He could coax a smile out of nearly anyone, even Micheline, and unlike the other aides he wasn't afraid to pat a shoulder or give a hug if he thought someone needed it. When two of the younger boys started swearing and shoving each other around, Ray gently pried them apart and talked to them in his soft, furry voice until they cooled down. With Ray around I felt safe, and I was grateful for that small comfort.

Visiting hours were after supper, and I braced myself in case my mother decided to put in an appearance. But the only one who showed up was Micheline's older brother – greasy-haired, plaid-shirted, and reeking of cigarettes – and I was torn between disappointment and relief. When I came back to my room, however, I found a suitcase full of clothes sitting at the end of my bed. Apparently my mother had dropped it off at the front desk earlier in the day. She'd also left a note, to say that she and my father would be coming to see me tomorrow.

I looked at the card for a long time. Heavy cream-coloured stationery, with that familiar liquorice-whip handwriting. It might have been a note to one of her real-estate clients for all the warmth it held: no 'Love' in the signature, no Xs or Os below it. Just letting me know we had an appointment, so I could be on my best behaviour.

I dropped it in the wastebasket and went to line up for my pills.

At midnight the ward was quiet, but I lay sleepless, staring at the ceiling. By then I was so delirious with exhaustion that I felt as though I were on another planet, and yet I still couldn't settle. Vague whispers and mutters ran around my brain, and I kept thinking about Tori. What I'd done to her, and what it might mean. What her family and friends must be going through, not knowing if she was dead or alive. What would happen to me, if the police decided to stop treating her disappearance as a missing persons case and started investigating it as a murder…

I got up and went to the window, laying my forearm along the sill and resting my chin on it. Shadowy pine trees blocked out most of the sky, but if I pressed my face against the plexiglass and looked straight up, I might be able to see the stars. I could feel their subtle warmth, listen to their tinkling music, and maybe feel a little less alone.

I tipped my head to one side and there they were: three stars, bright as a promise. But instead of giving off the crystal wind-chime noise that had soothed me since childhood, they sang an eerie, piercing harmony unlike anything I'd heard before. And their colours were strange, too. The first star burned blue neon, the second electric green, and the third…

I ransacked my vocabulary, trying to put a name to that elusive hue, and failed. It wasn't red, orange, yellow, green, blue, indigo or violet, or any of the million variations in between. It was something entirely new, a colour beyond ordinary perception.

And yet I was seeing it.

I jerked back from the window, rubbing my eyes. *I am not crazy,* I told myself. *I'm not.*

But after everything that had happened to me in the last couple of weeks, it was getting harder and harder to believe it.

THREE (IS YELLOW)

'I have good news for you, Alison,' said Dr Minta heartily, when he met me in the corridor the next morning. 'You've been doing so well these past couple of days, I don't see any reason to keep you in Red Maple.'

I hadn't been expecting to see him until after lunchtime, plus I'd only had about three hours' sleep the night before. So for a moment I could only blink at him, too dazed to follow.

'I'm having you moved to Yellow Poplar,' he continued. 'Your privileges will be limited at first, but if you continue as you have been—'

I understood now. He was trying to bribe me into giving up my appeal. But I couldn't see how I would be any happier in Yellow than I was in Red, and the danger of hurting someone would be just as great. 'I don't want to go to Yellow Ward,' I said hoarsely. 'I want to go home.'

'Alison.' Dr Minta's tone became paternal, and I could taste his condescension, cloying as a mouthful of toothpaste. 'I understand you'd rather not be here.

But I think you'll find being in Yellow Poplar a positive experience. Why don't you come for a walk with me, and let me show you around?'

He swiped his keycard and the doors *chunked* open, revealing a tantalizing glimpse of a sunlit corridor beyond. My resistance deflated, and I followed him out.

We visited the gymnasium first, where a couple of dull-eyed boys were shuffling around the basketball court. We watched them shoot air balls for a while, then moved on to the recreation centre to see the stack of battered board games and the ping-pong table with its missing net. In the adjoining room, a few more kids sprawled in front of the big screen TV, watching a video about drug and alcohol abuse. None of them looked thrilled to be there, but they didn't look particularly threatening either, and my anxiety about mingling with my fellow patients eased a little.

'This is our education room,' Dr Minta continued, leading me down the hall to another doorway. 'And there is the back of Kirk's head, which is the only part anyone gets to see of Kirk when he is on the computer. Say hello, Kirk.'

'Hey,' said Kirk, without turning. His hair was the colour of wet sand, feathering around his ears and over the nape of his neck. On the monitor in front of him, a video clip was playing. I grimaced and looked away.

'During the summer months, we offer tutoring to any patients who need it,' Dr Minta said. 'We can help you make up any work or exams you missed during the regular school year. Kirk, don't forget this door needs to stay open.' He wedged the doorstop back into place before leading me into the adjoining room. 'And here we have arts therapy. We offer sculpture, painting, drama and music—'

Music. It was the first good news I'd had since I got here. But though I saw a guitar, some bongo drums, and a few other instruments, there didn't seem to be any piano. 'I have a keyboard at home,' I said. 'Could I ask my parents to bring it here?'

Dr Minta regarded me with brows raised. 'So you're a pianist, are you?'

I had a sudden, unpleasant image of being forced to play in front of the other patients at some kind of psychiatric talent night. 'I'm…uh, still learning,' I said with a queasy twinge.

'Well,' said Dr Minta, 'we have to be careful about electrical cords, so I can't make any promises. But if you appear to be making good progress with your treatment, I'll see what I can do.'

Electrical cords. Of course. I'd forgotten that anything even remotely like a rope was taboo in this place, in case somebody tried to hang themselves with it. But my keyboard was my heart, my brain, my extra limb. Playing it calmed me, when nothing else could. Surely that ought to count for something, too?

After Dr Minta had shown me the cafeteria and the visitors' lounge, our next stop was the library. The collection was mostly reference works and self-help manuals, with a few literary classics for good measure. But the lilac walls and plum carpet conjured up a serene atmosphere that reminded me of my bedroom at home, and it had a comfortable-looking sitting area with the best view I'd seen in days – across the courtyard to the rocky, pine-dotted hillside beyond, with a tantalising glimpse of blue lake in the distance. I wanted to curl up on the sofa and drink it in, but Dr Minta was already moving on. I made a mental note to come back later.

'...And here's where we hold our group therapy and education sessions,' said Dr Minta as we passed through another room, where framed motivational posters crooned platitudes at a circle of empty chairs. 'We ask that patients attend at least two sessions a day, but you can participate in more if you like. I'll give you a schedule.'

In all my life, I'd only met a couple of people I trusted enough to tell about my feelings, and even my father and my best friend Melissa didn't know half of what went on in my head. The idea of opening up to a group of strangers seemed less like therapy to me than torture. But I had to at least pretend to cooperate if I wanted out of here, so I kept quiet and followed Dr Minta out.

We ended the tour in Dr Minta's office, where I chewed my way through a handful of jellybeans while he asked me how I was doing on my medication. But I'd already told him yesterday that it made me tired and restless, and he'd told me those symptoms were quite common and would eventually go away, so there didn't seem to be much point in going over it again. Nothing I said was going to make him take me off the pills altogether, and switching to a different prescription might make matters even worse.

'What about your mood?' he asked. 'How would you describe the way you're feeling right now?'

Knowing that I'd soon be facing off against him at my appeal, it was hard to confide in him even if I'd wanted to. I felt like anything I said, however innocent, was going to be used against me. 'I don't feel angry, if that's what you want to know,' I said. 'I don't feel like doing anything dangerous or violent. I'm just ...here.'

'That's good,' he says. 'But just because you're starting to feel better doesn't mean you're out of the woods yet. Considering how severe your symptoms were when you were admitted to St Luke's, and the persistence of those symptoms until just a few days ago—'

I was not going to let him talk me into withdrawing my appeal. Even if he thought he was doing it for my own good. 'I know I was acting crazy,' I said. 'But I'm over that now. It's done.'

'I hope you're right,' said Dr Minta. 'But remember, your symptoms only improved after you started receiving antipsychotic medication on a consistent basis. That's why I believe it's important to keep you at Pine Hills a little while longer, so that we can make sure you're really stable, and that you won't hurt yourself or anyone else again.'

Ever since my rights adviser told me Dr Minta wanted to keep me here for another four weeks, I'd wondered what I'd done to make him think I was dangerous. I'd thought he must be basing his decision on my records from St Luke's, but...

I reached into the jar of jellybeans – not even

looking this time, because I could sense their colours by touch. I pulled out a black one for strength, and a violet one for calm. Then I asked, 'What do you mean, *or anyone else?*'

Dr Minta was silent for a moment. Then he said, 'What do you remember about the afternoon of June 7th, Alison?'

'I don't remember anything,' I replied – and all the jellybeans I'd just eaten came rocketing back up my throat. I gagged, coughed, and swallowed hard until I'd got them down again. 'Sorry,' I panted, 'must have gone down the wrong way—' but a second surge of nausea nearly undid all my efforts.

'Let me get you some water,' said Dr Minta. I hunched on the sofa, breathing into my hands, until he came back and handed me a paper cup. But by then I'd realised what was making me sick, and though it shook me a little, I was pretty sure I could make it go away. I drank the water slowly, and then I said with perfect truthfulness, 'I don't want to talk about this right now.'

And just like that, my stomach was calm.

'Of course,' said Dr Minta. 'I don't want to press you into anything you're not ready for. But when you do remember what happened that day, or feel ready to talk about it…you can come to me any time. Any time at all.'

His voice was soft, but there was something hungry behind his eyes, and it made all the hairs on my skin stand up and quiver. Because I knew, now, why he was so determined to keep me here.

It wasn't because I'd done anything wrong. He just wanted to find out if I'd killed Tori, and if so, what I'd done with her body. He'd claimed that anything I shared with him would be confidential, but how hard would it be to phone in an anonymous tip to the police hotline? He might never be able to admit that he was the hero who'd solved the Tori Beaugrand case, but he'd have the private satisfaction of knowing the police would never have found her body without him…

'Feeling better now?' asked Dr Minta.

I couldn't say yes without throwing up; I was afraid even a nod might be dishonest enough to trigger my gag reflex. So I just gave a watery half-smile and looked at my feet until Jennifer arrived to escort me to lunch.

After two and a half weeks of semi-isolation, I found walking into the cafeteria at Pine Hills more than a little daunting. The room was tiny compared to the one at Champlain Secondary – it couldn't have seated more than forty people – but it still reminded me uncomfortably of the way I'd felt on my first day of high school. Were we supposed to go up to the counter in a certain order? Were there rules about where I could sit? Where did people get their trays? And – oh, no, there was a cash register at the end of the line. Did we have to *pay*? I looked around for Jennifer, but she'd already vanished. I was on my own.

'Hey,' said a voice, and I turned to see a boy about my own age standing there. He was tall and skinny like me, with dark blond hair and an impish curl to his mouth. For a moment, I wondered why his voice was familiar, and then I realised: I'd been introduced to the back of his head.

'Kirk, right?' I said. His name was spicy and elastic, like cinnamon gum. The letter *I* hinted at self-centeredness and *R* could be unreliable, but they couldn't compete with those forthright *K*s on either end.

'Yeah.' He ran a hand through his feathery hair, and the smile became a flash of teeth. 'And you're…?'

'Alison,' I said, relieved to have met someone so friendly and non-threatening. 'So what are the rules around here?'

'We all have our own special trays,' said Kirk,

leading me to a stack at the end of the counter. 'They're marked with a secret pattern of notches on the underside, and if you pick up somebody else's by mistake, they hunt you down and beat you to death with it.'

I raised my eyebrows at him.

'Aw, you're no fun,' he said. He grabbed two trays and slid them onto the rails. 'OK, here's all you really need to know: the lemonade tastes like pickle juice. The croissants are always stale. And don't eat the meatloaf, ever.' He caught the cafeteria worker's glare and winked at her. 'Oh, and you have to take at least two servings of fruits and vegetables every meal. The Canada Food Guide has spoken. Plus the nurses will snark you out if you don't.'

'Really?' I said.

'Serious. They're big on healthy eating here. And exercise. You don't exercise every day, you lose privileges. I dropped ten pounds once just trying to get back my computer time.' He reached for a ripe-looking peach, the only one in the bowl.

'Don't,' I said.

'What, you want it?' He held it out, but I shook my head.

'It's rotten,' I said. 'Look at it.'

'Huh,' he said, turning it over in his fingers and looking dubious. But he must have been used to humouring his fellow patients' quirks, because he put it back and picked up a banana instead. 'This one OK?'

I nodded, and he offered the fruit bowl to me. I resisted the impulse to rearrange it so the colours balanced, and picked out an apple. A bowl of vegetable soup, some crackers, and a muffin later, I followed Kirk to the end of the line, where to my relief the cashier merely glanced at our wristbands before nodding us through. Apparently she only took money from staff and visitors.

'Here we are,' pronounced Kirk, thumping his tray down onto one of the tables. At the far end, a heavyset boy lifted his head and regarded us with eyes mild as a cow's, then returned to poking at his salad. 'That's Roberto,' Kirk told me as we took our seats. 'He doesn't talk much since the meds kicked in. Welcome to Fine Pills.'

'You mean Bunny Hills,' said a skeletal girl with blonde hair, wriggling into the seat beside Kirk. 'That's what they call this place at the Regional Psych.'

Kirk snorted. 'Those pseudos at Regional, they think they're so hardcore. They're just jealous 'cause we've got all the prime chicks. Like Micheline.' He raised his voice on the last couple of words, leaning back in his chair for a better view. 'Right, Mish baby?'

I'd thought he must be joking, but there she was at the next table, all inky hair and sneering mouth, giving Kirk the finger. I hadn't seen Micheline at breakfast back in Red Ward, but assumed she'd just been too sick or stubborn to get up. I'd never imagined she was well enough to be transferred here.

'She loves me really,' confided Kirk. 'Oh, this is Cherie, by the way,' and with that he picked up his bagel and took an enormous bite.

'Hi,' said the blonde girl. She gave me a wan smile and began pushing her salad around her plate.

As we ate, the tables around us filled up with patients. Some were animated, chatting easily with those around them. Others sat with slumped shoulders, looking at their plates. One boy stared across the room with burning eyes, his fingers tapping out a persistent rhythm: *ratta-ta-tat, ratta-ta-tat.*

'Hey, Sanjay!' called Kirk, as a boy in glasses stumbled down the aisle toward us. 'Where you been?'

Sanjay lurched to a stop at the head of our table, his gaze wandering over Cherie, Kirk and Roberto before riveting itself to me. 'Who's she?'

'Alison,' said Kirk. 'She's new. Hey, want a space?' He nudged out one of the empty chairs with his foot.

'Space,' echoed Sanjay.

'The final frontier,' said Kirk helpfully. 'Or a place to sit, whatever. You gonna join us?'

The other boy didn't take his eyes off me. 'Don't know her.'

'Crap,' muttered Kirk. 'I thought we were over this,' and then more loudly, 'Go ahead and quiz her if you want, Jay, but can you get out of the aisle first? C'mon, grab a seat.'

Sanjay's eyes widened, white showing around the brown. 'Don't *know* her—'

With a sigh Kirk pushed his tray aside, ducked under the table and came up beside me, shaking the hair out of his eyes. 'There, take my spot. Cherie's OK, right? You know Cherie.'

Reluctantly, Sanjay sat.

'Can I do the questions this time?' asked Kirk. 'You tell me if I miss anything.' He turned to face me, sticking up his thumb in the manner of a fake microphone. 'All right, stranger, what's your name? First, middle and last.'

This was the weirdest dinner conversation I'd ever had. 'Alison Marie Jeffries.'

'Age?'

'Sixteen. Well, seventeen next month.'

'Ooh, I love an older woman,' said Kirk, mock-leering. 'Favourite colour?'

The colour of serenity, of feeling safe and confident and whole. On the piano, it was the B-flat below middle C; in the alphabet, the first letter of my name. 'Violet,' I said.

'So what's your psychosis?'

I hesitated.

'Oh, come on, like we're not all screwed up here,' Kirk said. 'You wanna know my special brand of crazy? I'm bi. And I light stuff on fire.'

Cherie rolled her eyes. 'He means bi-*polar*,' she told me. 'Heavy on the manic, in case you hadn't guessed. He's in and out of this place like it's his personal cuckoo clock.'

Kirk didn't even pause. 'Roberto's got major depression, Sanjay thinks his parents were brainwashed by aliens, and Cherie—'

'Wouldn't even be here if my doctor wasn't an idiot,' interrupted Cherie. 'I have a tumour in my stomach. That's why I can't eat.'

'Yeah, sure. Like we can't tell what your issues are, Skinny.' Kirk tipped his chair back on two legs and teetered there a second before thumping down again. 'That leaves you, new girl. You want me to guess? Bet I can get it in one try.'

'The doctors aren't really sure yet,' I said hastily, not wanting to know how crazy Kirk thought I was. 'I was fine until' – *until I killed Tori* – 'a couple of weeks ago, and then I had this big...panic attack, or breakdown, or something like that. They're still trying to figure it out.'

Kirk gave me a sceptical look, but he didn't question me further. He turned to Sanjay. 'So what do you say? Is she legit?'

Sanjay hunched his shoulders, which made him look like a cartoon vulture, and shook his head.

'Oh, yeah, I forgot.' Kirk tapped the back of my hand. 'Show him your arms.'

Until now, Sanjay's behaviour had struck me as simultaneously sad and funny. This, however, hit all too close to home. Feeling like I'd swallowed an icicle sideways, I stretched both my arms across the table, turning them palms up, then down again.

'See?' said Kirk. 'She's good.'

Sanjay relaxed. 'OK.'

'What was that about?' I asked.

I expected Kirk to answer, but to my surprise, Sanjay did. 'They look like us,' he said, 'but they're not really human. They're here to spy on us and use us in their experiments.'

'You haven't seen any of Them around here lately, though, right?' said Kirk. 'It's just Dr Wart.'

'It's *Ward*,' said Cherie, with an exasperated glance at Kirk. 'You think you're so cute.'

'I'm not?' asked Kirk, adding 'Ow!' as she kicked him under the table.

It took me a minute to realise who they were talking about, but then I remembered. He'd given me pills for my migraine when I first came in. 'The medical doctor, you mean?' I said. 'The one with the moustache like a dead mouse?'

Kirk hiccuped with laughter.

'It's not funny,' interrupted Sanjay, agitated. 'He's got the mark. He's one of them.'

My mouth went dry. 'Mark? What kind of mark?'

'Here.' He tapped the inside of his forearm. 'They all have it. But only I can see it. That's why they put me in here.'

I slid back in my chair, more disturbed than ever.

Sanjay was paranoid, anyone could see that. And yet his delusions and my experiences had at least one detail in common...

'I am so sick of Tori Beaugrand,' said Melissa bitterly, as we left the auditions for our eighth grade musical. 'She can't even sing, so how is it fair to make her Alice? I had that part wrapped.'

In the corridor behind us the custodian was running his floor polisher, filling my head with a wobbly green noise that tasted like mouthwash. 'I know,' I said distractedly. 'You did really well.'

And she had, though I'd found it hard to concentrate on her audition with Tori sitting just a few chairs away, buzzing at me. What I didn't say was that Tori was by far the better actress, much as I hated to admit it. Melissa delivered her lines like a talented thirteen-year-old girl pretending to be Alice in Wonderland; but when Tori opened her mouth she'd not only convinced me that she was Alice, she'd made me believe that I was in Wonderland, too.

'As if she needs another chance to show off,' Mel muttered, fumbling with the combination on her locker. 'She's already in the paper every other week for hockey, and I heard her tell Lara that her mom wants to get her into modelling – like I want to see her smug face every time I flip open a magazine? Ech.'

I wished I could assure her it would never happen, but I couldn't. Ron and Gisele Beaugrand were local celebrities in their own right, with plenty of media connections. Between their influence and Tori's looks, it'd be surprising if she didn't become a supermodel.

'And there was Brendan staring at her with his tongue practically on the floor.' Mel's running shoes hit the back of the locker, filling my vision with expanding rings of bronze. 'He didn't even look at me once.'

'That doesn't mean anything,' I said. 'Sure, Tori gets noticed, but have you heard the way the guys talk about her? It's not like they're interested in her personality.'

'Yeah, but that makes the whole thing suck even more,' said Mel, stomping into her winter boots and yanking a hat down over her curly brown hair. ''Cause right now they don't care about anybody's personality, as far as I can tell. And if they ever start caring – well, I can't exactly compete with Princess Victoria there either, can I?'

I couldn't disagree with that either, unfortunately. It would have been nice to dismiss Tori as a spoiled rich girl with nothing but looks to recommend her, but she'd learned people skills at her mother's knee, and even the bottom-feeders in the school's popularity fishbowl found her hard to dislike. If it hadn't been for the Noise and my loyalty to Melissa, I would probably have been charmed into liking her, too.

'You never know,' I said, grimacing as I zipped up the new jacket my mother had just bought me for Christmas. There was nothing wrong with the fit or the colour so I'd had no excuse to make her take it back, but I hated the ugly bile-yellow rasp of those metal teeth coming together. 'Maybe she'll end up going to a different high school.'

'Yeah,' said Mel slowly, savouring the idea. 'Really different. Like, on another planet.'

And then I'd never have to hear the Noise again. 'I wish.'

'Speaking of alien life forms, did you see Jenna's got blonde highlights now? She wants to be Tori so bad, she's turning into a clone.' Mel snorted. 'What's next, blue contacts?'

'And a pink tattoo,' I said.

'Huh?'

'Tattoo,' I repeated. 'Or whatever it is. That thing on her arm, you know.'

Melissa's eyes lit with unholy glee. 'Tori got a tattoo?

Are you kidding me? Where did you hear this? Whoa, her mom is going to flip when she finds out—'

'No, I mean the same one she's always had. How could you not notice? Looks like a sun with zigzag rays coming out of it. Kind of Aztec.'

'Um, Ali... I don't think so,' said Melissa. 'I was in the same swimming class as Tori last year, remember? I've seen her arm about a billion times. There's nothing on it.'

Her words hit me like a backhanded slap. I went rigid, the blood roaring in my ears. How could I have made such a stupid mistake?

Fortunately for me, Melissa hadn't stopped talking yet. 'She doesn't even get zits, for crap's sake. She's like some kind of walking Barbie.' She frowned up at me. 'When did you see this tattoo-thing on her?'

For one sickening moment I still had no idea what to say. Then I forced my face into a smile and smacked Mel on the shoulder. 'Psych! Had you going.'

'Uh, sure,' she replied. 'Ha ha. Except for the part where it wasn't funny.'

'I know,' I said. 'I blame the floor polish.' I shoved my hands into my gloves, to hide their trembling. 'Let's get some fresh air before I lose any more brain cells.'

Mel shuddered. 'Ugh, it's like minus thirty out

there. Where's a hot Mountie and a team of sled dogs when you need them?' She pulled her scarf up over her face, shoved the door open with her shoulder and vanished out into the snow.

I followed more slowly, arms wrapped around my aching stomach. Mel seemed to have already forgotten my lapse, so she probably wouldn't bring it up again. But it shook me to realise how close I'd come to betraying myself.

I'd figured out a long time ago that I was the only one at Diefenbaker Public who could hear Tori's Noise. I figured it was just another case of my senses doing strange things, or at least things that would seem strange to other people if they knew. But the mark on Tori's arm was different. It didn't come and go, or change shape or colour – it was just there, and had been from the first day I met her.

So what did it mean that nobody but me could see it?

'Ew!' burst out Cherie, startling me back to the present. She flung her just-bitten peach down onto the tray, spattering juice in all directions. 'It's rotten.'

Kirk's brows shot up. He looked at me.

'What?' I asked.

'The Force is strong with this one,' he intoned. He picked up the mangled peach and turned it over, exposing the soggy brown spot close to its core. 'Seriously, the x-ray vision's a neat trick. You'll have to show me how you do that some time.'

Nausea roiled inside me. I shoved back my chair. 'I have to go,' I blurted, and rushed for the door. Out the corner of my eye I saw Jennifer leap up to intercept me, but I didn't slow down. I flung myself into the girls' washroom, grabbed the toilet with both hands and threw up.

'You're not supposed to go anywhere without an escort,' said Jennifer sternly from the door.

'Sorry,' I panted, pushing my hair back out of my face. 'Bad stomach.'

Scowling, she took hold of my hand and turned it over, inspecting my fingers. I knew what she was looking for; I also knew she'd be disappointed. I might be thin and a picky eater, but nothing could convince me to make myself throw up on purpose.

'You OK?' she asked as she let me go.

I sniffed, wiping my mouth on the back of my hand. 'I think so. But…it would help if I could lie down.'

She nodded. 'I'll show you to your room.' She led

me down the corridor to a wing I'd never seen before, a broad, airy hallway with windows at the far end and several widely spaced doors on either side. The room she showed me was half occupied already, with an open suitcase spilling its contents out across the bed and a stuffed cow flopped against the headboard, and I could only hope my roommate would be someone quiet and not too scary. I crawled onto the empty bed, taking deep breaths to calm my churning stomach, while Jennifer adjusted the cordless blinds.

'I'm leaving the door open,' she said. 'I'd like you to keep it that way.' Then she left.

I closed my eyes and let my head fall back onto the pillow. *Get a grip, Alison*, I told myself. *What happened in the cafeteria is no big deal.* After all, it was hardly the first time I'd seen things that nobody else could see. Wasn't that the whole point of the conversation I'd had with Mel, that day back in eighth grade?

And yet this time, it hadn't been just a hallucination. Kirk thought I was crazy for telling him not to take that peach, and Cherie hadn't seen anything wrong with it either – until she bit into it and found the brown decay inside.

So what did that tell me about the mark I'd seen on Tori's arm? Had it just been my imagination conjuring up another excuse to dislike her, like the mark Sanjay thought he'd seen on Dr Ward?

Or had there really been something sinister lurking there, in the darkness beneath her skin?

FOUR (IS BLUE)

I'd been lying down for about half an hour, my mind
churning with new uncertainties, when my roommate
came barging in. Fortunately it wasn't Micheline, as I'd
feared. It was Cherie.

'Group therapy starts in five minutes,' she said.
'Jennifer says unless you're still throwing up, you have
to go. Which had better not give you any ideas, by the
way. I hate the smell of barf.'

'We all experience anger,' explained our therapist,
a round, earnest woman who'd urged me to call her
Sharon. 'It's a natural response to stressful situations, to
personal hurts and disappointments, to the wrongs and
injustices we see in the world around us. In this group,
we try to help everyone find ways to express their
anger without letting it become destructive.'

She gazed around the circle of bored, vacant and
sullen faces, then continued, 'One of the ways we can
deal with anger responsibly is to share our frustrations
with trusted friends who will listen and not judge.
I hope we can all be friends here, and give that gift of

open listening to each other. So Kirk, why don't you start? What makes you angry?'

'Anger's a waste,' said Kirk. 'I'm past that negative stuff. All you need to do is open your arms,' – he flung them out so enthusiastically that he knocked Sanjay's glasses off his face – 'and embrace the oneness of us all.'

Sharon sighed as she bent to pick up the glasses from the floor. 'Kirk, if you're not going to take this group seriously—'

'I'm absolutely dead serious,' he insisted, and launched into an explanation of how modern psychoanalysis was just reinforcing people's negative emotions and what the world needed was a radical new form of therapy that would make everybody feel good. I lost the thread of his logic at that point, but his grand scheme for reforming the mental health care system seemed to involve regular sex for all patients, unlimited access to energy drinks, and a giant outdoor rock concert featuring all his favourite bands. If Sharon hadn't cut him off after a couple of minutes, he would probably have talked the entire half-hour.

'Thank you, Kirk, that's very interesting,' she said. 'But I think it's time for us to give some of the others a chance. Sanjay, why don't you tell us what makes you angry?'

'I'm angry about being here,' said Sanjay softly.

Sharon leaned forward. 'Yes? Why is that?'

'Because I tried to warn my parents about the aliens, but they wouldn't listen. So the aliens injected them with mind control serum and put their mark on them. And then they sent me here, because—'

'You know why I'm angry?' interrupted Micheline in her rasping voice. 'I'm angry because I have to sit here listening to this crap, and all I want is a frickin' cigarette.'

'Let's use respectful language, Micheline,' said Sharon placidly. And then, to my discomfort, she turned to me. 'We're so glad to have you join us, Alison. Would you like to tell us about something that makes you angry?'

The last time I remembered being angry, Tori Beaugrand had died. 'I'd rather not,' I said.

'It doesn't have to be a big thing,' she encouraged. 'It's OK to start small.'

'I know, but I don't really…do anger. It never makes anything better. So I try not to get into it.' Or any other intense emotion, for that matter. Like grief, because there was no use wallowing in misery; you just had to accept that bad things happened and keep going. And love, because caring about anything too deeply was just asking to have it taken away.

Sharon crooked a finger in front of her lips. I could see she wanted to correct me, and yet it went against her therapeutic creed to tell a patient that anything he or she said was actually *wrong*. 'Well,' she said at last, 'we all have different personalities, and different ways of dealing with conflict. But I think it's possible for all of us to find ways to express our anger without it becoming unhealthy.'

Micheline spat out a bitter laugh, but Sharon ignored it. She turned to the patient on my left – a girl with drooping eyelids who looked about as full of buried rage as Eeyore – and began coaxing her to participate. And so the session dragged on, until I almost wished I could disintegrate myself and everyone else in the circle just to put us all out of our misery.

But Anger Management was just the beginning. Next up was an educational session called 'Understanding Your Medication', in which a nurse came in and talked about the various antidepressants, antipsychotics and mood stabilizers we were on, and how important it was for us to keep taking them consistently. She was running down a list of common side-effects – dry mouth, drowsiness, blurred vision and so on – when Kirk suddenly leaped to his feet and began doing a spasmodic song-and-dance routine to the tune of '*Glory, Glory Hallelujah*':

> '*I've got tardive dyskinesia,*
> *I've got tardive dyskinesia,*
> *I've got tardive dyskinesia,*
> *And now I can't sit still!*'

'Kirk,' snapped the nurse, 'sit down, or you're going to have to leave.' But the Eeyore-faced girl put up a tentative hand. 'What's tardive…whatever?'

'Dyskinesia,' said Kirk helpfully.

The nurse looked exasperated, but she could hardly refuse to answer. 'It's one of the *possible* side effects that *occasionally* happens when a patient has been on one of the *older* forms of antipsychotic drugs for a *considerable* period of time.' Her emphases left no doubt of how unlikely she thought this was to happen to any of us. 'It causes involuntary, repetitive movements—'

Kirk contorted his face into a grimace and poked out his tongue, blinking exaggeratedly all the while.

'This could happen to you, kids! So whatever you do, don't stop taking your happy pills!'

'That's it,' said the nurse. 'You're gone.'

Unfazed, Kirk got up and sauntered out of the door. But by then the damage had been done. I thought about the medications I was on, the side-effects I'd already experienced, and a chill settled into the pit of my stomach. Tardive dyskinesia sounded like the kind of thing that could ruin the rest of your life. What if taking Dr Minta's pills did that – or worse – to me?

I was sitting in the library after supper, watching the setting sun cast its long rays through the pine forest, when an aide came to the door. 'Alison? There's someone here to see you.'

I'd been expecting this, but I didn't feel ready for it. Licking my dry lips, I got up and followed her out, silently reminding myself to stay calm.

The visitors' lounge was tucked into a corner by the cafeteria, a low-walled triangle of glass blocks that offered little privacy to anyone sitting there. Especially not if he was standing, like my father; I could see his stooped shoulders and greying red hair from thirty feet away. As I approached, he turned, and I expected my mom – slight, brunette and fifteen years younger – to stand up and show herself as well. But she didn't. She wasn't there.

'Here we are,' said the aide. 'I'll be across the hall if you need me,' and with that she retreated, leaving my father and me alone.

'Hello, Alison.' He sounded hesitant, but then he usually did. His gaze wandered around the lounge, stuttering over the frayed upholstery, the dusty fake plants, the windows cloudy with fingerprints. 'How are you doing?'

'I'm OK,' I replied, and it only made me feel a little queasy to say it. Maybe I was finally getting used to the taste of my own lies.

'Really?'

His faded blue eyes were creased with anxiety. I could taste tears in the back of my throat, but I swallowed them. My dad had never been good at handling emotional outbursts, and I didn't want to scare him away. 'Yeah.'

'Well.' He let out his breath. 'That's good. For a while, you were…in pretty bad shape.'

'I know.' It must have been so hard for him, seeing me like that. I'd always been his nice quiet daughter, the one who could sit with him in his study while he worked on an article or graded papers, and not disturb him at all. 'But I'm better now.'

He patted my shoulder, then ambled over to one of the cleaner chairs and sat down. I followed. 'Your mother was hoping to come,' he said, 'but…it didn't work out this time. She's going to come another day.'

So either my dad had done something to upset her and she'd decided she couldn't stand to be near him, or else she'd simply chickened out. Maybe watching me thrash around in panic or lie there in a drugged stupor had been easy, compared to facing a daughter who might actually have something to say.

'What about Chris?' I asked. 'Is he going to come and see me, too?'

'Oh. Er. Well, your mother thinks it wouldn't be such a good idea to bring Christopher here. He's still young…'

Eleven wasn't that young, and my brother was hardly a sensitive child, but I got the message. My mother wanted to keep her screwed-up daughter and her normal son as far apart as possible. 'Right.'

'So, Alison…'

'Yes?'

'When do you think you'll be coming home?'

So my mother hadn't told him about Dr Minta's

decision, or my appeal. She'd kept him in the dark so he wouldn't interfere. *Oh, Dad.* I wanted to throw my arms around him and bury my face in his shoulder. I wanted to tell him everything, and beg him to help. But it wouldn't be fair to put him through that. If I pitted my parents against each other, all of us would lose.

'I don't know,' I said, struggling to keep my voice steady. 'They've got me on some medication, and I think they want to make sure it works out. I'm trying to appeal the decision, but...'

He made a melancholy noise of assent, and went quiet again. Then he said, 'Your friend Melissa's been asking about you. She wants to know if she can come and see you, now you're feeling better.'

Warmth spread through my chest. So Mel hadn't given up on me after all. She was a true friend, no matter what Tori – what anyone else said. 'I'd love that,' I told him. 'Tell her to come any time.'

My dad nodded, his big hands twisting in his lap. 'May I ask you something, Alison?'

Uh-oh.

'The police said you were the last person to see that girl, Tori Beaugrand, before she disappeared. And that you'd claimed...you'd said...'

91

'I said I'd made her disintegrate. I know. That's impossible. I'm not saying that any more.' Lying to him without actually lying was one of the hardest things I'd ever done. I just hoped he wouldn't force me to do it again.

'So…do you remember what really happened, then?'

Of course I remembered. No matter how many times I tried to push Tori's death to the back of my mind, the memory of that day still haunted me. But I could taste my father's hopefulness like powdered sugar on my tongue, and I knew that deep down, he still believed I was his good little girl. Maybe even believed, in spite of everything, that I was sane.

I couldn't bear to let him down.

'I'm sorry, Dad,' I said. 'I've tried to make sense of it all, to think of something that would help the police find her, but…I can't.'

He didn't seem disappointed. If anything, he looked relieved. 'That's all right,' he said.

We talked about safer things then, like the hideous pink-and-green bungalow my mother was trying to sell for one of her clients, and my brother Chris's plans to go to hockey camp that summer. My father had never been good with small talk, and he kept forgetting details and having to correct himself. But the fuzzy blue shape of his voice was such a comfort that I could have listened to him ramble on forever.

Not that I got the chance. It wasn't long before he ran out of words, and when he stood to leave, the room seemed to shrink around me. It was all I could do not to grab his arm and beg him not to go. 'When are you coming again?' I asked, as we walked to the exit.

'Next Tuesday, I think. Would you like me to bring you anything from home?'

I wanted to say *my keyboard*, and hope that when it showed up Dr Minta would let me keep it. But that was too much like open rebellion, and I couldn't risk that kind of black mark on my record. Not before I'd had my appeal, at any rate.

'Nothing right now, thanks,' I said.

My first night in Yellow Ward was peaceful enough – Cherie snored, but at least she slept soundly, and so far she hadn't done anything to make me anxious about sharing a room with her. But my bed was next to the window, and even through the cordless blinds I could hear the stars crooning, sense those nameless, alien colours that refused to go away. I tossed and turned all night, and by morning I felt as though I hadn't slept at all.

The next morning when I lined up for my pills, a nurse handed me an activity chart that looked like my high school schedule. I couldn't take in all that information right away, so I took the chart with me to breakfast. Cherie was already there, prodding unenthusiastically at her scrambled eggs, and I glimpsed Kirk talking to a silent Roberto in the corner. I didn't see Micheline, but then I hadn't expected to – last night at dinner she'd started yelling at one of the voices in her head, and they'd sent her back to Red Ward again.

I chose a table at the back of the cafeteria, where it was quieter, and looked over my new schedule. Dr Minta had arranged for me to finish my eleventh grade coursework, so I'd be spending three mornings a week in the education room under the supervision of the part-time teacher, Mr Lamoreux. In the afternoons, I'd be attending four different kinds of group therapy, plus something called 'Family Counselling' on Fridays – though there was a question mark beside that entry, and I hoped it would stay there…

'You have to be careful,' said a low, familiar voice from the aisle. Sanjay glanced around furtively, then set down his tray and slid into the seat across from me.

'Careful about what?' I asked.

'Them.' His voice dropped to a whisper. 'They know you can see the mark, too. Don't let them get you alone.'

My throat went dry. I'd never said anything to Sanjay about the mark I'd seen on Tori's arm. How did he know?

'I can hear people's thoughts sometimes,' he said seriously, as though I'd spoken out loud. 'And I can see the future. That's why the aliens want me. Because I know their plan.'

I looked at him helplessly. He seemed so earnest, so convinced of what he was saying. But even though I knew how lonely it felt to have a story that nobody else believed, I couldn't bring myself to agree with him just yet.

For one thing, his evil alien conspiracy theory didn't really hold together. One minute the aliens were trying to kill him because he knew too much, the next they wanted to capture him and use him in their experiments. First he claimed that the aliens disguised themselves as humans, but later he'd said they put their mark on humans and brainwashed them into doing their bidding. I'd heard him telling Roberto that the aliens came from a planet in the Horsehead Nebula, but I'd also heard him tell Cherie that they came from another dimension.

There seemed to be some new variation on the story every time Sanjay told it, and if anybody pointed out the inconsistencies, he'd just ignore them.

And yet when I'd passed Dr Ward in the corridor earlier this morning, the one Sanjay had accused of carrying the aliens' mark, my gaze had dropped to his arm before I could help myself. He'd been wearing a lab coat, of course, so I couldn't see anything. But when I raised my eyes again, he was giving me such a cold, probing look that my heart skipped, and I'd scurried into the library just to get away from him.

So maybe I wasn't quite as much of a sceptic as I'd thought.

After breakfast I went to the Education room, as my schedule instructed. Somehow Mr Lamoreux had got hold of all my textbooks from Champlain Secondary, so I could finish up the few assignments that remained before final exams. The implication that I'd be here long enough to do that bothered me a little, but it was a lot better than sitting in Red Ward doing nothing at all, so I took my physics textbook off the top of the pile.

I was still there an hour later, trying to wrap my brain around the principles of electromagnetism, when the message came. The Consent and Capacity Board had agreed to hear my appeal in five days, and in just a couple of hours my lawyer would be coming to meet with me.

So this was it. My chance to prove that I could control my behaviour without therapy or drugs, that I had enough clarity of mind to decide whether I needed those things or not. And if I made my case well enough, they might even let me go home.

Home. Even whispered, the word spread like maple syrup over my dry tongue. I'd always been a little embarrassed by the old split-level house I'd grown up in, but now I missed it more than anything. I missed slipping into my father's study and curling up in the armchair while he graded essays. I missed the taste of my mother's pot roast, which always had the right shape to it even when everything else between us was wrong. I missed the scuffle and thump of my younger brother practising his slap shot in the driveway. I even missed our fat, brainless cat jumping onto my chest in the middle of the night and breathing out amber waves of *fisssssh.*

Maybe it was irrational, but I truly believed that if I could just go home, everything would be all right. Sure, my relationship with my mother wasn't the greatest, but my bitterness towards her was an old ache that I'd lived with for years, nothing like the blind rage that had made me lash out at Tori. I couldn't imagine disintegrating her, any more than I could imagine doing it to my father or Chris.

Other people might be more of a problem. But even if my neighbours had seen the police taking me away to hospital, even if my schoolmates knew I'd been the last one to see Tori on the afternoon of June 7th, they had no reason to accuse me of murder – especially since the police weren't even calling Tori's disappearance a murder yet. If I just kept quiet and stayed out of sight, they'd probably leave me alone. And maybe once I'd had a few days to rest and get the drugs out of my system, I'd be able to work out exactly what I'd done to Tori, and how to stop it from happening again.

I just hoped the police wouldn't arrest me before I had the chance.

My lawyer showed up at two-forty that afternoon, more than half an hour late. He was a stout man with thin hair and a harried expression that reminded me of the White Rabbit, and I got the feeling that I was one client too many for his busy schedule. But he seemed to know the details of my case, and he also had a copy of my patient chart and a few other reports I'd never seen before. I leafed slowly through them, blinking at phrases like *flat affect* and *poverty of speech*, while he explained what would happen at my appeal.

It sounded similar to a court appearance, with both sides calling witnesses and presenting evidence to support their case. But the board would also consider some kinds of evidence that wouldn't necessarily be allowed in a formal trial, such as hearsay. The whole process would take about an hour, and once all the witnesses had been cross-examined and final statements made, the board would dismiss us while they made their deliberations.

'And within twenty-four hours, they'll notify you of their decision,' he said. 'Does all that make sense to you?'

I nodded distractedly, my eyes still on the file. Until now, I hadn't realised how many of the things I'd done and said, things that seemed perfectly innocent to me, had been taken down by Dr Minta and the nurses as proof of my mental illness. My reluctance to interact with the other patients on Red Ward, for instance, was antisocial behavior. When I'd tried to stay calm, that showed a lack of emotional response. My short answers and poor maths skills were evidence of disordered thought processes. I often seemed distracted, which suggested that I was experiencing auditory and visual hallucinations. And the one time I'd let my guard down enough to giggle in front of Dr Minta, he'd marked it down as 'inappropriate laughter'.

There was more, but I'd seen enough. I closed the file.

'So,' said my lawyer, 'do you have any questions?'

'I do, but...not about the appeal.' I took a deep breath, gathering courage. 'You've read my file, right? So you know I told the police I'd killed Tori Beaugrand, when I...when I was crazy?'

'Yes.' He paused, and I could tell he was trying to decide how fragile my mental state might be, and whether or not it was a good idea to ask if I'd actually killed her or not. But all he said was, 'So what's your question?'

'Could they charge me with murder, based on that confession? Even though they haven't found a body, or a weapon, or any other evidence that Tori's...not alive?'

'Ah.' He leaned back in his chair, lacing his hands together over his stomach. 'Well, I can't say for certain what the police will do, but I can tell you that the

Youth Criminal Justice Act is very strict about what it takes to get a valid confession from anyone under seventeen. First, the police would have to take you into a comfortable interview room and read you a lengthy statement of your rights – including the right to consult a lawyer, the right to have a parent present, and the right not to make any kind of statement to the police at all. You'd have to confirm that you'd understood everything they'd just told you, and then clearly state that you had chosen to waive those rights, before making your confession on video and audio tape. Is that what happened?'

I shook my head.

'Then no matter how many times you said you'd killed Ms Beaugrand, that statement would not be admissible in court. Especially in your case, because there are questions of mental health involved.'

'But could they still charge me, if they found other evidence? Like...Tori's blood on my hands, or on the ring I was wearing?'

'Without a sample of her blood for comparison, they probably wouldn't be able to tell if it was hers,' he said, 'only that it wasn't yours. They might be able to identify her DNA, but it would take at least a month, perhaps two, for those results to come back from the lab. And even if they did find a match, that wouldn't be enough evidence to charge you with murder, not by itself. Especially since so little time passed between the time Ms Beaugrand was last seen and the time you returned home. To lay a charge against you, the police would have to be able to explain how you murdered her and disposed completely of her body, in such a fashion that no trace could be found, in less than an hour.'

I let out my breath slowly. So as long as the police didn't find any more evidence against me, I should be safe. For now.

'So,' said my lawyer. 'Back to the appeal. Now you've seen what your psychiatrist has to say, do you still want to go through with it?'

It was a good question. Reading Dr Minta's comments in my patient file had shaken my confidence – he was the expert, after all, and he seemed to have no doubt that I was dangerously ill. And I couldn't deny that only a few days ago I'd been feeling and acting pretty crazy. What if I was really as deluded as Sanjay, and just didn't recognise it? What if I really did need the antipsychotics, antidepressants and anti-anxiety pills I'd been taking?

And yet…that would mean my mother had been

right all along. That her fears about me, her reluctance to get close to me, had been justified.

No. That, I refused to believe.

'Yes,' I told my lawyer. 'I want to go through with it. Just tell me what I need to do.'

FIVE (IS GREEN)

After two days on my new schedule, I'd been looking forward to the weekend. Not only because it would bring my appeal that much closer – *next Wednesday, next Wednesday*, chanted a little voice in my brain – but because it meant two days without group therapy or Dr Minta. By Saturday morning, two Yellow Ward patients had been discharged, four had gone home on weekend passes, and six more had piled into a van with a couple of aides to go shopping and see a movie. Pine Hills was so quiet I might even have found it pleasant, if I hadn't been trapped there with virtually nothing to do.

But the library was open, and although I still found it difficult to read I managed to dig up a few old books on tape – including, to my surprise, *War of the Worlds* by H.G. Wells. I wondered how a story about aliens invading earth had made it through the selection process, especially with people like Sanjay around. But it looked like it might be interesting, so I pulled out the battery-operated cassette player and slipped the first tape in.

The Martians had just launched their first attack against the helpless human race, and the narrator was fleeing the scene, when an aide knocked on the doorframe to get my attention. 'Alison? You have a visitor.'

Apprehensive, I walked out to the visitors' lounge – and there, to my relief, was Melissa.

'Ali!' she exclaimed, bouncing up and giving me a hug. 'Oh, wow, I can't believe how good it is to see you.'

I returned the embrace clumsily, blinking back tears. How could I ever have doubted her? 'It's really good to see you, too.'

'I wanted to come before, when you were at St Luke's,' she said, 'but at first they wouldn't let anybody in who wasn't family, and then I got totally swamped with exams. I'm really sorry it took me so long. Look, I brought you something.' She opened up the flowered tote bag at her feet and pulled out a box the size of a small dictionary. 'The nurses unwrapped it to make sure it was OK, but—'

I lifted the lid, and broke into an involuntary smile. 'Minties!' I exclaimed, inhaling until purple-blue pleasure hazed my vision. Forget therapy, a box of mint-flavoured chocolates and Mel were all I really needed to make me feel better. 'That's amazing. Thanks so much.'

'I brought you some stuff to read, too,' she said, hauling out a stack of magazines. 'They're pretty old, but I figured they'd probably be new to you, right?' She dropped them onto the chair beside me and sat forward, her brown eyes on mine. 'So how are you feeling?'

'A lot better than I was,' I said. 'I'm hoping that in a few more days, they'll let me go home.' I helped myself to one of the chocolates, letting its silky taste melt over my tongue, and offered the box to Mel.

'No, they're for you. But seriously…you think you'll be out soon? That would be fantastic.' She glanced around and shifted closer to me. 'So did you ever figure out what happened? Seeing those two policemen dragging you out of the house like that, and all the stuff you were yelling about Tori and how the colours were hurting you – it was really scary, Ali. I was so worried for you.'

Something cold snaked between my ribs. 'You saw that?'

'Well, yeah! I ran over as soon as I saw the cop car in your driveway. I thought maybe you'd had a break-in or something. But then I heard you screaming, and

I knew something was really wrong because I'd never heard you sound like that, ever.' She shuddered. 'I'm sorry. It must have been way more horrible for you than it was for me. If you don't want to talk about it, I'll understand.'

Somehow, just hearing her say that made me feel better. When Dr Minta said things like that they always sounded phoney, but Mel had been my best friend for five years, and I knew she really cared. 'It's OK,' I said. 'I haven't figured out what happened yet, but I'm working on it. I don't want it ever to happen again.'

Mel nodded. 'So, uh, I guess you know about Tori Beaugrand? Not that I think you had anything to do with that,' she added hastily. 'I mean, I know what you said at first, but there's no way.'

A sour taste blossomed in my mouth, like fermented apple cider, and I had to eat another one of the chocolates to cover it. 'I haven't really heard that much,' I said.

'Are you serious? It's practically the only thing anybody can talk about. They've had teams of volunteers combing the area, the police talked to just about every teacher and student in the school, they had dogs sniffing around the parking lot...but nobody's found a thing. It's like she vanished off the face of the earth.'

It would have been so easy to just nod, and let the subject drop. But I needed more details – and if anybody had them, Mel would. She'd dreamed of being a journalist ever since she was eight years old, and when she wanted information she knew how to get it. 'So…what did they find?' I asked. 'I mean, what do they know so far, about…what happened to her?'

'Well, she had detention with you after school, of course – what was all that about, anyway? I heard the two of you got into some kind of fight in the cafeteria, but nobody seemed to know why.'

It all seemed so pointless now. I'd accused Tori of one thing, she'd accused me of another, and then she'd shoved me and I'd shoved back, which was what got us both in trouble. But that was nothing compared to the fight we'd had later, the one that had destroyed everything. 'It wasn't important,' I said. 'Go on.'

Mel looked dubious, but for once she didn't push me to tell her more. 'Anyway, Tori told Lara and Paige that she'd meet them at the mall at three-thirty, but she didn't show up. So they waited a while and then Lara texted her, but she didn't answer. Then they walked back to the school looking for her, but all they found was her backpack lying by the side door, with her cell and all her ID and stuff still inside. And then – um, this part is kind of creepy –'

I knew what she was going to say. I'd been there, after all. 'It's OK,' I said.

'Well, there was blood. Not a lot, just a few drops and splashes, but Lara freaked and called Tori's mom, and then Tori's mom freaked and called the police. And at first the police thought Tori might have just skipped town, but everybody who knew Tori told them there was no way. So they started looking at other stuff. Like I heard there was a videotape that showed Tori leaving the school right after you did –'

My heart stopped.

'—but there was some kind of technical glitch and the picture cut out, so they couldn't get much off of that…'

Of course there had been a video; there were security cameras all around the school property. And if the tape showed Tori, it would also have shown me. How much of our fight had been caught on camera before it malfunctioned? Might it be enough to justify a charge of assault – or even of murder?

But if the police knew we'd fought, knew I'd hit her, why hadn't they come back to question me about what had happened? Were they waiting for Dr Minta to tell them I was well enough to talk about it? Was there a law that kept them from questioning mental patients without a doctor's permission, or something like that?

'Hello, Earth to Alison?' Mel was peering into my face. 'Did you hear me?'

'Sorry.' I shook myself back to attention. 'You were saying?'

'I was asking, when was the last time you saw Tori? Do you remember?'

I didn't want to lie to her. But how could I tell her the truth? She'd already heard me say it once, and I couldn't bear it if she thought I was still crazy. I needed her friendship too much. 'I…can't talk about it,' I said.

Mel leaned forward. 'Alison, this is me, OK? You can tell me anything.'

She had no idea how much I wished that were true. 'It's just too messed up, Mel. None of it makes any sense. I'm not even sure—' I took a deep breath, trying not to grimace as I lied. 'I don't even know what really happened any more.'

'But you don't still think that you killed her, right? You're not scared of…' Her voice trailed off as she caught sight of my face. 'You *are* scared.'

I couldn't look at her any more. I closed up the box of chocolates and put it down beside me, running my finger over the label.

'Wow.' Her voice was hushed. 'I knew you hated Tori, but…'

'No!' The word tore out of me, sharp with desperation. 'That's not what I mean! Even if I killed her somehow, do you really think I'd have done it on *purpose*?'

'Of course not,' she answered quickly. 'Ali, I know you. You're not that kind of person. I didn't mean it like that.'

Again, that acid taste in my mouth. I swallowed, wishing it would go away. 'Mel,' I said, 'you're not going to tell anybody what I said, are you?'

'What? No! Why would I do anything like that?'

My eyes prickled, and I closed them. 'OK,' I said hoarsely.

'I've got to go, my mom's waiting. But I'll come and see you again soon.'

'Sure,' I said, and forced a smile as I watched her go. But although the taste of untruth was still on my tongue, it felt different than before – less rancid and more bitter. And though it seemed impossible and

I wanted desperately to deny it, I knew what that flavour meant.

It was the taste of my best friend lying.

'Hey,' said Kirk, nudging me with one elbow. 'Are those chocolates?'

'Kirk,' cautioned a female voice on my other side, 'maybe you should leave her alone.'

I raised my head slowly, my eyes focusing. How long had I been sitting in the lounge by myself? I'd been so preoccupied thinking about my visit with Mel, I'd lost all track of time.

'Alison?' asked the aide gently. 'Is something wrong? Anything you'd like to talk about?'

What was I supposed to say? *Well, I've just found out my best friend thinks I'm a homicidal lunatic, and also that I can taste when other people lie.* I shook my head.

'Are you sure? Sometimes it can help to talk to someone who isn't involved—'

'Stop bugging her,' Kirk interrupted. 'She doesn't want to talk, OK? End of story. Hey,' he elbowed me again, 'I found some old Audrey Hepburn thing in the DVD box. Wanna watch it? You like old movies, right?'

It was true: black and white films didn't offend my sense of colour the way that modern ones did. I was surprised, and touched, that he'd noticed. 'Yeah,' I said.

'OK, let's do that then. We'll hang out, just you and me.'

'I don't know that's a good idea,' the aide began, but Kirk made a scoffing noise.

'I'm a pyro, not a rapist, OK? We'll leave the door open. Come on, Jill, you know there's crap-all to do on weekends, and it's only an hour until TV time anyway. Bend the rules for once.'

It wasn't the first time I'd been amazed by Kirk's boldness with the staff, but they all seemed to take it in their stride. I wondered how long he'd been coming here.

The aide sighed, and got to her feet. 'Oh, all right. Come along.'

I'd seen *Roman Holiday* before, but right now I didn't care. Kirk sprawled across one end of the sofa, while I curled up tight on the other, hugging a pillow. Every few minutes one of the staff glanced in to make sure we weren't plotting anarchy or tongue-wrestling on the floor, but other than that they left the two of us alone.

It would have been nice to imagine that Kirk was here to support me in my time of need. But he'd already helped himself to several of my chocolates and seemed to be enjoying himself thoroughly, so I found it hard to give him quite that much credit. Probably he'd just got sick of volleyball, or whatever activity they had going on in the gym at the moment.

I rubbed my eyes as they started to sting again. When Mel showed up, I'd dared to believe that she'd come because she cared about me, and for no other reason. Even when she started questioning me about Tori, I'd still managed to convince myself that she was only doing it for my sake. Because I needed so badly to talk to someone.

Not because she suspected I'd really killed Tori. Not because she wanted to be the first one to find out where I'd hidden the body. And definitely not because she planned to share that information with the newspapers – or the police.

She's just been using you, taunted Tori's voice in my head. *She's nobody's friend but her own.*

No. Tori had been wrong, and so was I, to even let myself think such a thing. Mel did care, and she would come back. And she wouldn't tell anyone what I'd said to her, especially since I'd asked her not to...

'Wow,' said Kirk. 'You're *ripe* for this guy, aren't you?'

I blinked back to attention, and realised that I'd been staring slack-jawed at Gregory Peck for the better part of a minute. 'Uh, yeah,' I said. 'But don't tell anybody.'

Kirk pretended to zip his lips, but the mischief in his eyes warned me I'd be hearing about this for a long time to come. 'So you're into older guys. Is this some kind of Freudian thing? 'Cause your father's, like, sixty?'

I opened my mouth to retort – and then the box of chocolates caught my eye. *Just* the box, because the wrappers inside were all empty.

He'd eaten my Minties. Every single one.

The next four days went by with agonising slowness, as the date of my appeal approached. Soon I was so anxious I could barely eat: I answered Dr Minta's questions in monosyllables, and in my group therapy sessions I didn't talk at all. Every night I prayed that the board would decide to uphold my appeal – and by day, I mentally reviewed all the arguments for why they should. I was old enough to make my own decisions, I hadn't done anything violent or destructive since I came here, and I was willing to keep taking my medication if only they'd let me go home. But deep down I feared they'd never let me go.

The night before the hearing I was desperate enough to take a sedative, but still I couldn't sleep. Breakfast tasted like gravel and sawdust, and when Jennifer showed up to escort me to the conference room, my heart was thumping so hard there was no space in my chest to breathe.

My lawyer met me in the corridor. 'So,' he said. 'Ready?'

I couldn't speak, but I gave a tight, nervous smile.

'Nothing to worry about,' he told me. 'You'll do fine.' He opened the door, and the two of us walked in.

The Consent and Capacity Board had already taken their seats along one side of the table, one man and two women, all wearing dark suits and sober faces. Dr Minta sat on the opposite side, alone for now. My lawyer pulled out a chair for me, and I sat down, pushing my hands between my knees to stop them shaking. The stenographer opened her laptop, and the brisk-looking woman in the middle spoke:

'This meeting of the Consent and Capacity Board has been convened to hear Ms Alison Jeffries' application for a review of her status as an involuntary patient, and also of a finding that she is not capable of making her own treatment decisions.' She introduced the other two members of the board, a psychiatrist and a community representative, before continuing, 'I'm Jeanne Menard, a lawyer by occupation, and I'll be the chairperson for this hearing. Let me state for the record that the Consent and Capacity Board is an impartial, independent body and is not affiliated with this hospital or any of the parties involved in this appeal.'

And so it began. It turned out that the Board had already read through all Dr Minta's documents – including not only Dr Minta's clinical observations and the certificate he'd issued to try and keep me here, but the police report from the night I was arrested, my patient file from St Luke's, a written statement from one of the nurses in Red Ward, and a letter from Gisele Beaugrand claiming that I had 'threatened and harassed' her daughter shortly before Tori disappeared. My lawyer tried to have that last letter, as well as the nurse's note, struck from the proceedings, but Ms Menard said they were both relevant, and overruled him.

Dr Minta then gave a brief summary of my case, describing how I'd been brought to St Luke's and the state in which I'd spent most of my first two weeks there before being transferred to Pine Hills. His voice was mild as butter as he talked about my 'psychotic state' and the 'delusions and hallucinations' that had caused me to injure myself, smash my mother's cell phone, assault a police officer, and nearly strangle the admitting psychiatrist at St Luke's with his own tie, all in just one day.

'And as you can see in the file,' he went on, 'there were several more incidents of violent and self-injuring behaviour during Ms Jeffries' stay at St Luke's Hospital. She showed little recognition of individuals, and her speech was fragmented and nonsensical. She could obey simple commands and carry out basic self-care with some assistance, but she was unable to speak coherently or show any insight into her situation until she had been receiving regular doses of antipsychotic medication for nearly a week. It is my belief that Ms Jeffries' mental state has improved only as a result of the medication, and that if she is allowed to discontinue treatment her mental health will seriously deteriorate, making her once again a risk to herself and to others. For that reason, I would like to continue treating her in hospital as an involuntary patient.'

'Thank you,' said Ms Menard, and turned to my lawyer. 'Do you have any questions for Dr Minta?'

My lawyer did his best, I'll give him that. He spent nearly ten minutes quizzing Dr Minta about various details of my case, trying to poke holes in his reasoning. But his arguments sounded petty even to me, and it was hard to imagine that the board would be convinced by them.

'Dr Minta,' asked the community representative, 'what makes you believe that Ms Jeffries is not suited to become a voluntary patient?'

'Her conversations with myself and some of the nurses indicate that she has an unrealistic view of her own mental health,' said Dr Minta. 'She believes that she has fully recovered from her psychotic episode and does not require further treatment or medication. If she were made voluntary, she would leave the hospital immediately.'

The community representative looked grave. 'Thank you, Dr Minta.'

'Are there any further questions?' asked Ms Menard, after a pause. 'No? Very well. Dr Minta, would you like to call in your witness?'

My lawyer had warned me about this moment, and I'd done my best to be prepared. But still my lungs constricted and my throat closed tight as an airlock, as the door opened and my mother walked into the room.

*

The night before my eighth birthday, I went to bed early, giddy with the thought of presents in the morning. It took me a long while to trick myself to sleep, and when I did, it was only to be shocked awake moments later by a thunderclap so loud it shook the house. It couldn't have lasted longer than three or four seconds, even with the storm right overhead. But to me that terrible noise seemed to go on forever. Pillars of rust and ochre loomed across my vision, threatening to topple and crush me flat. I held my breath, my small body rigid with alarm – but then the sound faded, taking the giant shapes with it.

I waited a moment, fearfully testing the silence, then tried to settle myself once more. But my head had barely touched the pillow when lightning fractured the darkness, stinging my eyes and searing my tongue like pepper. Then the clouds exploded and the rain came hissing down, pelting my window and my ears with bruising force. I cowered beneath the covers, not knowing which would shatter first, the glass or me.

Another crash of thunder, then more lightning, while the wind whipped the trees into a leafy froth and the rain continued to pound. I pulled the blankets over my head, wishing with all my might for the faceless giants and the horrible taste in my mouth to go away – but my senses refused to listen to anything but the storm. At last I flung the covers aside, fled down the hall to my parents' room and collapsed by the foot of their bed, sobbing.

'Alison?' said my mother sharply. 'What's wrong?'

I'd forgotten that my father wasn't there, that he'd gone to a conference and wouldn't be home until tomorrow. I'd made a mistake, but it was too late to fix it now.

'Maman, I'm scared. The storm, it's so loud—'

I tasted a buttery rustle of silk as my mother slipped out of bed to kneel beside me. I threw my arms around her waist and hid my face in her lap, hoping that this once she would hug me the way she used to, before I'd talked about gold stars and spoiled everything. But her body stiffened, and her hands closed on my shoulders, pushing me upright again.

'Alison, calm yourself,' she told me. 'Breathe in, deep – like that, yes – and out. And once more. There. Better?'

It wasn't. Outside the storm still raged, but I couldn't bear my mother's brittle touch any longer. I scrambled back into the corner, hugging myself for comfort. 'I don't want to go back to my room,' I said. 'I don't want to be alone.'

My mother sat back on her heels and looked at me, her fine features drawn with anxiety. 'It's…the thunder, yes?' she said. 'The noise, that's all that bothers you?'

She always sounded so much more French when she was afraid. 'Yes,' I lied.

Her dark head tipped to one side as she thought. 'Well, then,' she said, 'let me give you something to help you.' She rose and went to the dresser, treading carefully around me as she passed. 'This was your grandmother's,' she said, lifting out a long beaded necklace from the drawer. 'It calmed her sometimes. Maybe it will do the same for you.' She let it drop, and as the cross bumped into my palm I realised that it was a rosary.

'There are prayers to go with it,' she went on as another flash of lightning lit her face, making the strained lines around her eyes and mouth deeper than ever. 'But I can't teach them to you now. For tonight, just hold it in your hand and talk to the Blessed Virgin. She will ask Jesus to calm the storm, and help you not to be afraid.' Then, as I remained silent, 'Alison?'

'OK,' I said, gulping another breath. My legs trembled as I pushed myself upright, and the thought *of walking back to my room alone made my stomach cramp. Still, I knew better than to let my mother see just how upset I was, or give her any more reason to wonder why.*

'The storm will be over soon,' she told me as she guided me out into the hall. 'And tomorrow will be a beautiful day.'

I waited until her door had closed at my back, tongue sliding into the latch with a reproachful click. Then I ran back to my bed and dived beneath the covers. The rosary beads pressed against my palm, cold and comfortless, while outside the storm roared on.

I didn't pray that night. I just clutched my grandmother's rosary, and cried.

For the next twenty minutes she was the star of the hearing – Suzanne Jeffries, forty-three years old, neatly groomed and professionally dressed, a slight redness around the eyes her only sign of emotion. She told the board that even as a child, I had experienced hallucinations and shown signs of being unable to distinguish between fantasy and reality. I was intelligent, but found it difficult to concentrate in class and frequently had to do extra work at home to catch up. I had few friends – really just one, she said – and spent most of my spare time alone in my bedroom, playing my keyboard and reading 'strange' books about other worlds.

Dr Minta nodded soberly, as though this was just what he had expected. 'Did you have any other reason to be concerned about Alison's mental health?'

'Yes,' said my mother. 'There were a number of times when I expected Alison to be upset by some news she had heard, or something bad that had happened to her. But she showed very little reaction, or none at all.'

Then Dr Minta asked my mother to describe the state in which I had arrived home on the afternoon of June 7th, and in her low, faintly accented voice she told the board every detail. How I'd burst through the front door with blood on my hands and collapsed on the doormat, sobbing that I'd killed Tori Beaugrand. She'd tried to help me up, but I'd swatted her aside. I'd screamed when her cell phone rang, then grabbed it off the table and hurled it through the living room window. Then I'd attacked one of the police officers who'd come to investigate, and it had taken two of them to handcuff me and drag me outside, shrieking all the way.

'Would you say, Mrs Jeffries, that Alison's

behaviour made you fear for your own safety?' asked Dr Minta.

'Yes,' my mother replied, wiping her eyes with a tissue. 'Very much so. It was…terrifying.'

'Did you believe at that point that she had physically harmed another person?'

'I – I didn't know what to think. When she said she'd disintegrated Tori with her mind – I knew that couldn't be true, but…'

'Do you have any other children besides Alison, Mrs Jeffries?'

'I have a son, Christopher.' She twisted her wedding ring around her finger. 'He has – he is eleven years. Old.'

My mother always forgot her English grammar when she was nervous, probably because my grandmother used to punish her for speaking anything but French in her presence. I didn't know a lot about *Grandmère*; she'd died before I was born. But I knew she hadn't been an easy person to live with.

'And would you be concerned for Christopher's safety,' Dr Minta asked my mother, 'if Alison returned home?'

She lifted her head then, and those dark, haunted eyes met mine. I returned the look without flinching, though it wasn't easy. *Please don't do this to me,* I begged silently. *I would never hurt you or Dad or Chris. You have to know that.*

My mother bit her lip, and for a moment I thought I'd convinced her. But then she averted her gaze and said, 'Yes. I would be concerned.'

'Thank you, Mrs Jeffries,' said Dr Minta. 'I have no further questions.'

The hearing went on for another twenty minutes, but it might as well have stopped right then. I'd been planning to testify on my own behalf, but what good would it do? I couldn't deny I'd done all the violent, crazy things my mother and Dr Minta had described, even if I had a perfectly reasonable explanation for why I'd done them. Like how the high, wheedling ring of the cell phone had sounded, for a horrible instant, like Tori's Noise. And the psychologist's tie had been so orange-pounding-loud that it hurt me, and I'd only been trying to make him take it off.

My lawyer put up a good fight, but the leaden feeling in my stomach told me we'd already lost the battle. And when the board thanked us and asked us all to leave so they could make their deliberations, I felt as though I were staring down a long, dark tunnel with no end in sight. Disembodied voices murmured in the back of my brain, mocking my failure, and suddenly I was so tired I could hardly keep my eyes open. I gave a limp handshake to my lawyer, and headed for the door.

'Alison,' said my mother, catching my arm. 'Please, try to understand—'

I stopped and looked at her, knowing what she would see in my face: the expressionless mouth, the dead eyes. 'Dad can come to visit me any time he wants,' I said. 'But not you. I don't want to see you again.'

Then I pulled myself free of her and walked out.

The Consent and Capacity Board delivered their verdict later that afternoon. In their judgement, I was not competent to make my own treatment decisions, nor was I suited to become a voluntary patient. So for the next four weeks at least I'd have to remain at Pine Hills, and submit to whatever treatments Dr Minta prescribed for me.

It wasn't exactly a shock, but the news still hit me hard, and I spent the next two days in a state of hollow-eyed despair. For the first time in my life, the thought crossed my mind that I might be better off dead. Not that I had any real intention of committing suicide – in fact the idea had barely occurred to me before I shoved it into the dustiest, most cobwebby corner of my mental attic. But it made me realise that if I didn't find something to do with myself soon, I'd end up falling into a black hole of depression from which I might never escape.

It wasn't easy to stop brooding over my failure and start thinking about how to overcome it, but once I did, it wasn't hard to figure out where my appeal had gone wrong. I'd thought my best chance of getting out of Pine Hills was to convince the board that Dr Minta was mistaken about me. Only now did I realise that the person I really needed to convince, the one I should have been working on all along, was Dr Minta himself.

But how could I persuade him that I was capable of making my own decisions? In my mind, he was still the enemy, and he knew it. And no amount of pleading or reasoning was going to change his belief that I didn't really understand what was best for me, that my thinking was 'disordered' and only his magic pills could make it right.

Then it came to me. The perfect way to prove to Dr Minta, and my mother too, that I didn't need antipsychotic medication to keep me sane. It would take time and patience, but since I was going to be stuck here until the end of July anyway, what did I have to lose?

So when the nurse came around with the medicine cart that evening and handed me the familiar paper cups, I tossed the pills into my mouth and followed them up with a swig of water as usual. But it was only the water I swallowed, and the moment she stopped watching me I spit the tablets back into my hand.

I'd figure out what to do with them later.

SIX (IS PURPLE)

My second week at Pine Hills blurred into the third, and my fellow patients came and went. I'd just managed to talk myself into forgiving Kirk for the chocolate incident when he plummeted into a depressive phase, and started spending most of his free time in bed. Around the same time, Micheline came back to Yellow Ward, but then she found a paperclip in Mr Lamoreux's classroom and sliced up her wrist so badly she needed stitches. And a couple of days later, Sanjay sneaked out and got half a kilometre up the highway before anyone realised he was gone.

But even with all of that going on, I managed to stay out of trouble. Soon I was allowed to walk the halls without supervision and even enjoy courtyard privileges. I was still cutting back on my meds, but carefully – for the first few days I even broke the pills and took half, just to make sure the withdrawal symptoms didn't get too much for me. Little by little the fog over my senses began to lift, and the world regained its proper shapes and colours. During my sessions with Dr Minta, I kept my eyes down and said little, but every day I felt a little more alive.

Meanwhile my father came back to see me as promised, but not my mother, and the 'family counselling' part of my schedule remained mercifully free. I had an uncomfortable feeling that Dr Minta was working on that, though. He'd asked me to write a short essay about my childhood and turn it in by next week, so that we could talk about it at a future session.

Later that week, I was on my way to the cafeteria when I noticed a stranger standing by the nurses' station. From the back, he looked so ordinary that I almost passed by without a second glance. But then he turned and I stopped dead, my heart colliding with my ribcage.

His eyes were violet.

I'm not exaggerating. They weren't just blue or blue-grey. They were that deep bluish purple you only see when refracting light through a prism – or when someone is wearing tinted contact lenses.

And yet the man in front of me didn't look like he cared about fashion, or had even bothered to make its acquaintance. Not only was his shirt wrinkled and partly untucked, but he'd paired it with a shapeless cotton sweater vest and slacks in exciting shades like Old Filing Cabinet and Dryer Lint. His hair was the colour of a thunderstorm reflected in a mud puddle, and looked like he'd cut it himself with blunt scissors several weeks ago.

And yet he was clean shaven, and the apple-green tang of his scent told me he'd showered recently as well. His face was full of angles and wry humour, and he was younger than I'd thought at first – I guessed mid-twenties, though there was something ageless about him that made it hard to be sure. His gaze met mine directly, and as a smile deepened the corners of his long mouth I surprised myself by smiling back.

'Sorry to keep you waiting,' panted a familiar voice, and the man and I turned in unison as Dr Minta hurried toward us. I braced myself for the inevitable hearty greeting, but for once my psychiatrist didn't even seem to notice my presence. 'Konrad Minta,' he said, gripping the visitor's hand. 'Welcome to Pine Hills. Would you like a tour, or shall we go straight to my office?'

This obviously had nothing to do with me, so I gave the two men a wide berth and walked on. But I could feel those violet eyes on me all the way to the cafeteria, and as I picked up my tray I couldn't help wondering who the stranger was, and what had brought him here. Too old for a patient, too young for a parent, too sloppily dressed to be interviewing for a place on staff…a journalist, maybe?

'Hallo, bay-bee,' murmured a lecherous voice in my ear, and I jerked back, spilling iced tea all over my tray.

'Kirk, I swear—'

He gave me a look of wide-eyed innocence. 'What? I didn't say anything. It was him.' He pointed to Roberto, who was laboriously tweezing carrot sticks onto his plate. 'I know he looks innocent, but when it comes to women, he's the devil.'

'Uh-huh,' I said. 'And he can throw his voice, too.'

'A man of many talents,' agreed Kirk. 'So where you gonna sit?'

I shrugged, and headed for the nearest empty table. I was glad to see Kirk acting more like his old self again, but I didn't want to encourage him too much in case he started bouncing off the walls. 'How was Red Ward?' I asked, as we sat down.

'Suuuuuuucked,' said Kirk in a tone so low it was half belch, and then in his normal voice, 'But Ray told me to say hi.'

No wonder everybody loved Ray. I'd only been in Red Ward for two days, more than three weeks ago, and he still hadn't forgotten me. How did he do that? Not just remembering the names of all the patients he'd worked with, but the faces and personalities that went with them. It made me feel guilty that I wasn't more like that myself.

'So what've you been up to?' asked Kirk.

'Exams, mostly,' I said. Now that my mind was clearer, it hadn't taken me long to catch up on the schoolwork I'd missed. 'Today was World History.'

'Oh, yeah? How'd that go?'

'I think I did OK,' I replied, and took a quick sip of my iced tea. Truth was, I knew exactly how I'd done. Seeing everything I read in colour made it easier to remember, and if I'd thought about it hard enough I could probably have quoted the textbook word for word. But I didn't want to be that obvious, so I'd thrown in a few deliberate mistakes. The last thing I wanted was to be singled out as a prodigy – or worse, a cheater.

'There's no way you wrote that poem,' said Tori.

I turned, startled. Floating out of class on the lilac-scented cloud of my teacher's praise, I hadn't even heard the Noise until Tori was right behind me. 'What?' I said.

'You copied it from somewhere,' she told me, her voice barely audible above the familiar drone. 'I don't know exactly where, but I bet it won't be hard to find out. So if you don't want everybody to know you cheated—'

'I didn't cheat!'

Tori put her hands on her hips, which made her look annoyingly like an ad for designer jeans. 'This isn't just about you, you know. Lara's pretty upset that her poem didn't get picked for the competition, and I don't blame her.'

Until now I'd avoided Tori as much as I could, not even looking at her if I could help it – it was the only way I could stop her Noise from driving me crazy. At times I'd felt guilty for treating her so rudely, but now that Tori had finally lived up to her ugly burnt-umber name, I felt justified. 'It's not my fault your friend's jealous,' I said. 'And how do you know I didn't write the poem myself?'

'All that stuff about "martyred leaves whispering out their souls", or whatever? Please.'

This year, Champlain Secondary was participating in a province-wide poetry contest, and only the best poem from each school could be submitted. The prize for the winning student was two hundred dollars – just what I needed to finally buy the new keyboard I'd been saving for. So of course, I was determined to win.

I'd worked incredibly hard on that poem. I'd spent a whole Saturday afternoon hunched over my desk, scribbling and erasing one word after another, then crumpling up the page in frustration and starting again. I'd been almost ready to give up, convinced that nothing I wrote would ever be good enough – but the next morning I'd woken up with one perfect phrase in my head, and after that the rest of it came together like magic.

The poem I ended up with wasn't long, but it was the most emotional thing I'd ever written, and it had taken all my courage to turn it in. How was I to know my teacher would read it out loud in front of everybody? But once my embarrassment subsided I'd felt a shimmer of pride, especially when Mrs Mailloux said she and the other judges had chosen it to represent our school in the competition. And now Tori was trying to take that away.

'You're wrong,' I said. 'That poem is all mine, and if Mrs Mailloux thinks it's good enough to enter in the contest, that's her call. Not yours.'

Tori's lips flattened. 'Don't say I didn't warn you.' Then she strode away, leaving me wondering whether

I'd just called her bluff or made a very big mistake.

But a few days later Mrs Mailloux took me aside, and told me she had some bad news.

'There have been some concerns about the originality of your entry,' she said. 'And after looking at it again, the judges agreed that the language and imagery do seem a little too sophisticated for a student your age. I'm afraid we're going to have to pull it from the contest.'

I'd never forgotten the humiliation of that moment, when I realised that not only my good reputation but the prize I wanted so desperately had been stolen from me. Until then, I'd had no personal grudge against Tori. But from that day onwards, I hated her almost as much as Melissa did...

'Oh, hey,' said Kirk, jolting me from the memory. 'Got something for you.' He dug a piece of paper out of his pocket and dropped it onto my tray. 'Picture of your boyfriend.'

I unfolded the page and found a printed photograph of a grizzled, elderly Gregory Peck, wearing thick glasses and a baseball cap. 'Very handsome,' I said, forcing my voice to lightness. 'Nice to know you've made good use of your computer time.

But aren't you worried Mr Lamoreux's going to notice you fooling around online and kick you off?'

'For what? I didn't even have to hack through the nanny software to get it, and it's not like I'm printing off porn. Unless...' He grabbed the picture and turned it sideways. 'Ooh! I never saw *that* before.'

'What, in his beard?'

'I'll never tell,' he said, and waggled his eyebrows as he licked the last crumb from his fingers. 'So...you going to eat the rest of that sandwich, or what?'

I pushed my plate towards him. 'Go crazy.'

'Too late,' he said. 'But seriously, what are you waiting for, caviar? This is a nuthouse. Tuna salad's about as good as it gets.'

To me, the sandwich had tasted like moldy green zigzags. But supper would be blue and round. 'I'll hold out for the macaroni,' I said.

'You *are* nuts,' said Kirk.

As I walked out of the cafeteria, I barely noticed the police officer standing across the corridor. But when I took a second glance and realised who it was, I stifled a gasp.

It was Constable Deckard.

And he was talking to Dr Minta.

Hastily I backed into the girls' washroom, hoping that neither of them had seen me. If I put my ear to the door and listened hard, maybe I could make out what they were saying...

But all I heard was the dull clatter of trays and cutlery from the cafeteria, and the maddeningly loud laughter of two nurses in the hall. And when I dared to look out again, both Deckard and Dr Minta were gone.

They could have met by coincidence, I told myself. Police officers came in and out of Pine Hills all the time. They'd probably just been discussing the weather or last night's hockey game.

But deep down I was certain they'd been talking about me.

I was sitting in the library a couple of days later, gazing out the window at the steel-wool clouds and the pine trees dripping with rain, when Dr Minta appeared in the doorway and beckoned me over.

'I'd like to introduce you to someone,' he said.

My gaze slid past him to a pair of tranquil blue-violet eyes, and my heart did a little somersault in my chest. 'Uh...sure,' I said.

'This is Dr Sebastian Faraday, a graduate student in neuropsychology from the University of South Africa.'

He's here for a couple of months while he works on his thesis.'

Dr Faraday stepped forward, offering me the strong square palm and long fingers of a surgeon. 'Hello,' he said.

Just one word, yet it resonated through my bones like a cello. My muscles slackened, and my tongue felt thick and heavy. I couldn't speak.

Dr Minta gave a little cough. He murmured, 'Perhaps it isn't the best time…?'

'Sorry,' I said, collecting myself and thrusting my hand into Faraday's. 'Hello.'

He shook it once, in a professional but friendly sort of way, as Dr Minta continued, 'Dr Faraday is conducting a study, and he's looking for volunteers. I thought you might like to participate.'

If it involved listening to Dr Faraday talk, I thought I might, too. 'What would I have to do?' I asked.

'Nothing difficult or uncomfortable,' said Faraday. 'Just a simple visual test, where I show you a few pictures and you tell me what you see.'

Dark chocolate, poured over velvet: that was how his voice tasted. I wanted him to follow me around and narrate the rest of my life. 'That's all?'

'For now, yes,' said Faraday. 'At this point I'm just

looking for patients who might qualify for further testing. I'm sorry I can't pay you for your time, but at least it would be something different?'

His eyes crinkled as he spoke, as though he'd guessed how tedious I found my daily schedule and how glad I'd be for a chance to escape it. He was right, but still I hesitated. If I passed his test – or failed it – what would that mean? What if it proved there was something wrong with me?

On the other hand, it might also prove that there wasn't. And if I was going to convince Dr Minta to let me go, I needed all the support I could get.

'OK,' I said. 'I'll do it.'

Dr Minta showed us into an empty meeting room, excusing himself to attend to other business but leaving the door pointedly open. Nervous and excited at the same time, I pulled out a chair and sat down as Faraday hefted a battered leather briefcase onto the table. He snapped it open and rummaged through it, emerging at last with a pen, a digital timer and a notepad.

'Right,' he said, taking out a stack of laminated pages and laying them face-down between us. 'Let me know when you're ready, and we'll begin.'

'I'm ready.'

'Alison Jeffries, correct? Age sixteen?'

'Seventeen.' Well, close enough. I hardly even tasted the lie.

'Sorry.' He scribbled a correction. 'Now, have a look at this.' He picked up the timer in one hand, then lifted the first sheet and turned it toward me. 'Here's a diagram made of number symbols, with a shape hidden in it…'

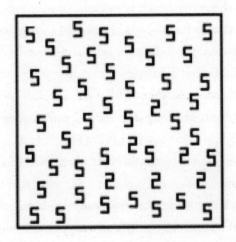

'It's a triangle,' I said. The answer was obvious: most of the page consisted of green fives, but off to one side sat a group of shiny red twos.

Faraday's brows went up. He turned to the next page, which was mostly twos with a few fives on one side. 'What about this one?'

'A diamond.'

'You sound confident.'

'You mean I shouldn't be?' I squinted at the diagram, but the diamond was still there. Was it my perception of shapes or colours he was testing? Either way, it seemed absurdly easy. He might as well have asked me how many fingers I had.

'Here's another,' he said, turning to the third page. This one was made up of 8s and Bs, which looked similar enough at first glance that it took me an extra second to recognise them. Still, once I'd adjusted to the font, the contrast was plain. 'Star,' I said, trying not to sound bored as he showed me the next few pages, each one more densely packed with symbols. 'Octopus. Spaceship.'

Faraday sat back, regarding me with the unabashed delight of a child who'd just unwrapped a model train set. 'Ms Jeffries,' he said, 'You've done well. Very well indeed.'

'Is that...a good thing?'

'Oh, yes. Excellent. I have a few more volunteers to test, but they'll have to be pretty quick to beat your score.' He fingered the unused timer, still smiling. 'So what do you think? Would you be interested in moving on to the next round?'

'What's involved?' I asked.

'Well, first we'd discuss your results from today's testing, and I can explain to you what they mean. Then I'd like to do an interview and have you fill out some questionnaires. Nothing too personal, though – and if you prefer, I'll keep your identity private.'

Nothing personal? Respecting my privacy? This man was like the anti-Dr Minta. 'Sounds good,' I said. 'When do we start?'

'Splendid!' Faraday put his hand over his heart and gave me something between a nod and a bow – a foreign gesture, but a respectful one. 'I'll just need you to sign the release form…and if all goes well, we'll meet again tomorrow.'

'He's gay,' pronounced Kirk over the lunch table, with all the conviction of an oracle.

'What?' I said.

'With a name like Sebastian Faraday?' He smacked his packet of crackers with the flat of his hand, then tore it open and dumped the pieces into his soup, where they drifted like ice floes on the greasy surface.

'Come on. It was fate.'

'Kirk, you haven't even met him—'

'Does he wear pink? Oh, sorry, I mean *salmon*?'

The sheer outrageousness of it cracked my annoyance, and I gave a splutter of laughter. 'Shut up.'

'He does!' The words bounced gleefully across the space between us. 'With tight jeans, and shiny Italian shoes—'

'No, he doesn't.' With an effort I managed to get control of my face again. 'Trust me. Actually he's pretty scruffy-looking, but…'

'But what?'

'His voice is gorgeous. And he's got the most amazing eyes.' I hadn't meant to say it, but it just slipped out. I hadn't meant to sound so dreamy about it, either.

Kirk made a face. 'No perving on the staff, please. So what did he do? Stick electrodes all over your forehead and make you play chess?'

'No, he just showed me some diagrams and asked me what I saw in them.'

'Sounds dumb.' Kirk's lip curled. 'Maybe I should have stuck with arts therapy.'

'He's testing you, too?'

'This afternoon, yeah.'

'Well, it doesn't take long,' I said. 'I don't think you'll have time to get bored. And once you've met him, you can tell me if you still think he's gay. But not,' I added firmly, 'until then.'

When I stepped outside for my daily walk, the rain was trickling to a stop, the puddles along the walkway broken by only an occasional ripple. A humid breeze misted my face and hands as I walked the familiar circuit around the courtyard, drawing deep breaths of the earthy-smelling air.

I'd never been much of an outdoor person before I came to Pine Hills. But after weeks inside those bland clinical walls, I felt as though I'd never take sunlight or fresh air for granted again. Unfortunately I could only go so far inside the compound before I had to retrace my steps, but if I ignored the fence and focused on the forest beyond, I could almost pretend that I was free.

Soon my strides carried me past the windows of the meeting room, where Faraday sat hunched over his laptop, all knees and elbows. I watched him out the corner of my eye, wondering what had brought him all the way to northern Ontario and what this study of his was all about. He seemed to think I had what he was looking for, but what did that mean? The diagrams had been so simple, the images inside them so obvious – it was hard to believe he couldn't find a hundred other patients who could do the same.

Unless it had something to do with my special perceptions, the ones that frightened my mother so much…but that seemed unlikely. Surely he wouldn't have been so relaxed and even happy about my test results if they'd shown anything so abnormal. Or at least, I hoped not.

Still, even if I was dubious about Faraday's research, I was definitely fascinated by the man himself. Not only was his voice amazing, but so was his name: violet to match his eyes, tranquil and playful at the same time, full of shimmering highlights and unexpected depths. And the *Sebastian* part wasn't bad either – all oregano and woodsmoke, with a hint of sensuality that made my skin flush just thinking about it.

But there was something else that drew me to Faraday, too. Some elusive quality about his face, or his colouring, that made him seem almost…familiar. And yet I was certain I'd never met him before. If nothing else, I would have remembered those eyes.

They weren't contacts either: no telltale edge around the iris. I had looked.

*

'So,' said Dr Minta at our next appointment, 'have you finished that essay I asked you to write?'

He meant the one about my childhood, of course. And since I knew I had to at least pretend to cooperate if I wanted him to think I was getting better, I'd forced myself to scribble down a few thoughts. I pulled the pages from my folder and handed them over.

Dr Minta's smile faded to a frown as he adjusted his glasses, and I could tell he was having trouble reading my handwriting. I probably should have written the essay on the computer, but Kirk didn't like it when I played with the monitor settings, and besides, typing always made me feel like I was tapping my skull with a very small hammer. I preferred handwriting, where every loop sent a flush of aquamarine up my arm as though I'd dipped it in a tropic sea.

In the essay, I'd described myself as the oldest child of an unlikely match between a university professor and a miner's daughter, a quiet little girl who'd had more books than playmates until Melissa Partridge bounced out of a moving van and announced that we were going to be best friends. To make Dr Minta think that I was opening up to him, I'd talked about a few social problems I'd had in primary school – mostly schoolmates accusing me of being snobbish, for reasons I'd never fully understood – and some of the quarrels I'd had with my little brother. I even mentioned the time I'd got disqualified from the school poetry competition in ninth grade, and how hurt and disappointed I'd been. But I hadn't told Dr Minta anything that my parents or my teachers didn't know. And I didn't say a word about Tori.

Dr Minta leafed through the essay, making little 'hmm' noises. At last he put the pages down and remarked, 'That's interesting, how your parents met. How do you feel about that?'

My father had been teaching at the university for nearly a decade when my mother enrolled as a mature student at the age of twenty-five. Apparently the irony of a course on Romantic poetry being taught by a shy middle-aged bachelor was lost on her, because halfway through the year she'd decided she was in love with him, and managed to convince him the feeling was mutual.

'I don't think it's important,' I said.

'The age difference, or the way their relationship began?'

'Either one.' After all, it wasn't like my dad had taken advantage of my mom; from what I could tell it was just the opposite. My father was a sweet man, but most of the time he acted like his body was only there to keep his brain from dragging on the ground. If my mother hadn't pursued him, he'd probably have spent the rest of his life single.

Dr Minta looked thoughtful. 'Would you say they have a good relationship?'

I shrugged. Sure, they didn't always get along, but it wasn't anything serious. It was just that my father was permanently bemused by my mother's emotional reaction to everything, and she was permanently frustrated that he was so laid-back. She worried constantly about her children's health and safety, while my father probably wouldn't have noticed if Chris and I had set the house on fire.

'Would you say they were good parents?'

I picked at a loose flake of leather on the sofa. 'Why are you asking me about this?'

'I'm just curious, Alison, because when I look at this essay, you mention how your parents met and had you, but after that you say almost nothing about them. Your father's been to visit you a few times since you came to Pine Hills, but the only time I've seen you and your mother together was when she acted as a witness at your appeal. And I've never heard you say that you love your parents or that you think they love you.'

'Of course I do,' I retorted, stung. 'And of course they do. Just because we don't say it with hearts and flowers—'

Dr Minta's palms went up. 'I'm not judging you, Alison. Only making an observation.'

Stay calm, I reminded myself. *Don't let him get to you.* 'If you're trying to find out if I'm an abused child,' I said, 'the answer is no.'

'Interesting,' said Dr Minta.

'What?'

'I didn't mention abuse or imply it. You were the one who raised the subject. Why?'

I was getting sick of this. Why was he even pretending to be interested in my family life? After seeing him talking to Constable Deckard the other day, I was more convinced than ever that all he really wanted to know about was Tori.

'Because it's the kind of thing psychiatrists like to talk about,' I said flatly. 'Can I go now? I have an appointment with Dr Faraday.'

SEVEN (IS OLIVE)

I paced in front of the library, nervousness fizzing inside me as I waited for Dr Faraday to arrive. Ever since supper last night, I'd been eavesdropping and asking questions, trying to find out if any of the others who'd taken Faraday's odd little test had been invited to participate in the next stage. As far as I'd been able to tell, I was the only one.

Seconds shaded into minutes, and the butterflies in my stomach had turned into biting horseflies, when a candy-pink squeal of delight rippled down the corridor towards me. Faraday had just walked in, and he'd come bearing doughnuts, which made him an instant hit with the nurses. They clustered around him like pigeons, dipping their hands into the box and cooing appreciation. Once they'd helped themselves, he crossed the hallway and offered the box to me.

'I'm afraid there aren't that many left to choose from,' he said.

I picked out an apple fritter, so sweet it made my fingertips tingle. No wonder the nurses had been pleased – unlike the pastries in the cafeteria, these were fresh, and premium quality. I chewed the doughnut slowly, savouring its fruity blue taste, as I followed Faraday into the library.

He pulled a stack of pages out of his briefcase and dropped them onto the table before piling himself into one of the chairs like an overgrown schoolboy, one long leg hooked over the arm and the other pulled up beneath him. 'Well, this is comfortable,' he said cheerfully. 'Better than that conference room, at any rate. Have a seat.'

He gestured as he spoke, and automatically my eyes went to his hands. They were almost as beautiful as his voice; it was easy to get distracted, looking at those hands. And with his sleeves casually rolled up to the elbow, I could see he had nice forearms, too – corded with lean muscle and dusted with fine hairs that in the sunlight looked almost silver...

'Ms Jeffries? Aren't you going to sit down?'

Embarrassed, I dropped onto the sofa. Then I recognised the papers scattered across the table between us, and frowned. 'Aren't these the same tests you gave me before?'

'They are. And now we're going to talk about what they mean.' He unfolded himself and reached for the first sheet. 'As you've already seen, all these diagrams are made up of graphemes – letters and numbers. As the tests went on, the graphemes on each sheet became smaller, and the shapes they formed increasingly complex.'

Complex? Maybe if you were in preschool. But I didn't want to contradict him, so I nodded.

'And yet,' he went on, excitement pinking his voice, 'you correctly identified each of the hidden pictures in under three seconds. None of the other patients I tested came close to that speed, or that accuracy.'

'*Hidden* pictures?' I asked. 'They didn't seem very well hidden to me.'

'Of course not,' said Faraday, 'because you saw the 5s and Ss, or the 8s and Bs, as different colours. But to the rest of the patients I tested, all those diagrams were simply black on white.'

A tendril of fear coiled around my throat. 'What are you saying?'

'Ms Jeffries…' He leaned forward, elbows braced on his knees and one long hand clasping the other. 'Have you ever heard of a condition known as synesthesia?'

Panic snaked through me, squeezing the breath from my lungs. I'd never dared to investigate why my senses were different from other people's – I'd been too afraid of what it might mean. Especially after the way my mother had reacted. But now Dr Faraday and his kindergarten pictures had defeated me, and I couldn't deny it any longer. I had a condition, and it had a name.

Synesthesia.

It sounded horribly similar to *dyskinesia.* Or maybe even, God help me, *schizophrenia.*

I knew I ought to ask how serious it was, and whether it could be cured. But even now, I couldn't bear the thought of giving up my colours: it would have been easier to ask Dr Faraday to take his pen and put out my eyes. All I could do was hope that my condition wouldn't get any worse...but I had a bad feeling that it was doing that already. Hadn't my perceptions been getting stronger – and stranger – ever since Tori died?

'Ms Jeffries?' asked Faraday. 'Are you all right?'

I couldn't speak. All I could do was look at him, helpless terror swimming in my eyes. *Please don't tell Dr Minta*, I begged him wordlessly —

But before I could even finish the thought, Faraday jumped to his feet and strode to the door. 'Nurse!'

It was too much. The dread inside me burst open, spilling into my mouth, and I hurled myself to the end of the sofa and grabbed the wastebasket just in time. Through the roaring in my ears, I heard Faraday curse in a language I'd never tasted before, and then he was crouching beside me, his hand light and warm on my shoulder, saying, 'Ms Jeffries. *Alison.* It's all right, I'm an idiot, I didn't think—'

'What is it?' asked Jennifer's voice from outside.

Faraday leaped up to meet her, planting his six feet plus of long limbs and broad shoulders in the doorway so she couldn't see into the room. 'I'm sorry to bother you,' he said. 'I thought I needed to borrow a pencil, but now I've found one. Never mind.'

If I'd had to listen to anybody but Faraday lie at that point, I would have thrown up all over again. Fortunately, I could live with the taste of chocolate liqueurs. I sat up gingerly, wiping my mouth on the back of my hand.

'Is everything all right in here?' Jennifer asked. She craned her neck to look past Faraday – but by then I'd kicked the wastebasket back behind the sofa, and there was nothing for her to see.

'Yes, we're fine,' said Faraday, and I managed to add with a weak smile, 'Thanks.'

She left, and I slid down in my seat, exhausted. 'Why...?'

Faraday looked apologetic. 'You seemed so tense, I thought it might help if I asked a nurse to bring us some tea. I didn't realise how alarming it would be to you, when I shouted.'

I slid my hands up to my face and into my hair, dizzy with relief. For a moment I'd been convinced he was going to tell the nurses about my condition, and they'd give me some horrible treatment and shut me up in Red Ward until all my colours and shapes went away forever. But he'd protected me, lied for me, instead. What did that mean?

'I'll get you some water,' he said. 'Just wait. And try to relax.'

I closed my eyes and concentrated on breathing until Faraday reappeared and handed me a paper cup. I sipped the cold water gratefully, swishing it around my mouth to get rid of the sour, yellow taste of my own bile.

Faraday sat down again, one foot on the chair seat and fingers laced around his ankle. It was as though he'd never had a mother to scold him for putting his shoes on the furniture – or indeed anyone to tell him how grown men were supposed to behave. 'Do they treat you so badly here?' he asked.

'Badly? No.' The staff could be clueless and insensitive at times, but on the whole, they meant well.

'Then why...?' He gestured to the wastebasket.

'I don't,' I faltered, and then, 'I can't,' and finally, 'I'm sorry, I can't explain it very well. It's just...if the nurses think I need to calm down, they'll give me drugs, and I don't want that.'

'You seem to be doing a fine job of calming yourself down,' he said. 'Which is remarkable, considering how upset you were just a few minutes ago. But there's really nothing to be worried about, Ms Jeffries.' He shifted closer, his eyes holding mine. 'Synesthesia may be somewhat unusual, but it doesn't mean there's anything wrong with you.'

'It...doesn't?'

'Not at all. About four per cent of the population – one in twenty-three people – have some form of synesthesia, and it doesn't keep them from living normal lives. All it means is that your senses are interconnected, or cross-wired, so that when one sense is stimulated one or more other senses respond at the same time.'

'Like seeing letters as coloured, even when they're printed in black and white?'

'Exactly. Associating numbers and letters with colours is one of the most common forms of synesthesia. But there are many other kinds as well.

Seeing sounds, tasting words…'

Up to that point I'd felt like I was lying on a morgue slab watching my own dissection. Now the blood came rushing back into my body. 'So you can have all those things, and it doesn't mean anything bad? It doesn't mean that you're…crazy?'

'Well, some people with synesthesia do suffer from mental illness as well, but there's no direct relationship between the two. Why, did someone tell you otherwise?'

'Not exactly. Just that my…someone I know was really upset when I talked about the things I was seeing.'

'Ah,' said Faraday. 'Well, it is true that people who've never experienced synesthesia tend to be sceptical or suspicious of those who have it. Many synesthetes learn to keep their impressions to themselves for fear of being thought liars – or insane.'

I nodded.

'But there's been a great deal of scientific research done into synesthesia in the past decade or so, and it's become widely recognised as a legitimate neurological phenomenon. There's no reason anyone should be afraid of you for having it – and certainly no reason for you to be afraid of having it yourself.'

I wanted desperately to believe him. Not only because he knew a lot more about synesthesia than I did, at least in theory, but because he was the first person I'd met in weeks who talked to me as though I were sane.

But what would he say if I told him what I'd done to Tori? Would he still think my synesthesia was harmless then?

'Ms Jeffries, I realise it may not be easy to talk openly about your sensory experiences, especially if you've been conditioned to keep them private. But I think your psychiatrist ought to know—'

'No!'

Faraday didn't say anything, but his face was a question, and I had to explain. 'It's just…I'm still trying to get a handle on this synesthesia thing myself. There's so much I don't know yet, and I need more time.'

'You mean,' said Faraday, 'you'd like this to stay between the two of us?'

'Could it?'

'Certainly,' he said, with a smile that sent a ripple of golden warmth through my body. 'But let me tell you what I'd like to do. If you're willing, I'd like to keep meeting with you on a regular basis – say three times a week, as your schedule and mine allow. There are many different forms of synesthesia, and every synesthete's sensory associations are unique, so recording all your impressions could take some time. But you'd be free to ask me whatever questions you like, and I'll do my best to answer them. Would you like that?'

Strange, how Faraday kept asking if I still wanted to cooperate. I'd said yes to him twice, I'd signed the forms, so what made him think I'd back out now? But it was nice to be reminded that I still had a choice, that he considered talking to me a privilege and not a right. It made me want to talk to him, open up to him, in a way I'd never done with Dr Minta.

'Yes,' I said. 'I'd like that.'

'So this Dr Faraday guy wants to keep testing you?' Cherie asked as she, Kirk and I sat down around the card table. 'What for?'

'He thinks there's something unusual about the way my brain works,' I said, and then as Kirk opened his mouth, 'Don't say it.'

Kirk smirked and began dealing out the cards. 'Nice of you to save me the trouble.'

Behind us, Sanjay and Roberto were playing ping-pong at about half normal speed, while most of the others had crowded around the TV to watch a sitcom. I was a little surprised that Cherie had agreed to play Cheat with the two of us – usually she would have been in front of the TV, too.

'You go first,' said Kirk.

I picked up my hand, studied it, and suppressed a grimace. Two-thirds of the cards were red, which meant that everything except the king and the two of diamonds were labelled in the wrong colour. 'Ace of clubs,' I said, putting it down.

Kirk pulled a couple of cards out of his hand. 'Two twos.'

I'd been trying to get over my habit of judging people by the colour and taste of their names, but it was hard when my instincts were so often right. There seemed no point telling myself that the *R* in the middle of Kirk's name didn't make him untrustworthy when the game had just started and he was already cheating.

Still, it wasn't worth calling him on it yet. I looked at Cherie, who said, 'Two threes,' and laid them face down on top of the pile.

'So,' I said to Kirk in what I hoped was a casual tone, 'now you've seen Dr Faraday's idea of fashion, do you still think he's gay?'

'With that accent? Yeah, no question. Only now

I think he's gay and lonely.'

Cherie giggled.

'One four,' I said, then added, 'But you do have to admit he's got incredible eyes.' Kirk shrugged, and I looked at Cherie for support. 'Don't you think so?'

'I dunno,' she said. 'I didn't really notice.'

Disbelieving, I was about to ask how anybody could *not* notice – and then I realised. They didn't see Faraday's eyes as violet, any more than they'd seen the bruise on the surface of that peach. Once again, I was alone with my weird perceptions...but at least now I had a name for them, and reason to hope that they might not be a bad sign after all.

Kirk tossed out another card. 'One five. So how long is this guy going to keep picking your brains?'

'I don't know. Until he's got all the information he needs for his study.' Or until Dr Minta released me, whichever came first. After all, he couldn't keep me here indefinitely...or at least, I hoped not.

'Three sixes,' said Cherie.

'You were in there with him for a long time today,' Kirk said to me, not even noticing her bluff. 'You missed arts therapy.'

'How do you know that?' I demanded. 'You aren't even in my arts group.'

'Roberto told me. Two sevens.'

I glanced at the pile and decided that yes, it was worth it. 'Cheat,' I said, and with a grunt of annoyance Kirk scooped up all the discards and added them to his hand. Which served him right, because Roberto wouldn't have said anything if Kirk hadn't asked him first. 'Since when are you so interested in my schedule?' I asked. 'Did Dr Minta make us swim buddies when I wasn't looking?'

'Ha ha,' said Kirk, eyes fixed on his cards. But there was no humour in his face, and his laughter was all sharp points. Cherie touched his arm, but he shook her off. 'Are you going to play or not?'

She sighed. 'One seven. Kirk, just let it go, all right?'

There was something going on here I didn't understand. 'Do you know something about Dr Faraday that I don't?' I asked Kirk. 'Because you're acting…kind of weird.'

'No, I don't know anything. I—'

'Kirk,' said a gruff voice, and we all looked up to see one of the male aides standing there. 'Van's here. Time to go.'

'Van?' I said blankly.

'*Crap.*' Kirk slapped his cards down on the table and

shoved back his chair. 'Guess I lose. See you around.'

'Kirk, what's—'

But he was already gone.

'It's no big deal about Kirk being discharged,' Cherie told me as we walked to the cafeteria for supper. 'He'll be back in a couple weeks anyway. They ship him out, he goes off his meds, and next thing you know he's jumping up and down naked on top of the bus shelter, yelling that he can fly.'

'So why doesn't he keep taking the pills then?' I asked.

Cherie shrugged. 'He says they make him feel like a zombie. He'd rather ride the emo-coaster than be flat all the time.'

I was silent, watching her out the corner of my eye. How long would it be before Cherie was discharged as well? She'd put on a good fifteen pounds since I'd met her, and now she looked a lot more healthy. Scars still mapped her body, and I'd noticed her habit of biting her fingernails until they bled, but I'd never seen her try to seriously hurt herself in all the time I'd been here – unlike, say, Micheline.

'He was jealous, you know,' she said, breaking into my thoughts. 'I think he kind of liked you.'

'Who?' I asked.

'Kirk, of course.' She gave me an incredulous look. 'You really do live in your own little world, don't you?' Then without waiting for an answer she grabbed a tray and marched up to the counter, leaving me alone.

I ended up sitting with Sanjay, twirling spaghetti around my fork while he explained to me the aliens' secret plan. Apparently they were transmitting mind-altering waves through people's cell phones, using the Big Nickel – the world's largest replica coin, which stood on a hillside just a few kilometres away – as an amplifier. He also told me about a scientist at Laurentian University who had invented a helmet that made people see God, or sometimes aliens, which he said proved that God was actually just a super-intelligent alien being who had brainwashed people into worshipping Him. I listened politely, but I could just imagine what my devoutly Catholic mother would have said to that.

'I have a question,' I asked Faraday at our next meeting. 'If there's no connection between synesthesia and mental illness, why are you studying psych patients?'

'That's a good question,' he replied. 'And I hope that one day, I'll be able to answer it for you. But at this point I think it would be better to keep that information confidential, in case it influences your response.'

Which seemed to be the truth, as far as I could tell. Though admittedly, I was a little distracted by the silvery curves that looped around his words, and the way his voice felt like a warm hand stroking the small of my back.

Still, I wasn't so charmed by the way he sounded that I hadn't noticed a few of the less attractive things about him. The acrid scent that sometimes wafted from his skin, for instance. How his outfit, while clean, never seemed to change. Or the shadows beneath his eyes that suggested he needed more sleep than he'd been getting. Not that those couldn't be explained away as the effects of jet-lag, light packing, and too much institutional soap – but even so, they made me wonder.

On the other hand, Faraday had met me in a mental hospital, watched me vomit into a wastebasket, and still gone out of his way to assure me that having synesthesia didn't mean I was insane. I owed him for that. So I swallowed my curiosity and said, 'OK.'

'Excellent. Now, why don't we start by talking about your alphabet?' He reached into his briefcase, and took out a sketchbook and a box of coloured pencils. 'Could you give me a rough idea of the colours you see when you look at, or think about, each letter?'

I sorted through the pile, and wrote a large *A* at the top of the page in blue before overlaying it with violet. Not exactly the shade I saw in my mind, but at least it didn't make my skin crawl. '*A* is calm,' I said, half hoping to surprise him, 'and confident, and always in control.'

'Is it friendly?' asked Faraday. 'Or more of a distant sort?'

He didn't seem fazed by the idea that letters had personalities as well as colours. So apparently that was normal for synesthetes too. 'It's not unfriendly,' I said. 'Just a little reserved. It's my favourite letter.' I didn't add that *Sebastian Faraday* had five of them – more than anyone else I'd ever met.

He scribbled a note on his pad. I glanced over to see what he'd written, but I couldn't recognise any of the symbols. They were mostly green, though, and gave me a tugging feeling in my left shoulder. Some kind of shorthand?

'Go on,' he said.

I examined the pinks and reds with a critical eye, and decided on a light application of magenta with a haze of candy red around it. '*B* is female,' I said as I drew the letter, 'and extroverted. It's something of a Southern belle, if you know what I mean. *C*—' I set the red pencil down, hesitated between the light blue and the light purple, and finally chose the latter, '—is lavender, sort of translucent and silky. It's shy, and it doesn't have any gender.'

'Do any of these letters have tastes?' asked Faraday. He was leaning across the table with his chin propped on one hand, obviously fascinated.

'Some do,' I said. '*A* tastes like blueberries – the kind that grow wild around here, not the big watery ones you get in stores. *B* is like those candy hearts they sell around Valentine's Day. And *C* doesn't have a flavour exactly, it's more like a very light perfume. Then there's *D*.' I began to layer shades of blue and green, trying to get the right intensity of teal. '*D* has hidden depths, it's sort of mysterious…'

Over the next thirty minutes I worked my way through the alphabet and all the numbers from zero to nine, while Faraday jotted more notes in his indecipherable script and asked questions that showed he was paying close attention to everything I said.

Not even Dr Minta had ever given me that kind of audience, and it was hard not to feel flattered – even though I reminded myself it was all in the interests of science.

'Wonderful,' said Faraday, when I had finished. 'Thank you, Ms Jeffries.'

'Call me Alison,' I said. After the wastebasket incident, it seemed ridiculous to be formal – especially since he'd already learned more about the workings of my mind in three sessions than I'd told anybody else in my entire life.

'Oh, well, in that case, you can call me Sebastian,' he said. Then he caught me looking at him as though he had sprouted tentacles from both ears, and added in a more cautious tone, 'Or perhaps not?'

No, definitely not. Calling him *Faraday* without the formal title was familiar enough for me; I couldn't possibly call him *Sebastian* without blushing.

'You're…the strangest psychologist I've ever met,' I said, when I got my voice back.

He rubbed the back of his neck, looking sheepish. 'Yes, I suppose I am. I'm afraid neuropsychology's always been more of an academic subject for me – I'm not really experienced in dealing with the public.'

I smiled. I couldn't help it. 'That's OK,' I said. 'I don't mind.'

'So how are things going with you and Dr Faraday?' asked Dr Minta. 'Do you enjoy the testing? Have you learned anything interesting about yourself?'

I bit my lip. Maybe Faraday was right, and I ought to tell Dr Minta that I was a synesthete. But I'd kept that part of myself secret for so long, and with good reason, that talking about it felt uncomfortably like stripping naked. Besides, there were things about my cross-wired senses that even Faraday didn't know yet – like the nameless colours that still haunted the edges of my vision, or the cosmic orchestra that tuned up outside my window every night. Until I had more confidence that all my perceptions were harmless, and that there was no connection between my synesthesia and what I'd done to Tori, it might not be safe to discuss it with anyone else.

'It's hard to put into words,' I said slowly as my brain scrambled for a semi-truthful answer. I could lie now without making myself sick, but that didn't make the taste any less unpleasant. 'Just...he said that the way my mind works is unusual, but he doesn't seem to think that's a bad thing.'

'Ah,' said Dr Minta sagely. 'And you found this encouraging because…?'

'Maybe it's OK for me to be different,' I said. 'In some ways, I mean.'

The words were so inane I nearly choked on them. But Dr Minta nodded, as though I'd said something profound. 'Yes,' he said. 'You should be proud of your uniqueness, Alison. You're an intelligent, creative young woman, and you have a lot to offer the world. All you need to do is open up a little more, and give the rest of us a chance to get to know you.'

It was definitely time to change the subject. 'Speaking of being creative,' I said, 'have you thought any more about whether I could bring my keyboard?'

Now that the drugs were mostly out of my system, I could read again, and I'd been working my way through some old favourites my father had brought from home, like *Dune* and *Watership Down*. But not even the pleasure of a good book could make me forget how much I missed my music.

Dr Minta's smile faded. 'Oh. Yes,' he said, and I knew then that he'd forgotten about it. 'Well, as I said before, there is the problem of the cords, so it would have to be set up in a supervised area, and locked up securely whenever you weren't using it. I'd have to talk to the nurses, and see what they think…'

Which was an answer in itself, because the nurses already had enough to do. 'Never mind,' I said colourlessly.

'No, no,' Dr Minta said. 'I've just thought of an idea.'

The gleam in his eye made me wary. 'What is it?' I asked.

'Well, music is obviously important to you, and I would very much like to hear you play. I used to be in a band myself, did you know?'

Always these little kernels of self-revelation, tossed out with a flourish, as though he expected me to pounce on them like a hungry duck in the farmyard. 'No, I didn't,' I said in my most indifferent tone, though my fists had clenched and my insides were spiralling like a drain. I had always been good at hiding behind words, but music left me transparent, and the last thing I wanted to do was give Dr Minta a private concert.

'Perhaps we could set up your keyboard in here,' he continued, his round face alight with inspiration. 'I could bring my guitar, and we could improvise together.'

If the idea of playing for Dr Minta had been bad,

the idea of playing *with* him was even worse. Lightning flashed around the edges of my vision, and my temples began to ache. 'I'm sorry,' I said, 'can we talk about this another time? Because I really need to go.'

He looked surprised. 'Well... I suppose, if you—'

'Thanks,' I told him, getting up and heading for the door. 'I'll see you later.'

Only he didn't, and neither did anyone else, because I spent the afternoon in bed with a migraine.

EIGHT (IS BROWN)

Fortunately, Dr Minta didn't bring up the subject of music again. I could tell that he wanted to, especially at our next session, but I managed to distract him by mentioning that I was missing Kirk, and we spent most of our time talking about that instead.

Kirk had been Dr Rivard's patient (or as Kirk oh-so-sensitively liked to call her, 'Dr Retard'), and the details of his case were confidential, so Dr Minta couldn't tell me where he'd gone or how he was doing. But he did say that Kirk was a survivor, and that he was smart enough to come back to Pine Hills if things got too much for him, so if I hadn't heard anything it was probably good news.

Unfortunately, my concern also led Dr Minta to ask whether I'd been in love with Kirk, which caused me to choke on my licorice jellybean and cough sticky black particles all over his sofa. But once I recovered I managed to explain that no, he was only a friend. A *younger* friend. Dr Minta looked dubious at that, but he didn't press the point. Instead he gave me an extra helping of bland sympathy and the suggestion that I try to make some new friends, which made me feel more desolate than ever.

But no matter how depressing I found my sessions with Dr Minta, I always looked forward to spending time with Dr Faraday – and I wasn't the only one. I saw him at the nurses' station, nodding sympathy as Marilyn complained about her staffing issues; I saw Sharon talking animatedly to him over coffee; I even saw him with Roberto at one point, although they didn't seem to be having a conversation so much as a friendly mutual silence. For someone who was only at Pine Hills three afternoons a week, Faraday did a surprisingly good job of appearing omnipresent.

Still, he spent more time with me than anyone else, and I liked it that way. Especially since I still had so many questions about my synesthesia, and he was the only one I knew who could answer them. In our last few sessions, we'd talked about my near-photographic memory, the way certain sights and sounds made me feel as though I were being touched, and how I felt pain as orange while pleasure came in shades of purple and blue. According to Faraday, all those things were quite normal for a synesthete, which was was reassuring. But I hadn't yet dared to ask him about the thing that worried me most – the fear that my sensory abilities had something to do with the way I'd disintegrated Tori. And that if I got angry enough, or scared, I might do it again.

'What fascinates me,' Faraday said towards the end of our fifth session, 'is that you have so many different forms of synesthesia at once. Do you sometimes find it overwhelming? When you hear a particularly loud noise, for instance?'

For a moment I was tempted to tell him the truth. Not about killing Tori: I couldn't bear to have him think of me as a murderer. But the way my senses had overloaded afterwards, and how it had landed me here. Faraday had always been so easy to talk to, willing to accept even my most evasive answers without judging me or pressuring me to say more, that I could almost believe he'd understand this as well. I lifted my head, met those inquiring violet eyes with my own...

And lost my nerve completely. 'Sometimes,' I mumbled, and looked away.

'Before we go,' said Sharon at the end of our Wednesday life-goals session, 'Cherie has an announcement to make.'

With obvious reluctance, Cherie got to her feet.

'Uh, I'm going home tomorrow,' she said. 'So I guess this is my last session with you guys.'

Sharon beamed, and led the rest of us in a ragged round of applause. 'Does anyone want to say something to Cherie about her achievement?'

An awkward pause followed, while Sanjay muttered something about tracking devices and Roberto studied his thumbs. Finally I said, 'Congratulations, Cherie.'

She gave me a wan smile, which broadened unexpectedly into something more genuine. 'Hey, Kirk!' she exclaimed, and when I looked around there he was, hanging from the doorframe like Spider-Man and flashing his manic grin.

'Kirk,' said Sharon, 'please get down.'

'Oh, come on,' he said, sliding down the frame and bounding over to sling an arm around her shoulders. 'Don't fight it. You know you love me.'

For an instant Sharon's disapproving expression wavered, but she kept it under control. 'You know the rules, Kirk.'

'Yeah, yeah,' he said, releasing her only to spin around and grab Cherie instead. 'Hey, Skinny, did I just hear you got the green light? Score!' But she barely had time to blush before he looped his other arm around me, fingers digging into my ribs as he pulled me against

178

his side. 'But you're gonna stick around, right, Ali? 'Cause I came back just for you.'

'Kirk,' said a cool soprano voice, as Dr Rivard appeared in the doorway. 'I'd like you to come with me, please.'

'She can't get enough of me,' he stage-whispered. 'See you later, my lusty wenches.' Cherie squealed as he pinched her, and I slapped his hand away before he could do the same to me – but he only winked as he sauntered off.

'Back again,' muttered Cherie as we left the therapy room, her eyes following Kirk's bouncing figure down the corridor. 'Seriously, this is the third time just since I came. It's like he *enjoys* it here.'

I'd never seen Kirk quite this manic before. He acted like a happy drunk, but there was a wild, almost desperate look in his eyes. I wondered what he'd done, or threatened to do, before they brought him in.

'His life outside must be pretty horrible if that's the case,' I said.

Cherie gave me a scornful look. 'Right, and my life's all rainbows and ponies? Like that has anything to do with it. Once I'm out of here, I'm *never* coming back.' She quickened her stride and broke away from me, heading for the TV room.

I watched her go, shame creeping over me as I realised that tonight would be Cherie's last night at Pine Hills, and that even after four weeks as her roommate, I still didn't know much about her. True, we'd only had one therapy group in common, and even in our free time we lived by different schedules – she liked to stay up late and sleep in as long as the nurses would let her, while I often went to bed early just because I couldn't think of anything better to do. But I could have at least tried to get to know her. And I hadn't.

I hadn't really tried with Kirk, either. We'd bantered back and forth, and for a while he'd been the closest thing to a friend I had in this place. But we'd never talked about anything important. Maybe Dr Minta was right – I was too reserved and cautious, too fearful of letting others in. Just because I'd had a few bad experiences with people didn't mean that it always had to be that way, and maybe I just needed to find the courage to open up to someone. To let them know me as I really was, the way I'd always longed to be known.

It wouldn't be easy. But I knew where I wanted to start.

*

'I've been wondering,' I said to Faraday the following morning, trying to keep my voice light even though every muscle in my body was screaming at me not to do this. 'Have you ever heard of someone's synesthesia changing? Like...getting a lot stronger, all of a sudden?'

Faraday propped his long legs up on the library table, one ankle crossed over the other. The sunlight slanting through the windows behind him chased gold across his broad shoulders and kindled odd, glittering lights in his hair. 'Well,' he said, 'some drugs have been known to temporarily cause synesthesia or make synesthetic experiences more intense. Is that the sort of thing you mean?'

'Not really,' I said. 'I mean that if a synesthete had some kind of, uh, stressful experience, could it affect them in that way? Or even give them new kinds of synesthesia they'd never had before?'

Faraday looked thoughtful. 'I've heard of people losing synesthesia due to depression, or even with age. But to suddenly develop new sensory modalities... I'd have to look into it.' He gave me a sidelong look. 'What kinds of synesthesia are we talking about? Theoretically.'

Theoretically was good; I liked that. It made it

easier to pretend I wasn't really talking about myself. 'Like...seeing colours that aren't on the regular spectrum. Or knowing a piece of fruit's rotten inside, when nobody else can see anything wrong with it. Or...' I braced myself, and took the plunge, 'being able to taste when somebody's lying.'

His brows rocketed up. 'Really?'

'Sort of,' I said, heat blooming in my face. 'I don't mean like mind-reading or anything. You might be able to tell that someone isn't telling the truth, but not what they were lying about. Or why.' And it had to be a deliberate deception, not just a joke or a mistake. But I'd said enough already.

Faraday frowned, and anxiety flickered inside me. But when he spoke, his voice was mild. 'I can't say I've heard of anyone who could do those things before,' he said, 'but there is a certain logic to it. We know, for instance, that some birds and insects perceive a far greater range of colours than we do, including the ultraviolet spectrum. That kind of vision might make it possible to perceive slight differences in hue that others miss. And it's also been demonstrated that when a person lies they give out subtle bodily cues, and their heart rate and blood pressure are affected. So, if someone happened to have unusually well-developed vision *and* a high degree of sensory overlap…' He ran a finger beneath his lower lip, looking thoughtful. 'Then yes, perhaps they would be able to sense those kinds of things.'

I sat rigid, afraid to move in case the whole scene vanished and I woke up in Red Ward. *A certain logic to it*, he'd said, and, *yes, perhaps.* And he'd meant it.

'Alison?' Faraday reached across the table, fingers hovering over mine. 'What is it?'

'You,' I said hoarsely. 'You…you don't think I'm crazy. You don't think I'm making this up.'

'Does that surprise you?'

'Of course it does!' Where the anger came from I didn't know, but it was better than tears. 'You're a psychologist—'

'Neuropsychologist.'

'—and I'm a patient in a mental hospital. You're supposed to think I'm crazy. You're even supposed to be worried that I'm dangerous. How do you think I ended up here – that I just got off at the wrong bus stop? I *killed* someone.'

An enormous silence crashed down between us. I sat immobile, appalled at my own self-betrayal. But Faraday didn't jump to his feet and shout for help, or even look alarmed. He just regarded me steadily for a moment, and then he said, 'How?'

Surprise blanked my senses. 'What?'

'How did you do it? The killing, I mean.'

'Wh— Why are you asking me this?'

His eyes met mine, serene as a trusting child's. 'Because, to be quite honest, I'm finding it difficult to imagine you hurting anyone. So you're going to have to explain to me how it happened.'

I couldn't look at him any longer. I got up and walked to the window. The clouds outside were the colour of bone, the birch trees delicate as nerve fibres. I leaned against the glass and closed my eyes.

'I couldn't stand to be around her,' I said hollowly. 'Nearly everybody I knew thought she was perfect, but right from the beginning I sensed there was something wrong about her...'

'You don't tell anyone about this,' Tori hissed at me. 'Get it? I swear, if you even say one word, I'll make you sorry.'

It was the night of our high school's Spring Cabaret – our last chance to raise money for the big year-end trip to Toronto. The stage band, drama club and choir had been practising for weeks, and everyone had pitched in to help – from the art students who'd spent hours decorating the gym, to the mysterious technical wizard who had fixed our ageing sound equipment and set it up with professional skill last night.

I was especially glad for that last one, because it made my job easier. Mr Adams, the music director, had asked me to play audience during the dress rehearsal and help make sure every microphone and every speaker sounded right. I'd taken that task so seriously that I'd drawn up a whole chart for our sound technician, Dave – how the main mike had to be at four when Tori was introducing the numbers and eight when Lara sang her solo because her voice was so much softer, that kind of thing. And I'd made especially sure that the microphones for the jazz choir worked, because the medley they were singing was one I'd arranged myself.

The gym was filling up, the backstage crowded with nervous performers, and the Cabaret was about to start when Dave came running up to Mr Adams in a panic. He'd taken a last-minute trip to the washroom, only to find when he came back that somebody had taken his sound board and cut all the cords for the microphones too.

I didn't even wait to be asked. I sprinted upstairs to the music department and flung open the door of the equipment room – only to find Tori crouching on the floor, surrounded by smashed-in speakers and tangled wires. Her upswept hair had tumbled out of its pins, the hem of her angel-white dress was grey with dust, and she clutched the two halves of a broken microphone as though she'd just pulled it apart.

I was so shocked that for a few seconds I couldn't even hear the Noise. All I could do was stare, unable to comprehend why Tori would do such a thing. Not just because she'd been on the committee that put the Cabaret together in the first place, but because Lara Mackey's solo was the opening act, and Lara had been Tori's best friend since seventh grade. Sure, they'd had a bit of a quarrel when Tori started dating Brendan, but—

She didn't give me time to finish the thought. 'Don't tell anyone,' she snapped. Then she flung the ruined microphone aside and stormed out.

I knew what would happen next. Tori would brush off her gown, fix her hair and glide backstage, ready for her role as emcee. I'd be left to report to Mr Adams that we had no sound equipment. The Cabaret would go on, because it was too late to cancel, but when Lara came out for her solo, the jazz band would play right over her. She'd be humiliated, and once again, Tori Beaugrand would be the star of the show.

I'd had enough of this. I grabbed the microphone Tori had dropped, and went to find Mr Adams. He didn't believe me when I told him Tori was the one who'd destroyed the equipment – in fact he snapped at me to stop wasting his time with my ridiculous accusations. But Lara overheard us talking, burst into hysterical sobs and fled out the side door, leaving the band to play without her. Everyone was flustered, and the Cabaret was a disaster.

I managed to avoid Tori all the rest of that night and the weekend that followed. But as soon as I walked into school the next Monday, she grabbed me by the arm and breathed in my ear, 'You are so dead.'

And by the end of that day, as I lay shuddering on the asphalt with Tori's blood on my hands and her dying screams still tearing at my ears, I almost wished she'd been right...

'She started the fight,' I said to Faraday. 'Pushing me around and shouting at me, telling me things – things I didn't want to hear. And at first, all I wanted was to get away. But she wouldn't let me go, and the more she pushed me the angrier I got—'

I was in the moment now, the library around me fading into the parking lot outside Champlain

Secondary as my merciless memory supplied every detail. I'd struck out at Tori with both hands, not even knowing or caring where I hit. It was sheer bad luck that she'd ducked away from my left fist as it came down, and ended up taking a solid hit to the face with my right. I'd felt her nose crack, there'd been a sickening gush of blood, and when I panicked and tried to stop the flow with my hands she'd shoved me away —

'Alison,' said Faraday softly. 'Stay with me. What did you do?'

'I don't...' The lie made my stomach heave, but it was my last chance to escape. 'I can't remember.'

'Yes, you do. Otherwise, why would you think you killed her?'

'It doesn't make any sense.'

'Try me.'

'You'll think I'm crazy.' *Maybe I am.*

Faraday didn't reply. But I could feel his eyes on my back, and the silence between us stretched thinner and thinner until finally, I broke.

'She...disintegrated.' I turned around and sank onto the windowsill. 'The Noise – it got so loud I felt like my head was splitting open, and I could feel it... her...everything, all at once, and she screamed as she came apart but I couldn't make it stop, and I could still hear her screaming even after there was nothing left of her—'

I couldn't go on. I hunched over, and buried my face in my hands.

'No wonder,' Faraday said, with a tremor in his voice that might have been shock, or revulsion, or excitement, or all three. 'No wonder they thought you were insane.'

And now he thought so, too. I'd ruined everything – but the pain of reliving what I'd done to Tori was even worse. I clenched my teeth, willing myself to think of Bach concertos, old movie clips, lines from Shakespeare, radio commercials. Anything but the memory of Tori Beaugrand with her bloodied face and her body twisted in anguish, shrieking—

Faraday crouched in front of me, so close I could feel his warmth. 'But I don't,' he said. 'Alison, do you hear me? *I believe you.*'

NINE (IS BLACK)

I believe you.

If it hadn't been for the gentle weight of Faraday's hand on my shoulder, I'd have thought I was hallucinating. I'd dreamed of hearing those words for so long, it was almost too much to accept that I was really hearing them. 'You do? But...why?'

'I can't explain,' he said. 'Not in any way that would make sense to you, not yet. But I believe that what you've told me about Tori is the truth, and that it happened exactly the way you remember it.' His fingers tightened briefly, reassuring. 'Now. Do you believe me?'

I licked my dry lips and nodded.

'Good,' he said, and let me go.

Dazed, I watched him walk back to his chair and sit down. I expected him to say something else, but he didn't. He just sat there, waiting, until my chest filled up with words and I felt like I'd explode if I didn't let them out.

'It was my fault,' I said. 'I didn't mean to kill her, but somehow I did. And I knew it wouldn't be right to deny it. I was in so much pain I could barely think straight, but I tried to tell my mother, and then the police, what I'd done. They didn't believe me.'

'Even though they knew that Tori had disappeared?' asked Faraday. 'And that you were the last one to have seen her? I'm surprised the police didn't question you more closely, once you were lucid again.'

'They tried,' I said, 'or at least Constable Deckard did. But by then I'd blanked it all out, and I couldn't remember anything. And when I did remember, I knew there was no point in telling the same story over again. So I just let them go on thinking that I'd forgotten.' I got up from the windowsill and walked back to my chair. 'But I don't know how much longer I can do that. The police have been looking for Tori for weeks now without finding anything, and I'm sure they suspect that I killed her, even if they can't figure out—'

'Alison,' said Faraday, 'you didn't kill her.'

The words speared through me, and my head whipped around. He regarded me with an expression at once grave and compassionate, like Jesus on a Sunday School poster, and I stared into his impossible eyes until I felt my own beginning to burn. 'But you said...you told me you believed...'

'I said I believed that Tori had disintegrated. I never said I believed you were responsible.' He leaned forward, pinning me with his gaze. 'You might be able to sense some things that ordinary people can't – that's a logical application of synesthesia, at least in theory. But blasting someone to atoms simply by thinking about it? Where would you get an ability like that?'

'But people don't just disintegrate—'

'No, but people don't just make other people disintegrate, either. What made you believe that you could? Have you ever disintegrated anything else?'

'No!'

'Well, then,' he said, 'perhaps it's time you tried. Let's do an experiment, shall we? How about this wastebasket?' He picked it up from beside the sofa and set it on the table between us. 'You can stare at it or shout at it or do whatever you think you did to Tori, and—'

I recoiled. 'I can't.'

'Why not? Do you need to be more frightened? More angry?'

Couldn't he see that I was terrified already? I shook my head.

'Think about it,' Faraday said. 'It would take an incredible amount of energy to disintegrate even the tiniest object, let alone a human being. Where would all that energy come from? It can't have been inside of you, or you of all people would have sensed it. And besides, that much energy would have destroyed you long before it got to anyone else.' He set the wastebasket down, his violet eyes sober. 'I'm sorry, Alison.'

'Sorry.' It was a struggle to push the word past the tightening noose in my throat. 'What for?'

'Because you've been treated like a criminal, you've treated yourself like one, and it should never have happened. After hearing your story, there's no doubt in my mind that you are not only sane...but innocent.'

I couldn't take any more. I jumped up, ignoring Faraday's protest, and fled. Blindly I stumbled up the hallway towards the courtyard exit, desperate to find a place where I could cry and not be seen—

The sob that burst from my lips was streaked with orange, as though it had cracked a rib on the way out. I shoved the door with my shoulder, pummelled the glass with my fists, slammed a hip into the bar, but it refused to open.

'What's going on?' asked Jennifer sharply. I spun around and she stepped back, palms up in a careful non-threatening gesture. 'Easy, Alison. I just want to help.'

How many weeks had I been here without causing the staff even the slightest trouble? And yet all I had to do was rattle a door to make them nervous. 'I want outside,' I choked. 'I want to be alone.'

Jennifer glanced back at Marilyn, sitting behind the nurses' station, and an unspoken message passed between them. 'OK, look,' she said. 'There's some work being done on the courtyard right now, so how about I take you back to your room, and we'll get you lying down.'

'I can't. Cherie—' She'd be packing, getting ready to leave. I couldn't stand to look at her, not when she was going home and I couldn't.

'It's OK,' Jennifer assured me. 'She's gone. It'll be just you and me for now, all right?'

Miserably, I nodded. She took my elbow as though I were ninety, and together we shuffled back towards the residential wing. As we passed the library I stiffened, but Faraday was no longer there.

'Try to relax,' said Jennifer when we reached my bedside. She punched the pillow into shape, lifted my feet onto the bed as I slumped sideways, and drew the blanket around my shoulders. 'Would you like me to call Dr Minta?'

'No,' I mumbled into the pillow. All he'd be able to offer me was fake sympathy or antidepressants, and I didn't want either.

Jennifer hesitated, then sat down on the edge of the bed. 'I know it must be hard,' she said, 'starting all over with a new roommate. Especially – well. Anyway. But I know you'll do fine.'

It was the longest speech I'd ever heard her make, and the kindest. If she hadn't been so wrong about the reason I was upset, I might have felt grateful. As it was, I ignored her.

'Fine,' said Jennifer, her usual briskness returning. 'You can rest until lunchtime. But after that they'll be coming in to inspect the room, so—'

I rolled over. 'What?'

'For Micheline,' she said. 'She's been doing a lot better lately, but we have to check the room carefully to make sure she can't hurt herself.'

'Micheline?' I sat up, my stomach convulsing. 'You're moving her? You're putting her in here?'

Jennifer was taken aback. 'I thought Marilyn had told you. I thought—' She left the sentence unfinished, but I could see the rest of it clearly as if it had been written across her forehead: *I thought that was why you were upset.*

'Oh, God,' I moaned, not sure if it was a curse or a prayer. 'I'm going to throw up.'

And I did.

Jennifer must have requested a lunch tray for me, because it showed up an hour later in the hands of Simone, a middle-aged aide with a face like a basset hound. She thumped it down on the desk beside the bed, said, 'Fifteen minutes,' and left.

Even now that my stomach had settled, I didn't feel much like eating, but I managed to nibble a corner off the sandwich and force down a few crackers. Then I lay down again, but I couldn't sleep – not now that I knew Micheline might show up at any moment. And especially not with Faraday's last words still seared across the back of my mind.

Not only sane…but innocent.

I should have been happy, or at least relieved, to hear him say it. But right now all I could think was how stupid I'd been. For six weeks now, I'd blamed myself for Tori's death, and lived in fear of the terrible power inside me. I'd told myself I had to get out of Pine Hills, for everyone's sake – but all my attempts to regain my freedom had failed, and now I knew why.

First I'd appealed Dr Minta's decision prematurely,

with hardly any evidence to back up my case. Then when my appeal failed I'd turned my back on my mother, the only one with the power to overrule Dr Minta, and told her I didn't want to talk to her again. After that I'd decided to take myself off my meds, which wasn't a bad idea in itself; but what I'd done with my pills was more than just risky, it was reckless. It was the kind of thing people did when they *wanted* to be caught.

It had taken Faraday to make me realise the truth, but I saw it clearly now. All along I'd been sabotaging myself, because deep down I still thought of myself as a murderer, the kind of person who didn't deserve to be free.

Yet painful as it was to realise the extent of my own self-delusion, there was another thought that disturbed me even more. If I hadn't disintegrated Tori…then who or what had?

Faraday seemed to think there was an explanation that didn't involve me, but I couldn't think of any. And just because he believed in my innocence didn't necessarily mean he was right. What if I had killed Tori after all, and then hallucinated her disappearance because I was just that crazy?

I was still brooding over that question when the

door opened and the cleaning staff came in. They pulled out the empty bed that had once been Cherie's and took off the mattress, examining every corner and cranny of the frame. They inspected every inch of the room, and the bathroom as well. Then they made me get up so they could go over my bed, and last of all they searched my suitcase so they could make sure I wasn't hiding any sharp objects. It was humiliating that they wouldn't take my word for it, but I knew that protesting would only make them suspicious. So I stood back and watched as they tossed all my clothes into a pile and dumped my toiletries all over the floor.

At last the two of them left and Simone returned, bringing Micheline with her. Her head was down and her black hair hung limp over her forehead, but her mouth was as sullen as ever.

'Meet your new roommate,' Simone told her. 'And you better get along with this one.' Then her mournful brown gaze swivelled to me, and she said, 'You gonna stay here?'

It was then that I realised why the staff had decided to move Micheline in with me. I'd established myself as a calm, responsible patient, unlikely to provoke Micheline or otherwise add to the nurses' worries. In a way, it was a vote of confidence.

That didn't mean I had to like it, though. And judging by the glare she gave me, Micheline didn't think much of the arrangement either.

'I was just leaving,' I said.

'Alison, may I speak to you for a moment, please?'

I turned at the sound of Dr Minta's voice – and my stomach flipped. Standing beside him was Constable Deckard.

'I...I'm supposed to be in group therapy,' I said.

'It'll only take a few minutes,' said Dr Minta. He beckoned me into his office, and I followed. We all sat down, and the constable took off his hat – as though that could make him any less intimidating.

'Ms Jeffries,' he said in his soft but unnerving voice, full of blue shadows and glints of hidden steel. 'I've been hearing from Dr Minta that you've made very good progress over the past few weeks. Since you're starting to feel better, I'm wondering if you might have remembered anything that could help us in our investigation.'

I swallowed. What was I going to say?

'But before I go any further, Ms Jeffries,' the policeman went on, taking out his notebook, 'it's my duty to let you know that you are under no obligation to make a statement, and that if you do make a statement it could be used against you in court. You have the right to ask that a lawyer be present, and to call a parent or guardian to be present as well, before you answer any questions...'

'Wait,' I said. 'Are you arresting me?'

'Not at this time,' said Deckard. 'I'm just trying to make sure you're fully aware of your rights before we talk any further.' He flipped a page in his notebook. 'And I have about eight pages to go, so if you don't mind...'

The wry note in his voice disarmed me, and for a minute I almost liked him. But I had nothing to say that he would want to hear, especially not on the record. 'I'm sorry,' I said, 'but there's no point. I don't know what happened to Tori.'

'You mean you still don't remember?'

'I can't help you,' I said. That much at least was true.

Constable Deckard regarded me narrowly for a moment. Then he pushed back his chair and rose. 'I'm sorry to hear that, Ms Jeffries,' he said. 'But perhaps it will help you to hear about a couple of things we've learned in the course of our investigation. One is that we've just received the DNA test results from the blood we found on your fingers and in your ring shortly after you came home on June 7th. I think you can guess what those results are.

'The second is that we have two witnesses who say they saw you and Ms Beaugrand fighting just outside the northwest door of Champlain Secondary School, shortly before she was reported missing. And we also have part of that fight on videotape.'

My muscles dissolved into water. I stared at him, too shaken to speak.

'Does that jog your memory at all, Ms Jeffries? Is there anything more you'd like to tell me?'

Then he waited. And waited some more, while the silence grew so thick and heavy that I wanted to scream. But I clenched my teeth and pressed my lips shut, and at last Constable Deckard said, 'I'll give you time to think about it. And the next time we talk, maybe you'll have decided that you do remember something about what happened to Ms Beaugrand, after all.' He closed his notebook, picked up his hat, and with a curt nod to Dr Minta, walked out.

I sat rigid, my hands knotted in my lap. So the police had enough evidence now to confirm that I'd hurt Tori badly, if not killed her. For some reason they still weren't ready to press charges against me yet, but that could change very quickly – all it might take was one more piece of evidence. And the bitter irony was that even though I now knew I was innocent, I was no closer to clearing my name than I had been before.

'I apologise, Alison,' said Dr Minta. 'I didn't expect him to speak to you quite so, er, strongly. Are you all right?'

Anger flared inside me. I wanted to shout *how dare you*, to tell him that he had no excuse for springing Constable Deckard on me that way. But I couldn't, because I needed him to believe that I wasn't dangerous.

So I pushed the bitterness down, into the black pit of my stomach along with my regret and my grief and my fear, and I said, 'I'm fine. May I go now?'

I made it – just barely – through my Life Goals session and was in the gym trying to hold a yoga pose when Jennifer appeared in the doorway and said, 'Alison, your mom's here.'

I lost my balance and thumped onto the mat. 'My...are you sure?'

Please let it be someone else. Anyone else.

'Yes, I'm sure,' she said testily. 'Hurry up, please.'

Which was how I ended up sweaty and dishevelled

in the visitors' lounge, face to face with my mother for the first time since my appeal. I watched her delicate nostrils flare as she took in my unbrushed hair and sloppy appearance, and I knew I must look every bit as crazy as she thought I was.

'I'm sorry to bother you,' she said, her French-Canadian accent as strong as I'd ever heard it. 'I know you probably don't want to see me, but—'

If she'd made the effort to come here, it had to be important. Maybe even urgent. 'Is something wrong with Dad?' I asked, my heart beating faster. 'Or Chris?'

My mother looked blank. 'No...no, nothing like that. I just... I needed to talk to you about something. Could we...?' She gestured to the chair across from her, and reluctantly I sat down.

'I hear you're doing well,' she said.

That was more than I'd heard, but Constable Deckard had said much the same. Was there some reason Dr Minta had been giving glowing accounts of my progress to everyone but me? 'I hope so,' I said.

'So the medication you're on...it's helping you? You're not seeing or hearing...anything?'

I didn't know how to answer that, so I gave a weak smile. Fortunately that seemed to be enough, because the tailored line of her shoulders relaxed as she went on: 'Melissa came by yesterday, looking for news about you.'

'Oh,' I said, not really wanting to get into the subject. Thinking about what Mel might be doing, or who she was talking to, was more than I could take at the moment.

My mother looked down at her hands, pale against the dark serge of her skirt. 'I'm sorry, Alison. I haven't been a very good mother to you.'

Oh, no. Why did she have to do this to me now?

'I should have taken you to a doctor earlier,' she said. 'Before it came to this. I just thought...hoped... that you'd outgrown your...problem. You seemed to be doing so well...' Her sniff stroked charcoal across my vision. 'And when they took you to St Luke's, so frightened and angry, and in such pain...I realised what a mistake I'd made. Seeing you that way...it was unbearable.'

'Mom, don't.' My voice barely sounded human, it was so rough. But she didn't even seem to hear it.

'I couldn't put Chris through that,' she went on. 'It's too much to ask of a boy his age. No one should have to live with that much uncertainty... That much fear.'

I didn't say anything.

'Alison?' She reached out and put her cold, trembling hand on mine. That was when I knew that whatever she had come here to tell me, it couldn't be good.

'I'm sorry,' she whispered again. 'Please try to understand. I have to do what's best for all of us.'

I wanted to ask her what she was talking about, but my chest felt like it had filled up with cement. I couldn't deal with this, not after everything else that had happened today. I bowed my head, the thin curtain of my hair sliding down to hide my face, and clenched my hands together.

'Alison?' She touched me again, and when I didn't answer, she got up and hurried across to the nurses' station. She spoke too softly for me to see her words, but I knew what she must be telling them: *Alison seems depressed. Isn't there something you can do to help?*

Get me out of here, I wanted to scream at her. *I wouldn't be in this place if it weren't for you. You always treated me as though I were on the verge of going crazy and hurting someone, until I almost believed it myself. And now you've finally got me locked up, all of a sudden you're pretending to care how I feel?*

But I didn't say any of those things. I just sat there, with my chin on my chest and my messy hair hanging down, until my mother left and an aide came to coax me back to my room.

I didn't go to the cafeteria for supper that night. I didn't eat the food they brought me, or take the pills they offered. I didn't move when Micheline came in and swore at me for leaving my stuff all over the floor, or pay any attention when she thumped onto her bed and started muttering to herself. I just lay there, facing the wall, as the sky went dark and the windows filled up with the cries of a million lonely stars.

Because by then, I'd realised what my mother had been trying to tell me.

'Rough night?' said Dr Minta sympathetically.

I shrugged. My eyes felt gritty from lack of sleep, but I hadn't washed my face, or brushed my hair, or changed my clothes. There seemed no reason to bother.

'Would you like to talk about it?'

'No.'

'Your mother came to see you yesterday, I hear. How did that go?'

I didn't answer.

'Did she say anything you'd like to share with me?'

'No.'

Dr Minta sighed. 'Alison, I may as well tell you that I asked your mother to come. I felt it was important for her to take responsibility for her decision not to allow you to come home, and to tell you in her own words why she made it. I hoped that perhaps when she'd had a chance to see you and talk to you in person, she might change her mind, but…' He lifted his hands helplessly.

'You're going to release me,' I said. 'Aren't you.'

'I am, yes. I may not be entirely satisfied with your emotional progress, Alison, and I would strongly encourage you to keep taking your medication. But you've expressed no suicidal or violent impulses since I began treating you, and you've had no conflicts with staff or fellow patients that would justify my keeping you here.'

'So I could have gone home, except…'

Except my mother doesn't want me there, because she thinks I might hurt my little brother. And my father's too weak to stand up and tell her she's the one who's crazy.

'There are alternatives,' Dr Minta assured me. 'We

have a transition house in New Sudbury, close to your old neighborhood. You'd be with other patients in recovery, receiving excellent care and much more freedom than we can give you here.'

Close to your old neighborhood. So I could have all the negatives of going back there – the stares, the whispers, the tense encounters with Tori's friends and family – and none of the comforts.

'I know you've been wanting to go home for a long time now,' said Dr Minta. 'I'm sorry we weren't able to make it happen. But it's still good news, Alison. And once your mother sees how well you're doing, she may change her mind. Don't lose hope.'

I was too tired to argue with him, so I just nodded. I was on my feet and halfway to the door when a thought came into my head, and for once I just turned around and said it.

'Do you think I killed Tori Beaugrand?'

Dr Minta looked uncomfortable. 'It's really not my place to pass judgment on legal matters, Alison.'

'I'm not asking for an official statement. I just want to know – from what you've seen of me – is there anything that makes you think—'

No, I was not. I was *not* going to cry in front of Dr Minta.

'I think,' said my psychiatrist in a carefully beige tone, 'that you are a reserved and cautious young woman who has suffered a great deal and is extremely lonely. And I think it would help you to talk openly about the trauma that provoked your mental-health crisis, whether that was committing a violent act – or merely witnessing one.'

So at least he was willing to consider that I might not have killed Tori. But it was still a long way from Faraday's *not only sane, but innocent.*

'Thank you,' I said, and shut the door behind me.

'Hey.'

I looked up from the book in my hands to find Kirk standing over me. His eyes had lost some of yesterday's fevered brilliance, but his grin remained a disturbing fraction of an inch too wide.

'Did you miss me?' he asked as he kicked off his shoes, flung himself down on the other end of the library sofa and dropped his feet into my lap.

'Dirty socks and all,' I said, pushing his feet off again. 'Where did you go?'

The question came out more baldly than I'd intended, but Kirk didn't hesitate. 'With my mom and her fat loser boyfriend, to start. Then Porkface threw a party for his biker friends and the police came in and cleaned the place out. Mom went off to detox, and I got farmed out to some creepy born-again family who made me go to church with them. Seriously, acting crazy was the only way I could think of to get a break.'

Judging by the taste, at least half that story was pure fabrication. I wondered which half, and why. 'So you...what? Pretended to be possessed?'

'No, I lit their dog on fire.'

I stared at him.

Kirk whooped with laughter. 'You went for it! Oh, man, that's beautiful.'

'Ha,' I said dryly.

'I love to hear the sizzle when it hits their skin,' he went on, widening his eyes like a demented scientist in an old sci-fi movie. 'Yip yip yip yip yip—'

'That's disgusting,' I said, but only because I knew it was expected, and probably the only way to get him off the subject. 'So how long are you back for?'

'I dunno. Until they figure out I'm wasting the taxpayers' money and kick me out again. What have you been up to? Still letting Dr Fairly-Gay pick your brains?'

'No, he's been giving me fashion advice,' I said.

'You like him, don't you? You think he's sexy.'

I was speechless.

'Sure you do. You and your kinky old guy thing.' Kirk snickered, then abruptly turned serious again. 'So what about me, huh? I'm sexy, too.'

This was not a conversation I wanted to have. I cast an imploring glance at the library door, but although I caught a faint scent of voices in the hallway, there were no aides in sight. Why was it that when I wanted to be left alone the staff interrupted me every few minutes, but when I could actually use some help, they were all busy?

'I've been thinking,' said Kirk, sliding over and slinging his arm around my shoulders. I stiffened, but he only gripped me tighter as he went on, 'You and me, we're the only sane people in this place. We should get together.'

Sandwiched between his wiry body and the end of the sofa, I couldn't move. 'OK, I get it,' I said. 'You're hilarious. Do you mind? I'm getting squashed here.'

'I'm not even joking.' He leaned closer, his breath scalding my cheek. 'So what if I'm younger than you. I'm not a kid. I've done stuff you probably never even heard of.'

A bubble of hysteria swelled in my chest. 'I'm sure,'

I said, squirming in a fruitless attempt to get free. 'But—'

'Yeah, I know, you're all uptight. But you've gotta cut loose sometime.' His hand caressed my arm with nauseating familiarity. 'Besides, I've got a plan. You write music, right? And I make videos, right? So when we get out of here, we get an apartment together and go into business. We can do commercials and promos and stuff, we'll make lots of money, it'll be great. What d'you say?'

'Kirk, I can't—'

'Oh, right, the Tori Beaugrand thing. But even if they send you to jail, they can't put you away forever, right?' He nuzzled my neck. 'It's OK, Ali. I'll wait for you.'

He knew. He knew about Tori.

Terror jolted through me, giving me strength. I writhed out of his embrace, cracking both my knees on the table as I slid off the sofa and crashed to the floor.

'What the—' For an instant Kirk looked startled, but then he broke into a grin. 'Gonna make me work for it, eh?' he said gleefully, and before I could scramble to my feet he lunged, grabbed my shoulders, and mashed his lips against mine.

I opened my mouth to scream and instantly regretted it. I pushed against his chest, beat his shoulders with my fists, but I couldn't break his hold. Desperately I wrenched my head aside, gasping, 'Stop, please, no—'

It seemed to take a lifetime of struggling and pleading, but finally the message got through. Kirk let go of me slowly, his face incredulous. 'You mean it?' he said. 'You're not messing around?'

I couldn't answer. All I could do was hug myself and gulp sobbing breaths. I felt violated. I felt ashamed. I felt weak. I hated what Kirk had done to me, I knew I ought to tell someone – and yet even now, I couldn't make myself do anything about it.

'So what is it with you?' demanded Kirk. 'I've been hitting on you practically since you got here, and you were fine with that. But when I finally make a move, suddenly it's not OK? You already got a boyfriend or something?'

For a wild moment I was tempted to say yes, to let him save face. Maybe then he'd accept his defeat and leave me alone. But my wits were still skittering around like a frightened hamster, and I didn't have the strength to lie. 'No,' I stammered. 'I just – I don't want to be with you. Not – that way.'

'So you'd rather be with nobody than with me? Way to make a guy feel good.'

'I'm sorry.' No, I wasn't. And yet I couldn't *not* say it.

'Yeah, I'll bet.' He flung himself back onto the sofa, not looking at me. 'Fine. I'm done with you. Get out.'

I'd gone to the library to escape, to be alone. And then Kirk had shoved himself into that private place and desecrated it, and left me with nowhere safe to go. I staggered out of the room and down the corridor, head throbbing and my skin flushing hot and cold. It wasn't until I reached the cafeteria that I realised I was going in the wrong direction.

But if I wanted to get back to the residential wing – *oh, please let Micheline be watching TV, please don't let her be still in our room* – I'd have to pass the library again, and Kirk was in there. He might see me, and come after me, and try to touch me again…

My stomach heaved. I couldn't do it. Which was why I was still standing in the middle of the corridor, paralysed, when the fire alarm above my head went off.

I'd never felt pain so loud. It felt like someone had smashed my skull open with a sledgehammer, flayed the skin off my arms, and poured bleach down my throat, all at once. Convulsing in agony, I collapsed to the floor.

Not this, not again, not now—

Doors flapped open and slammed shut, like the valves of a pounding heart. Footsteps splattered blue onto the fluorescent orange shriek of the alarm, and the air thickened with shouting voices:

'*Smoke in the library! Code Red!*'

'*Get the patients outside!*'

I was trapped in a kaleidoscope, spinning out of control. Sounds crashed against my ears, lights flashed before my eyes, a million colours burned my skin—

'Alison, is that you?'

Don't let them see you like this—

'What's she doing?'

Drowning, choking, coming apart—

'Call a Code White. We need help, *now*!'

Alien shapes loomed over me, their high-pitched voices stabbing into my brain. I dug my fingers into the wall, struggling to pull myself upright, but my feet refused to hold my weight.

Have to get away—

'Hold her down!'

A giant hand closed around my arm, grinding my bones. Sparks of panic fired all over my body, and in a surge of wild adrenaline I kicked out with all my strength—

Something cracked beneath my foot, and my eardrums rang crimson as my captor howled. I wrenched myself free of his grip and stumbled forward, only to trip and crash to the floor/wall/ceiling again. More hands grabbed at me, pinning me like an insect on a card, and my mouth filled with the rusty taste of blood as the needle bit home.

Home for a long time you've been wanting to go now, echoed Dr Minta's voice in my head. *Make it happen we weren't able to I'm sorry.*

No, I wailed silently as my freedom spiralled away, taking my consciousness with it.

PART TWO:

PRESENT SENSE

TEN (IS VULNERABLE)

I lay on a bed in the hospital wing, surrounded by morning sunlight and the smell of my own stale sweat. It hurt to breathe. It hurt to have a pulse. I wanted to die.

'...another psychotic episode,' Dr Minta was saying quietly just outside the curtain. 'It took four nurses to restrain her, and one staff member was seriously injured as a result.'

'How could this happen?' The voice was my mother's, a wavering mauve pulse of distress. 'You said her medication was working—'

'Unfortunately, that wasn't the case,' said my psychiatrist. 'We found this envelope in the library, when we were investigating the fire. The pills inside match Alison's prescription. It appears she'd been hoarding them for a couple of weeks at least.'

I'd saved up those pills so carefully, ready to drop them onto Dr Minta's desk at just the right moment. That envelope had been my insurance, in case he decided not to let me go – the ultimate proof to him, my mother, and everyone else that I didn't need drugs to keep me sane.

Except that now I'd ended up convincing them of exactly the opposite.

'I've done my best to impress upon Alison the importance of taking her medication,' Dr Minta continued, 'but there's only so much I can do. Perhaps if you were to talk to her, Mr Jeffries—'

'Oh,' my mother sobbed. 'Oh, Alan. Please.'

At first I heard only pained silence. Then came a shuffle of footsteps, and my father stepped into view. He looked so old to me in that moment, so lost and frail, that I knew his faith in me had finally broken.

'I'll see what I can do,' he said heavily.

I gave up then. I didn't even pretend to be asleep, and when my father sat down by my bedside and took my limp hand in his, I didn't protest or try to explain. I just listened quietly to everything he said.

And then I behaved like a good little mental patient, and took my pills.

'I knew you were concerned about the side effects of your medication,' said Dr Minta, when my parents had gone. 'But I wish you had come to me to discuss your options, instead of taking matters into your own hands.'

'You're not going to let me go now,' I said. 'Are you.'

He looked grave. 'Do you think I should?'

I slumped back against the pillows. 'I didn't mean to hurt Ray. I didn't even know it was him. I was just scared.'

'Fire is a frightening thing,' said Dr Minta. 'You weren't the only patient who was upset by the alarm. However, you were the only one who panicked violently enough to break the leg of a 220-pound man. I'm afraid I can't feel comfortable about releasing you.'

I had nothing to say to that. My instep still throbbed orange from where I'd kicked Ray, and though Dr Ward said it was only a bad bruise and not a fracture, it would be days before I could put my full weight on it.

I wanted to tell Ray I was sorry. I wanted to beg for his forgiveness. But he was gone.

'Now,' Dr Minta continued, 'why don't we talk about the reason you decided to go off your medication?'

Because it was all about the pills, of course. It had nothing to do with being threatened by a police officer, hearing my own mother tell me she didn't want me back in the house, or being sexually assaulted by a boy I'd thought was a friend. Never mind all my senses going into overdrive at the sound of a fire alarm.

I knew it wasn't fair to blame Dr Minta for not knowing about my synesthesia. But I also knew that telling him wouldn't make any difference. He'd still want to give me drugs, to make sure I didn't lose control of myself again. And he'd still consider me a danger to myself and others.

Because I was.

'It's good to see you again,' said Faraday as the two of us sat down in the visitors' lounge. 'Thank you for agreeing to meet with me – I thought you might not want to, after the way our last session ended.'

I hadn't seen Faraday since the day he'd told me I was innocent, and now that conversation seemed like it had happened a hundred years ago. I'd spent most of the past week in Red Ward, and after four days and nights in that dismal space, coming back to Yellow Ward had felt like stepping through a portal to another world.

And yet Faraday hadn't changed. He'd trimmed his hair and traded one drab and rumpled outfit for another, but his voice had lost none of its richness, and those violet eyes were compelling as ever. 'I heard what happened,' he said. 'I'm sorry, Alison.'

I didn't bother to ask how he'd found out. That flattering attentiveness of his made people want to confide in him, and by now he probably knew the names and life stories of everyone in the place. A ripe morsel of gossip like me going ballistic in the corridor and breaking Ray's leg would hardly have passed him by.

Still, he seemed to be waiting for a response, so I shrugged. My head felt thick, all my senses overlaid by a greasy film, and my mouth was a dry cavern. Speaking would have been too much effort.

'Alison.' He nudged his chair closer to mine. 'Tell me. What went wrong?'

He sounded concerned. But Faraday wasn't a therapist, only a researcher. Of course he'd been curious when I'd told him I'd disintegrated Tori – who wouldn't be? But there was no reason he should want to hear about the rest of my problems. I shrugged again.

'I don't mean to pry,' said Faraday. 'I just wondered if it had anything to do with your synesthesia.'

Of course. I should have realised. He needed the information for his study. 'The fire alarm,' I said tiredly.

'It went off right beside me.'

Faraday let out his breath. 'I thought as much,' he said. 'Even ordinary synesthetes can sometimes find loud noises painful, but for you it must have been unbearable.'

His understanding was more than I could take. I looked away, past the blurry window to the mist-covered courtyard beyond.

'And when Ray and the other aides tried to restrain you,' Faraday went on in the same musing tone, 'you panicked and fought. But you were wild with pain, not anger. You weren't trying to hurt anyone.'

I gave a croaking laugh. 'Did anyone tell you all the things I did before I got here? How I assaulted a police officer? Smashed my mother's cell phone? Nearly strangled the psychiatrist at St Luke's? Dr Minta says it's psychosis, you say it's synesthesia – but either way I act crazy and people get hurt, so what difference does it make?'

Faraday was silent. Then he said, 'Your synesthesia is exceptionally strong, and you were under tremendous stress. I don't think anything you've done was unreasonable under the circumstances, even if the results were…unfortunate.' He touched my hand. 'I'm not afraid of you, Alison. Let me help you.'

His fingers rested on mine so lightly that I could hardly feel it, and yet that touch sent a shiver through my whole body. 'How?' I asked. 'You don't work here. You're not even a real—' I stopped myself before I could say something we'd both regret, and went on, 'I don't understand why you'd want to help me. I'm just another patient in your study.'

'Oh, no.' He breathed the words. 'You are much more important than that, Alison.'

Warmth rose in my face. Even through the fog of antipsychotics and antidepressants, I could taste the truth in his voice. But did he really mean that the way it sounded?

Faraday drew his hand away. 'I want to help,' he said. 'It may be premature to try and do anything just yet, but if you give me some time, and permission to look at your records, I believe I might be able to convince Dr Minta to let you go.'

'How?'

'By correlating your incidents of violent behaviour to the sensory stimuli that triggered them. If I can demonstrate that there's a cause-and-effect pattern instead of just random psychotic episodes...'

'You mean,' I said, 'you want to tell him about my synesthesia.'

'When the time comes, yes. If I can make him understand that you were in pain when you had those violent reactions, that you were only trying to protect yourself, and that it could all have been prevented if you'd been allowed to retreat to a quiet place, then perhaps he'll realise that he's been mistaken. That you aren't dangerous – or at least you wouldn't be – if he treated you as a synesthete instead of someone who's mentally ill.'

'But it's not just him,' I said. 'It's the police, too. Constable Deckard said they had witnesses and a videotape of me fighting with Tori, and that the DNA tests showed it was her blood on my hands. And then my mother said she didn't want me back in the house—'

'I understand,' said Faraday. 'But I may be able to help you with some of those problems as well. Let me look into it, and I'll see what I can do.'

It seemed too good to be true. 'I don't understand why you're doing this,' I said.

Faraday leaned back in his chair and studied me for a moment, his face unreadable. Then he said, 'Well, let me put it this way. I know how hard it is to be alone in a strange place, and longing for home.'

Oh. 'You must miss South Africa,' I asked.

'Sudbury is…pretty different.'

His mouth twitched up at one corner. 'You could say that,' he said. 'But right now, I'm content to be here. And to help you. If you'll let me.'

I'd lost faith in myself, and everyone else I'd ever trusted had let me down. But here was Faraday, picking up my shattered confidence and handing it back to me. His offer seemed improbably generous – and yet, what did I have to lose?

'OK,' I said, a little shyly. 'And…thank you.'

As I headed back towards my room I felt strangely light, as though I were on a spaceship and someone had turned down the artificial gravity. The discovery that Faraday had stopped being a remote observer and turned into a friend was still floating in front of me like a shimmering rainbow soap bubble, and I was afraid to look at it too closely in case it burst.

But my mood sobered quickly when I saw what was left of the library. The entrance was draped in plastic sheeting, with barriers and caution tape around it for extra security. Not that anyone would want to go in there now. The floor was a dirty snowdrift of ash and loose paper, the only furniture a giant bin full of scorched and water-stained books. What Kirk had started, the sprinklers had finished. My favourite place, my refuge, destroyed.

But where had Kirk got the matches? And what had he been thinking when he set my book on fire and dropped it into the wastebasket to watch it burn?

The only way to know for sure was to ask him. But I hadn't seen Kirk since I got back to Yellow Ward, and I wanted to keep it that way. The memory of his hot breath on my skin, his hands pawing my body, still made me feel sick inside. Not to mention the careless way he'd mentioned Tori, as though it were common knowledge that I'd killed her...and as though it didn't bother him at all.

All my life I'd believed that my unusual senses gave me insights into other people, that I could tell something meaningful about them by the taste of their names or the shape their voices made in my mind. But after everything that had happened in the past few weeks, I didn't know who or what to trust in any more.

I could only hope that Faraday would keep his word about helping me. Because if one more person let me down, I really *would* go crazy.

That night at supper, I'd filled up my tray with lasagna and salad and was heading for an empty table when a familiar voice spoke at my elbow. 'Hey.'

A slow burn kindled in my stomach. I gripped my tray tighter and kept walking.

'Ali, wait!' He tried to grab my arm, but one of the male aides stepped between us. 'Leave her alone, Kirk,' he warned.

'I just want to talk to her, I'm not gonna make any trouble. I only need a minute, Dr Rivard said I could—'

I hesitated.

'Look, Ali, I know I screwed up,' Kirk said quickly, trying to dodge around the aide and get to me. 'But what I did, with the library – it wasn't to get back at you. It was like…I get all wound up inside and I feel like I'm gonna explode unless I burn something. I needed to light something real bad, and the book was right there, and it just kinda…happened. So can we still be friends? And forget about…that other stuff?'

I'd never seen Kirk so anxious – no longer a cocky teenager, just a scared little boy. He must have realised I hadn't told the nurses or Dr Minta what he'd done to me, and now he was trying to smooth things over before I changed my mind and turned him in.

This was my cue to feel ashamed of myself for being angry with him, and tell him everything was OK.

Because that was what I'd done when he ate all my chocolates. It was what I'd always done with Mel whenever she'd hurt me. And it was what I ended up doing with my mother every time the two of us had a fight. After all, my feelings weren't normal, couldn't be trusted, didn't really matter compared to other people's. Even now I could hear a traitorous little voice in my head nagging, *It's not like he did anything that bad to you, you know. You're just being oversensitive.*

But I was tired of pretending I didn't care, that I couldn't be hurt. I might not be ready to pour out my feelings to the world, but I'd had enough of trying to ignore them.

I folded my arms.

Kirk's eyes reddened, and for a horrible moment I thought he was going to burst into tears. 'You've gotta understand,' he said, on a hysterical rising note. 'I didn't know you'd freak out like that! It wasn't my fault!'

'Enough.' The aide held up a warning hand. 'You've said your piece. Back to your seat.'

'But—'

I didn't stay to hear the rest.

'I called my lawyer this morning,' I said to Faraday as

we sat down in the conference room with the long table between us. 'I told him what Constable Deckard said, but he still doesn't think the police have enough evidence to charge me with murder yet.'

Faraday nodded. 'I thought as much. Especially since there was such a brief interval between the time you and Tori left detention and the time you arrived home. It's difficult to imagine how you could possibly have got rid of her body in that space of time.'

'But people still think I killed her,' I said. 'I know they're talking about it. Even if the police don't charge me, what kind of life am I going to have when I get out of here? How can I go back to school, or get a job, when...'

Wait, what was I doing? He didn't need to know all that. I cleared my throat and said, 'Never mind. Sorry.'

Faraday folded his hands together and propped his chin on them, his eyes searching mine. 'Do you have anyone you can talk to? Besides Dr Minta, I mean?'

I gave a mirthless laugh. 'Are you kidding? I can't even talk to him.'

'Someone in your family, then? Your mother?'

'Definitely not my mother. She's been convinced that I was crazy since I was six years old.'

'Because of your synesthesia?'

It still hurt to think about it, even now. I nodded.

'And yet,' said Faraday, 'synesthesia often runs in families. So it's possible that one of your relatives has it as well.'

'Not in my family,' I said.

'Are you certain?'

I wasn't, but it didn't matter. My mother didn't talk much about her childhood, but I knew she'd been an only child and that both her parents had died of cancer, one when she was little and the other when she was in her late teens. And my father's relatives all lived out on the East Coast, so even if one of them turned out to be a synesthete, what good would that do me?

'Well,' Faraday said after a moment, 'if you can't talk about your situation, is there anything you can do to take your mind off it?'

'The medication I'm on makes it hard to read,' I said. 'I don't really like watching TV. I used to play my keyboard a lot, but – Dr Minta won't let me bring it—'

A lump dislodged itself from the middle of my chest and swam up into my throat. I couldn't finish the sentence.

Quietly Faraday got up from his seat, came around

the end of the table, and offered me his handkerchief. I stared at that crumpled white square, my throat clenched tight and my eyes stinging like I'd washed them with soap. Then his hand came down on my shoulder and the warmth of that touch – so clumsy and so comforting at the same time – dissolved me completely. I grabbed the handkerchief, buried my face in it, and cried.

Faraday just stood there, letting it happen, and after a moment he took his hand away and moved back to his chair. It was the right thing to do: the door was open, and we both knew the rules. But in my mind I took his hand and held on to it and leaned against his side, and he stooped down and put his arm around my shoulders, and I clung to the comfort of that imagined embrace until the grief moved through me, out of me, and was gone.

'All right?' asked Faraday, as I straightened up again.

'Yeah,' I said thickly. I put the handkerchief down on the table between us, and he took it back. His fingers were rough and calloused, yet there was a strange elegance in the way he folded up the damp cloth and tucked it back into his pocket. Who even carried a handkerchief any more? It made me wonder, not for the first time, what kind of life he'd left to come here.

'Alison,' Faraday said, 'you don't have to tell me anything. But if you ever want to talk to someone…' His gaze met mine. 'Then I'm here.'

It wasn't the words: Dr Minta had said the same thing any number of times. It was the way he looked at me when he said it. Not like he was trying to imagine how lonely and frightened I felt or how desperate I was to be understood, but like he *knew*.

'I do want to talk,' I said thickly. 'I just…I don't know where to begin.'

Faraday folded his hands together and sat forward, not taking his eyes off me. 'Take as much time as you need,' he said. 'I'm listening.'

ELEVEN (IS INTIMATE)

I hadn't thought I was going to say much to Faraday, especially not at first. Maybe just one or two things, and save the rest for later. But once I started talking, it all came out in a rush: missing my music, hating therapy, longing to get out of Pine Hills yet not knowing where else I could go. I told him why I'd gone off my medication and how miserable it made me feel to be back on it again. I told him about Mel, about Micheline, about my mother. I even told him, so help me, about Kirk.

And still the words kept flowing, in such a blur of tastes and colours that it made me dizzy. I felt as though I were looking down at myself from some great height, appalled at my own lack of self-control, and yet I couldn't have stopped talking any more than I could have held back the tide. All I could think was that Faraday hadn't had a clue what he was letting himself in for.

But he didn't interrupt me. Now and then his brows twitched surprise or his lips thinned into a frown, but for the rest of the time he stayed calm, just taking it all in. As the hour crept on I expected him to start glancing at his watch, but he never did. He sat there, giving me his full attention, until I was done.

'Do you feel better?' he asked.

Oddly enough, I did. Not that any of my problems had gone away, but the ache in my chest had eased. 'Yes,' I managed to say. 'And…thank you. I'm sorry I took up so much of your time.'

'No, Alison,' Faraday replied. 'There's no need to apologise. It was my pleasure.' And with another of his odd little hand-on-heart bows, he picked up his briefcase and left, leaving me staring in hazy bewilderment after him.

It wasn't so much that he'd said it. It was that he'd really meant it.

By the middle of that week the dry mouth, nausea and headaches that accompanied my medication had subsided, leaving me with just the old, hateful fogginess and fatigue. Occasionally I heard voices – disembodied murmurs that always seemed to be coming from just around the corner, or in the next room – but since they had no colour or taste, I could ignore them.

Meanwhile Kirk had taken to leaving little presents around for me – pictures of animals in silly outfits or celebrities in embarrassing poses or vice versa, occasionally interspersed with staff members' old yearbook photos. Where he managed to find a picture of a long-haired Dr Minta perched on a bar stool with his guitar I'd never know, but I crumpled that one up quickly.

I suspected Kirk thought that if he could make me laugh, we'd be friends again. But when I barely glanced at the pictures and didn't return his hopeful grins, when I waited to get my meals in the cafeteria until he'd already sat down, when I avoided him in the corridors and never came into the recreation room while he was there, even he had to get the message. Or at least I hoped he would. Eventually.

Dr Minta noticed the estrangement, of course, but he put it down to me still being upset over what Kirk had done to the library, and I didn't correct him. He reminded me that Kirk was already being punished for setting the fire, with more penalties and consequences to come, and that perhaps I would feel better if I allowed myself to forgive him and move on. Especially since Kirk seemed to be the only person I'd really connected with since I got here, and I'd been such a good influence on him overall, it seemed a shame…

I heard him out politely, and assured him I wasn't harbouring any malice, but I didn't agree. Until Kirk admitted he'd wronged me and apologised, instead of making excuses or trying to distract me with jokes, I had no intention of going near him.

Yes, I was lonely. But not lonely enough to make myself vulnerable to someone who'd hurt me once and might well do it again.

The only person I could trust now, the only friend I wanted, was Faraday.

The room I shared with Micheline was dark, or as dark as I could make it by turning my back to the window and pulling the blankets over my head. But even so, I couldn't sleep. Not knowing my roommate was still awake.

During the day, I usually managed to keep clear of Micheline, except for the occasional group therapy session. But at night, there was no escape. And the constant foul-mouthed muttering, her unpredictable moods, and the way she thrashed around noisily in her sleep made her just as unpleasant a roommate as I'd feared she would be.

She wasn't thrashing or muttering right now, though. She was making a sound I'd never heard her make before: a snuffling, wheezing moan like the last gasp of a wounded animal.

I sat up, tentatively stretching out my senses. Micheline lay huddled with her back to me, the blankets balled up around her feet. Her shoulders jerked in little spasms, as though she were struggling to breathe – or crying.

It was almost easier to believe she was having an asthma attack. I got up, cautiously, and padded over to her bed. Her eyes were scrunched shut, her mouth wide open, but still she made no sound except those horrible strangled sobs.

I glanced back at the door. She wasn't actually causing trouble, so it seemed like betrayal to call for a nurse. But that only left me to try and comfort her – and the last time I'd tried to talk to somebody who was crying, the conversation had not gone well.

I'd never been at such a huge party in my life. Tori's house was enormous, and between the visiting concert band and the bands from our own high school, there had to be at least a hundred and fifty people here. Music boomed from the basement, giggles floated out of the indoor pool, and the kitchen was packed with teachers and parents too busy munching canapes and arguing about the economy to care what the rest of us were doing.

Where was Mel? She'd convinced me to come to this party, but I hadn't seen a trace of her yet. I scanned the living room and study, made a quick lap of the pool, then climbed the stairs past a row of Tori's baby photos to check the upper floor. But all the bedroom doors were shut, and it didn't seem likely that she'd be behind any of them. I headed back down and peered out of the front window, but all I saw was a long line of cars curving away into the gathering dusk. Discouraged, I was about to give up and go home when I heard the familiar ear-piercing buzz of Tori's Noise, overlaid by three female voices all talking at once:

'—kind of friend you are!'

'What are you talking about? I didn't do anything—'

'Come off it, Tori, we both saw you kissing Brendan.'

The last voice, to my surprise, was Mel's. I followed it through a doorway and found Mel and Lara facing off against Tori in the laundry room, an acute triangle of accusation. Lara's eyes were red, her face smudged with the ruins of her makeup. Mel looked righteously indignant. Tori, on the other hand, just seemed confused.

'I didn't even think you liked him,' she said to Lara.

'I only said that because you said you didn't like him! If I'd known you were lying—'

'I wasn't! I didn't like him at first, but then—'

'Liar.' Lara's voice trembled with rage. 'You're such a liar.' She whirled and fled out the back door. Mel gave Tori a scathing look and went after her.

'Mel?' I called, but she didn't answer. The door slammed shut, and Tori and I were left alone, staring at each other.

For a minute I thought she was going to hit me, she looked so furious. She knew I'd overheard the fight. She knew it was none of my business. She knew that my best friend was out in the yard trying to console her best friend, and for all I knew she thought I'd put Mel up to it.

But she didn't move. She just stood there, breathing shallowly. Then she spun around to face the wall, and as her shoulders heaved I realised that Tori Beaugrand was crying.

I stood there awkwardly, not knowing what to do. Sounds tumbled in from the rooms beyond: the bright clink of glasses and the dull crunch of potato chips, Mr Clarke's fluorescent-pink bleat of a laugh. But the Noise was louder than all of them, and as it needled into *my brain, all my instincts told me to flee.*

But it didn't seem right to just walk out on her. I cleared my throat and said, 'Is there…um…anything I can do?'

She whipped around, eyes wet and incredulous. 'Are you screwed in the head? You think I'm going to believe you give a flying—' Then she straightened up and said coldly, 'You really think I'm that stupid.'

I was taken aback. 'What?'

'Like I don't know it was you who's been going around telling people I was a crack baby my parents adopted out of pity? Nice try, Ali-snob.'

My face heated at the old, hated nickname. Yes, I'd always been something of a loner, but that didn't mean I was full of myself. 'What are you talking about?' I asked, but she ignored me.

'What business is it of yours, anyway?' she snapped. 'I don't even know how you knew I was adopted, let alone why you had to make up a big story about it. How would you like it if I went around gossiping about you?'

Where was all this coming from? Sure, I'd remarked to Mel last week after family studies class that I didn't know why Tori didn't just admit she'd been adopted – to me, the difference between her vibrant colouring and the much more ordinary hair and skin tones of her parents made it obvious she wasn't their natural child. But it had just been an offhand remark.

'I didn't say those things about you,' I said. 'I wouldn't do that.'

'Right,' snapped Tori. 'Sure. So what am I supposed to believe now? That you just feel bad for me and want to make friends? And then I tell you what's going on with me and Lara, so you can spread it all over the school and make yourself feel important? Sorry, try again—'

'Victoria? Are you all right?'

We both froze as the door opened and Gisele Beaugrand stepped in. She took one look at her daughter's face, set down her glass on the washing machine and swept Tori into an embrace. 'Sweetheart! What's wrong?'

Ash-blonde hair, ice-blue eyes, skin like ivory silk – even in her late forties, Tori's mother was stunning. But it wasn't her beauty that made my throat close up, it was the protective, maternal way she held Tori as she demanded, 'What's going on here?'

'It's nothing, Mom.' Tori squirmed, reddening. 'I'm fine.'

'You don't look fine.' Gisele turned Tori towards the

light. 'Who did this? Is this girl bothering you?' She turned to glare at me. 'Are you the one who's been harassing Victoria at school?'

I flinched. 'I was just—'

'Leaving,' said Tori between her teeth. 'Weren't you, Alison?'

She was upset, and somehow it was my fault, and I didn't know what to say. The words came out automatically: 'I'm sorry.' Then I fled.

I spent all night worrying about how bad that apology must have sounded, how guilty it made me look. Tori really thought I'd been spreading nasty rumours about her? No wonder she hated me. And now her mother did, too.

But then Mel came bouncing over, and told me Lara and Tori had made up again, and the rest of the party had been great. And when I tried to tell her what Tori had said to me, she laughed it off and said it was just a misunderstanding, she'd get it straightened out.

So I tried to forget about it, and for a few weeks I succeeded. But then Tori died, and I ended up at Pine Hills, and when I tried to appeal Dr Minta's claim that I was dangerous, he'd produced a letter from Gisele Beaugrand saying I'd threatened and harassed her daughter...

For a few more seconds I hovered by Micheline's bedside. Then I backed away to my own bed and lay down again. She hadn't asked for my help, or given me any reason to think she wanted it; and if I'd done anything personally to upset her, she would have let me know.

So I turned my back to her, pulled the blankets around me and shut my eyes. But it was a long time before Micheline's sobs subsided, and even longer before I could get myself to sleep.

If Micheline knew I'd heard her crying in the night, she gave no sign of it. The next morning she was back to her old belligerent self, stomping out to the courtyard right after breakfast and wafting back in on a cloud of nicotine. Technically she wasn't supposed to smoke, but depriving Micheline of cigarettes was just asking for trouble, and besides, her older brother kept smuggling them in. So in the end the staff just looked the other way and pretended they didn't notice.

That afternoon I went to the conference room to meet Faraday, but he wasn't there. After waiting ten minutes and hunting around Yellow Ward for another five, I found him at the nurses' station, helping a frazzled-looking Marilyn with her computer. It turned out he was something of an expert, and he'd just finished solving a network problem that she and the tech support people had been struggling with all day.

'You should have access now,' he said, getting up and holding the chair out for her. 'But let me know if you have any more trouble.'

'You're an angel,' Marilyn said fervently. 'I thought I'd never get my updates done. Can we keep you?'

Faraday smiled. 'I'll be around for a while yet,' he said. 'Ready, Alison?' and we walked back to the conference room together.

'I didn't know you were so good with computers,' I said as we sat down.

'Oh. Yes.' Self-consciousness gave his voice a twist of lime. 'They're a hobby of mine.'

'You should get along well with Kirk, then. He'd be on the computer all day if they'd let him.' Not that he couldn't find a way to get online whether he was allowed or not. I was pretty sure he'd lost his computer privileges after he set fire to the library, but he'd still slipped a printout of an owl wearing a top hat onto my breakfast tray that morning.

'But you're not interested?' asked Faraday.

I shook my head. 'I use it sometimes for school, but

I don't like looking at pictures or videos on the computer. The colours are all wrong, and it bothers me.'

'Wrong? How so?'

'They aren't...' I cast around for the right words. 'They aren't *enough* somehow. You know how when some people first take up painting they don't know how to mix colours properly, and all their pictures end up looking all garish and cheap? It's like that when I watch TV. It doesn't matter so much if I'm watching a cartoon, but if the show's supposed to be realistic, it's just too—' I broke off then, because Faraday was looking at me with a kind of awestruck envy, as though I'd told him I had superpowers. 'What?'

Faraday grabbed his laptop, pried it open, and began clicking away, muttering something about RGB monitors and how this probably wasn't going to work. But after a minute he spun the monitor around to face me, revealing a deep orange screen with a small word typed across it in a slightly greener shade. 'Can you read what that says?'

'Tetrachromacy,' I said slowly, tasting the syllables.

'Yes! I knew you were exceptional, but this! This is amazing!' I'd never seen Faraday so excited. He leaped up and seized me by both shoulders, and for a heart-stopping moment I thought he was going to kiss me. 'Alison, if I'm right, then it's no wonder you can see things nobody else can see. You're a tetrachromat.'

I licked my lips, trying to calm the fluttering inside me. 'And that means…?'

'A tetrachromat is a person – excuse me, a woman, because human tetrachromats are inevitably female – with four colour cones for vision instead of the usual three. That gives you a far greater ability than the average person to distinguish different hues, perhaps even see into the ultraviolet range. And that's why you could see that incredibly subtle difference between the background and the word I typed, even though the whole screen would look like a solid orange square to anyone else.'

The rotten peach, I thought dizzily. The mark under Tori's skin. I really had seen those things. Even without synesthesia, I would still have seen them.

'And that's why movies and television programs – or images on a computer screen – look wrong to you. A tetrachromat synesthete! Do you have any idea how amazing that is? Tetrachromats are rare enough, but you're one in a billion – maybe one in ten billion—'

'Dr Faraday?'

248

'—I could spend the rest of my life studying you and there wouldn't be a moment wasted. The ramifications for information processing alone—'

'Faraday,' I repeated, and then desperately, '*Sebastian*.'

His eyes widened, and he stopped talking. I'd never seen him look so young.

'I'm glad to hear this,' I said. 'It explains a lot. But not everything. And the part it doesn't…kind of scares me.'

Faraday sank back into his chair. 'Go on.'

'If you're right, then I've had this tetrachromacy all my life, just like my synesthesia. So why, after Tori died, did my perceptions suddenly get so much stronger? And why can I sense things now that I never could before?'

The exultation on his face faded. 'I don't have an answer to that,' he said. 'Until we know exactly what happened to Tori and why, I'd hesitate even to guess. But…don't be afraid, Alison. You have an incredible gift. Gifts.'

'Well, I didn't ask for them,' I said bitterly. 'And a lot of good they've done me. I wish—'

I wish I could give them back, I almost said, but I couldn't finish the sentence. Even now my cross-wired senses and overcomplicated eyes brought me more pleasure than pain, and I couldn't imagine living without them. But twice in less than two months, my sensations had become so overwhelming that I'd lost control – and the last time it had happened, I'd broken Ray's leg. To say that my feelings about my abilities were mixed would be an understatement.

I cleared my throat. 'Never mind,' I said. 'I'm just being stupid.'

'No,' said Faraday, 'I am. You're not a laboratory specimen, Alison, and you have every right to check me when I get carried away. It's just...' He shook his head. 'You're so much more than I ever imagined I'd find, when I came here. So remarkable, in so many ways.'

'Yeah, well.' I gave a short laugh. 'Welcome to the one-woman freak show.'

'That wasn't what I meant,' he said.

He wasn't lying. I looked up in surprise, and his cheekbones darkened a shade. So did mine, and then we both looked away.

TWELVE (IS RECKLESS)

I turned seventeen on the hottest day of August, a day reeking of pine sap and screaming with cicadas, while the sun seared the black rocks to charcoal. I came back from my walk around the courtyard red-faced and limp with sweat, to find that both my parents had come to see me. I left them waiting while I took a shower.

'You're…looking well,' said my mother, when I came in. I'd sleeked my damp hair back into a ponytail, and put on a fresh T-shirt and the only pair of jeans I owned that still fit.

'Where's Dad?' I asked.

'He'll be back in a minute. He has to…arrange something with one of the nurses.'

Oh, no. Not a lighted birthday cake and the staff all gathered around singing. On his own my father would never dream of humiliating me that way, but with my mother, anything was possible.

'In the meantime,' my mother said, 'why don't we open your other presents? There's one here from Melissa—'

Who hadn't come to see me again, despite her

promises. I took the package and dropped it beside me unopened.

'And one from Chris, and one from your father and me.' She handed them over and sat back, smiling nervously.

I unwrapped the smallest present first, to find a wooden puck with my initials carved into it. It had been sanded as smooth as an impatient eleven-year-old could make it, and stained to a glossy finish. I ran my fingers over it, and tasted a slow spiral of caramel. 'Thank Chris for me,' I said. 'Tell him I really like it.'

The other present turned out to be a sweater – soft, feminine, and very November, which made my teeth clench. What was my mother trying to tell me? That by the time winter came, I'd still be locked up here where I belonged? But I'd barely formed that thought when I saw the book of piano music lying in the bottom of the box. If I'd thought the first part of the gift was cruel...

My father cleared his throat. 'Suzanne? We're ready.'

'Come,' my mother said, getting up and beckoning me after her. I followed her out of the lounge and down the hallway to the arts therapy room, where Jennifer joined us with the key. She unlocked the door, flicked on the light—

And there it was. My keyboard, set up and waiting for me.

After I'd gabbled thanks and blown my nose and hugged both my parents as hard as either of them would let me, they said goodbye and Jennifer went back to her duties – though not before reminding me to keep the door open while I was practising and to lock it behind me the moment I was done. I assured her I'd be careful, but the moment she was gone I switched off the lights and eased the door half-shut. If I kept the room dark and the volume low, I might be able to play without anyone interrupting.

Picking my way around scattered easels, drama props and cheap instruments, I sat down on the piano bench and poised my hands above the keys, summoning up the memory of my last composition. Melody came first, icy-bright as sherbet; then the tropical hues of harmony, and the dusky tones of the bass clef. Louder notes projected themselves at the front of my mental stage, while softer ones lingered in the background. Holding the musical picture in my mind, I lowered my hands and began.

My fingers were clumsy from lack of practice, and

at first they kept slipping off the keys, spoiling the symmetry of the piece with random blotches of colour. But after a few minutes my muscles warmed up and the song began to flow, notes leaping out of the keyboard and splashing luminous across the air. Confidence returning, I started to improvise – a twist of syncopation here, a shower of arpeggios there – working my way from one end of the keyboard to the other in the sheer delight of seeing the notes again. At last I shifted into a minor key and slowed down, letting my fingers speak of all the emptiness I'd been feeling, the yearning for freedom and home.

Abandoned to the passion of music, eyes closed and body loose, I'd lost all sense of time when an uncomfortable awareness crept over me that I was no longer alone. Someone had slipped in the door while I was playing, and stood there watching me for…how long? I let my fingers fall from the keys, feeling fuchsia all over.

'Please don't stop,' said Faraday. His voice sounded uncommonly hoarse. 'I didn't mean to disturb you.'

'No, it's OK.' I rubbed my damp hands against my thighs. 'Is it four o'clock already?'

Faraday moved closer, touching the A-flat key so

gently it didn't make a sound. 'When did this arrive?' he asked.

'Just today. My parents brought it, when they came.'

'Well, good,' he said. 'Maybe we can use it in our next session, when we talk about the way you perceive music.'

'Is that how you convinced Dr Minta to let me have it?'

Faraday didn't answer, but he stiffened, and I knew my reckless shot had gone home. 'I thought it must be you,' I said. 'I couldn't imagine how else my father could have got permission to bring my keyboard here. Especially after I turned Dr Minta's offer down.'

'He made you an offer?'

'Sort of. He suggested I set up the keyboard in his office. So he could watch me play.' Even now, the idea made me shudder. 'I can't believe you got him to agree to this.'

'I didn't.'

'What?'

'I didn't talk to Dr Minta. I talked to Marilyn. She suggested the arts therapy room would be the safest place to put it, I assured her I'd take responsibility if there were any objections, then she called your father and…here we are.'

I was dumbstruck. He'd actually done that? Gone behind Dr Minta's back and put his own study in jeopardy, just for me?

'But don't let me keep you from playing,' Faraday said. 'We can have our meeting tomorrow. Happy birthday, Alison.' He turned to leave.

I caught his hand.

Faraday went still. His fingers tensed, but he didn't pull away.

'Sit down,' I said softly. 'I want to play something for you.'

I drifted into the cafeteria that evening on a current of pure bliss, glowing with the exultation of making music. Not to mention the memory of Faraday sitting beside me on the piano bench, so close I could feel the heat of his body and his breath stirring my hair as I played, listening to a song I'd composed that very moment, just for him.

I hadn't told him that, of course. When the music stopped, I'd been afraid even to look at him, sure that he could hear my rapid heartbeat as clearly as I could see his steady teal-green one. When he'd slid away from me and got up, the wanting inside me had ached so hot that I'd had to stifle a whimper. Inwardly I'd berated myself, not just feeling more than I should but for coming so close to showing it.

And then Faraday had put an arm around my shoulders and said in that low, delicious voice of his, 'Thank you, Alison.'

Even if I hadn't been three-quarters in love with him already, that would have been enough to tip me over the edge. The sensible part of me had any number of things to say about what a bad idea this was – he was a researcher and I was his test subject, he'd be going back to South Africa in a few more weeks, and for all I knew he might not think of me in a romantic way at all – but for once, I wasn't listening. Because the excitement of being close to him had sliced through all the fog and fatigue that hazed my brain, and for the first time in longer than I could remember, I felt fantastic.

When I'd filled up my supper tray and carried it to my usual seat, I found more birthday gifts waiting for me: a chocolate cupcake from the nurses, a small package of gourmet jellybeans from Dr Minta, and a piece of white paper folded into quarters. I helped myself to a couple of jellybeans before opening the letter. It consisted of one line, in a familiar uneven scrawl:

I saw you with him today. Does Dr Mental know?

The bottom dropped out of my stomach, and the candy in my mouth turned sour. I crumpled up the paper and shoved it into my pocket, but I couldn't erase those taunting words from my mind.

What had Kirk seen when he glanced in the door? The two of us sharing the piano bench? The way Faraday had hugged me, however briefly, at the end? Or had just spotting us alone together in a dimly lit room been enough?

Sick as I felt, I forced myself to finish the rest of my meal and walk out of the cafeteria as though nothing had happened. But even though Micheline managed to go to bed quietly for once, I did not sleep well that night.

'Alison, I'd like you to come in for a moment, please.'

Dr Minta sounded even more serious than usual, and his face held no hint of a smile. Apprehension curdling inside me, I followed him into his office and sat down in the morning light.

'I'm going to come straight to the point here,' he began as he pulled his chair around to face mine. 'I'm beginning to be a little concerned about your relationship with Dr Faraday.'

Don't panic, I reminded myself. 'What about it?' I asked.

'I've noticed that you've become quite friendly with him, and he with you. It's also come to my attention that he's been visiting you outside of your regular testing sessions.'

'He only did that once,' I said, trying not to sound defensive. 'To make sure I was OK, after...what happened with the fire.'

Dr Minta studied me, his expression sceptical. Then he said, 'But you have become attached to him. Isn't that so?'

Deep breaths, Alison. 'I like Dr Faraday,' I said. 'He's been kind to me, and he's taught me a lot about how my brain works. But...' I braced myself, knowing the next two words were going to taste terrible. 'That's all.'

Dr Minta's mouth flattened. 'Alison, I don't think you're telling me the truth. Or perhaps it would be fairer to say, I don't think you're being honest with *yourself*.'

I didn't say anything.

'It's not unusual for patients to develop strong

feelings towards their therapists,' Dr Minta went on, 'or even to fall in love with them. An experienced psychologist would be aware of the danger and make sure to keep proper boundaries in place, but Dr Faraday is young, and I'm afraid that in your case he may have been…unwise.'

'I don't know what you mean.'

'Alison, you were seen together in the arts therapy room, with the lights off. Do I have to go any further?'

If I hadn't known this was coming, I might have lost my nerve and confessed everything. But thanks to Kirk's spiteful little note, I knew exactly where Dr Minta was getting his information. And if it was a case of Kirk's word against mine…

'My parents brought my keyboard yesterday, as part of my birthday present,' I said. I was pretty sure he knew that already, and probably wasn't too pleased about it either, but I wanted to make my story sound as innocent and above-board as I could. 'I was practising, and Dr Faraday heard it and came in. He sat down, we talked about music for a while, and then he left again. The lights were dimmed because I wanted to practise in private, but the door was open. I don't see the problem.'

Dr Minta sat back, and I could see that my confidence had unsettled him. 'Well, if you say that nothing inappropriate has taken place between you and Dr Faraday, then I'll take your word for it. But I strongly feel it would be best for you to keep your interactions with him on a professional level. And to stick to your regular meeting place and times from now on.'

He didn't say *or else*, but he might as well have. And I knew that if I'd won this round, it was only because Dr Minta trusted Kirk's word even less than he trusted mine.

'Do you hear me, Alison?' persisted Dr Minta.

'Yes,' I said quietly. 'I hear you.'

I'd thought Kirk would be disappointed when he found out his attempt to get me and Faraday in trouble had failed. But as he walked into group therapy the next afternoon, he was practically scintillating with energy. When Sharon prompted him to talk he fired out syllables like popcorn, rattling on about how *some* people liked to be judgmental and look down on him when he screwed up, but he didn't care because all that mattered was staying real and being true to himself. Unlike some other people who acted like they had it all together, but were really just pseudos who'd get what they deserved in the end.

I'd heard Kirk go off like this before, so I didn't pay much attention to the words. What bothered me more was the triumphant glint in his eye. Why was he so pleased with himself all of a sudden? Did he know something that I didn't?

I tried to tell myself it was just the drugs making me paranoid, and that nothing would come of it. But when Faraday showed up half an hour earlier than usual and pulled me out of yoga class to talk to him, I knew with icy certainty that my instincts had been right.

'What is it?' I asked. 'What's wrong?'

'We have to hurry,' he said, taking my elbow and steering me down the corridor to the conference room. Once we were inside, he shut the door, took me by both shoulders and looked straight into my face. 'Alison, do you trust me?'

Violet should always be tranquil and self-assured, but what I saw in Faraday's eyes at that moment looked disturbingly like panic. 'I – yes,' I said. 'Of course.'

'Then listen.' His hands framed my face, smoothed the hair back from my temples. 'You're not insane. You're not a murderer. And what you saw happen to

Tori was real. Don't let anyone make you forget that.'

Tremors ran all over my body, and my insides knotted. I wanted to beg him to tell me what was going on, but I already knew the worst: he was going away, and I'd never see him again. 'Faraday—'

He leaned his forehead against mine and closed his eyes. 'I'm so sorry,' he murmured. 'If I could have told you…if only there'd been more time…'

The door banged open, and the two of us leaped apart. Dr Minta walked in, with a security guard and one of the larger male aides close behind. 'Excuse me, Alison,' he said, 'but I'm afraid this conversation is over. Mr Faraday has an appointment with me.'

Nobody would tell me what was happening. Was Dr Minta upset that Faraday had gone behind his back to get me my keyboard? Or was it something else – something worse? I tried to wait outside Dr Minta's office, but Jennifer shooed me away. Then I sat down in the lounge, where I could keep an eye on the main doors and hopefully catch Faraday before he left again. Time slowed to a drip, seconds swelling into minutes. No one came.

After about a quarter of an hour the sheer tedium of waiting became more than I could bear, and I picked up a dog-eared women's magazine someone had left on one of the tables. It turned out to be one of the old back issues Mel had brought for me weeks ago. She'd said it would be new to me, but as I leafed through the pages, some of the pictures and articles struck me as familiar. Maybe I'd read this one in my dentist's office or something? I turned another page, my eyes went to a box labelled 'Poetry Corner'—

And the phrase *'falling leaves, splendid in death as martyrs'* pierced straight into my brain.

It was the poem I'd entered in the school contest two years ago, back in ninth grade. The words printed here weren't exactly the same ones I'd written, but they were close enough. Too close for me to deny any longer that I'd been wrong, and Tori Beaugrand had been right...

I flung the magazine back onto the table and got up, unable to bear my own company any longer. I'd been so convinced my poem was original, so upset that anyone would even suggest it wasn't. How many other times had I lied to myself and others, and never known it?

The aides had changed shifts now, and Jennifer was gone. I hurried back to Dr Minta's office. The door was shut, the lights turned off. There was no sign of Faraday. I kept walking.

'—told you there was something creepy about that guy.'

I stopped short. The words were Kirk's, tumbling out the door of the recreation room just ahead.

'But how did you know?' someone asked him. 'What made you look?'

'I was just messing around, looking for old photos and stuff,' said Kirk. 'I googled him and got his page at the university, and at first it seemed legit, but when I got a couple clicks deep I realised it was totally spoofed. I mean, he'd done a good job and everything, most people wouldn't even notice, but the address wasn't the same as the real University of South Africa site. And he had all these PDFs of papers with his name on them, but when I did a text search I found the same stuff credited to a bunch of other people. So I showed Dr Minta, and he called the university, and it turned out they'd never even heard of the guy.'

Faraday. He was talking about Faraday.

'You mean he was doing tests on Alison all this time and he wasn't even a real scientist?' A girl's voice, ginger with horrified fascination. 'What are they gonna to do to him?'

'Probably send him to jail,' said Kirk. 'They're not letting him back in here again, that's for sure. Screwing around with a teenage girl who's messed in the head already – there's gotta be a special hell for that.'

The floor tilted away beneath me, and I staggered into the wall. Black monoliths loomed up before my eyes and burst into orange flame. Someone was prying my ribcage open, tearing out my heart.

Faraday.

THIRTEEN (IS BROKEN)

'You going to eat that?' demanded Micheline when she came in, jabbing a finger at the untouched dinner tray by my bedside.

I shook my head. I'd spent half an hour vomiting in the bathroom, and the last two hours in the foetal position under the blankets, shivering uncontrollably. Food was the last thing I wanted.

Micheline pulled the tray over to her side of the desk and started tearing into a bagel like she hadn't eaten in days. Her face looked bloated, her hair limp with grease, and she stank of sweat and nicotine, but for once her eyes were bright. 'I hear that Faraday guy screwed you over pretty good,' she said between chews. 'Bet you don't feel so special now, eh?'

'*I think he had some kind of perverted thing for her,*' Kirk had told the other patients, his voice dark with relish. '*If you know what I mean.*'

'Shut up,' I rasped. I didn't care if Micheline swore at me or spat in my face or strangled me and shoved my body in the closet. Nothing she did could hurt me more than I was hurting already.

'Make me,' retorted Micheline, popping another piece of bagel into her mouth. 'Come on, you're such a tough girl, breaking Ray's leg and all, you can take me easy.'

'*I knew it,*' Sanjay had blurted. '*I knew there was something wrong with him, he wouldn't answer the questions or show me his arms, he was one of them all along...*'

'You know your problem,' Micheline continued, leaning back on her elbows, 'you think you're better than everybody. You're not crazy like the rest of us, right? It's all a big mistake and you're so misunderstood, boo hoo.'

My stomach heaved again, acid scorching the back of my throat. I pulled the pillow over my head, but I couldn't shut Micheline out.

'So this guy shows up, and he acts like you're something special, and you buy into it 'cause it's exactly what you want to hear. And he makes you feel so good you'll do anything he wants, screw the rules, it'll be your little secret—'

'*He was a con artist,*' Jill had told me, when she brought my meal tray. '*He knew how to manipulate people, how to win their trust. It wasn't your fault. He fooled all of us.*'

'Bet he's done this before. Bet he does it all the time.'

'Shut up!' I shrieked into the pillow. 'You don't know what it's like! You don't know anything!'

'You are so stupid,' said Micheline with contempt. 'I know *exactly* what it's like.' She slid off her bed with a thump, crouched beside me and went on in a harsh whisper, 'Where do you think Kirk got those matches?'

I raised my head slowly. 'What?'

'Heh.' She bared her yellowed teeth at me. 'That got your attention, didn't it? Bet you thought I hated him. Bet you thought he never looked twice at me. 'Cause I was just that freaky schizo who kept cutting herself, right? And he was always hanging around with you, doing that flirty thing. Nobody knew, we were that good.'

What was she saying? That she...and Kirk...?

Micheline leaned on the desk, staring out the window at the fading sunlight. The malice in her eyes died away, and her expression became hard and remote. 'He said...nobody could know. He said if the staff found out we were together, they'd break us up and send me to Regional. So if it seemed like he was coming on to you or Cherie, I shouldn't be jealous. 'Cause he was only doing it to protect me...'

I sat up, watching her warily. Was this the truth? Or was it only what she wanted to believe?

'He promised me,' Micheline went on softly, running her wrist back and forth along the edge of the desk, 'that as soon as the two of us got out of here, we'd be together. But—' Her hand curled into a fist, and her voice cracked as she went on, 'He lied.'

'Micheline...'

'He lied. He lied. He *lied*—'

The words were punctuated by thuds as she drove her fist repeatedly into the painted concrete wall, blood spidering along her knuckles and dripping onto the floor. Then her breath hitched into sobs, and she collapsed.

She loves me really, teased Kirk in my memory.

I got up, aching inside and out, and went to find a nurse.

'I realise this will be difficult for you to hear,' said Dr Minta as we sat together in his office the next morning, 'but Sebastian Faraday is not, and never was, a legitimate neuropsychologist. His credentials, his references, his connection to the University of South Africa – all were false. As was the study he concocted in order to get close to you.'

He paused, but I had nothing to say. I slumped in my chair, staring at the eight-coloured carpet.

'Alison, I know we've talked about this before, but I have to ask you again because it's very important. Did he ever say anything to you that made you uncomfortable? Did he ever touch you sexually?'

His fingers resting on mine, so gentle I could barely feel them. His hand on my shoulder, too briefly. The way he'd put his arm around me after I'd played for him, and then that last desperate press of his forehead to mine as he said goodbye.

'No,' I said dully.

'Did he pressure you to disclose personal information about yourself, or your family? Your involvement with the police?'

Everything I'd told him had been of my own free will. Because he was listening, because he believed in me, because he really seemed to care. I shook my head.

'Then I'm surprised he was so persistent in coming to see you,' said Dr Minta. 'Because when I confronted him, he claimed he was a journalist working undercover to investigate your case for his magazine.'

'His...magazine?'

Dr Minta picked a business card off his desk and handed it to me. It read, in sleek italic letters:

PARANORMAL RESEARCH QUARTERLY
Sebastian Faraday, Editor / Chief Reporter

There was a phone number and an e-mail listed underneath, but the characters wobbled and swam so much that I could hardly read them.

'I deeply regret that you've been exposed to this,' said Dr Minta. 'I should have been more thorough about investigating his credentials – but all the documents he submitted seemed in order, and I never suspected anyone would go to such lengths—'

'What happened to him?' I asked hoarsely. 'Faraday. Where did he go?'

'He was escorted from the grounds by our security staff, and warned that if he attempts to return, we will notify the police.'

My surprise must have shown on my face, because Dr Minta gave a little cough and went on, 'Without being able to accuse him of any actual crime, it was the best I could do on short notice. However, the hospital board is developing a protocol for preventing such incidents in future, and I plan to assure your parents—'

'My parents.' I sat up straighter. 'Do they know?'

'Not yet. I thought it would be best if I asked them to come in, so we could all sit down together to discuss it.'

'Please don't tell them.'

His brows rose, but behind the curiosity I glimpsed a betraying flash of relief. He gestured for me to continue.

'I know my mother,' I said. 'She'll blame herself, because she knew I was working with Dr – with Faraday and didn't question it. But she'll also blame you and the staff at Pine Hills for not protecting me, and she'll want to take it to court. It'll be all over the papers, and not only will it hurt this hospital's reputation, it'll draw even more attention to me and my family. I don't want that to happen.'

'Well,' said Dr Minta. 'I can see your point. If you'd rather not involve your parents in this matter or make it public knowledge, then I'm prepared to respect that decision. But...what about Sebastian Faraday? Aren't you concerned he'll try to contact you again?'

I knew it. He didn't really care about accountability, he just wanted to make sure he didn't look incompetent. 'It's over,' I said. 'He's gone. I just want to put the whole thing behind me.'

Dr Minta nodded gravely. 'I am truly sorry, Alison. I know you liked him, as did many of us. The staff are in shock as well. He seemed so…genuine.'

Offering me his hand to shake, his long mouth quirking in a smile. Draping himself over a chair with the carelessness of a boy half his age, and then speaking with the insight of a man three times older. Giving me his handkerchief while I cried, listening to me pour out my troubles, and then making me feel like I'd done him a favour by doing it.

'Yes,' I said huskily. 'He did.'

When I left Dr Minta's office, I wanted nothing more than to go back to my room and hide. Every step I took away from the residential wing felt like a heroic effort. But I had to hold myself together just a little longer, because I had something important to do.

After the nurses had taken Micheline to the hospital wing the other night, I'd spent a long time thinking about what she had said to me. Not about her relationship with Kirk, but what she'd told me about myself. And once I'd struggled past the denial and the anger and the self-pity, I'd realised she was right. I had been arrogant, and stupid as well. It was time to stop fighting the system that kept me prisoner, and find a way to work within it – even if that meant sacrificing my secrets and my pride.

The education room was quiet, the long tables all empty. Mr Lamoreux sat at his desk, marking worksheets. I didn't envy him the task. One patient had turned half the maths questions into psychedelic doodles, while another – I suspected Sanjay – had turned the sheet over and drawn up a meticulous chart of all the 'Accidents, Injuries, and Other Surprises' he'd ever had.

'How can I help you, Alison?' Mr Lamoreux asked without looking up. Either he hadn't heard about Faraday or else he didn't care, which was fine by me. I didn't want any more pity.

'Can I use the computer?' I asked. 'I need to do some research.'

I walked out of the classroom forty minutes later with a sheaf of printouts and a headache so fierce I had to spend most of the afternoon in bed. But for once it was worth it, because I'd found all the information I needed. Scientific papers, newspaper articles, forums bubbling with conversation. All of them proving that at least some of what Faraday had told me was true.

I spent the rest of the day going over the printouts, committing the most important details to memory. All night I rehearsed the words I planned to say, willing myself to ignore the frenzied pounding of my heart, the way my insides recoiled at the beginning of every sentence.

And then in the morning I dragged myself out of bed, splashed my face with cold water, and went to tell my psychiatrist about my synesthesia.

'Alison, I…I don't know what to say.'

I'd never seen Dr Minta so flustered. He pulled off his glasses and rubbed his eyes, then returned to blinking at the articles I'd handed him. 'So this… sensitivity of yours…you claim that's the reason for your violent episodes? That you simply became… over-stimulated?'

'My synesthesia gets a lot more intense when I'm under pressure,' I said. It wasn't the whole truth, but it was as close to it as I could expect him to understand. 'The fight I had with Tori…it was pretty emotional, and we'd been building up to it for a long time. I felt guilty for hitting her, and I was scared I'd get in trouble, and by the time I got home I was so upset that every little thing set me off. Sudden noises, bright lights, people touching me or even just talking to me – it all hurt so much, I would have done anything to make it stop. And when I couldn't get the peace and quiet I needed to calm down, my brain just sort of… short-circuited, I guess.'

He seemed to be listening, so I went on to explain all the stresses and upsets that had led up to my latest attack, including what Kirk had done to me in the library right before he set the fire. The only detail I left out was that Micheline had given Kirk the matches. I owed her too much to betray her confidence like that.

When I was finished Dr Minta sat back in his chair, rubbing a knuckle across his moustache. 'You've given me a lot to consider, Alison. Especially now that I know about Kirk's behaviour… That matter will certainly have to be addressed. You understand that I can't keep something like that confidential? That I'm required to report any incidents of sexual harassment or abuse between patients that come to my attention?'

'I understand,' I said.

Slowly Dr Minta leafed through the printouts on his desk. 'I'd like to keep these and go over them in more detail,' he said. 'I had heard of synesthesia before, but never realised it could be so debilitating. You say you've had this condition all your life? Why didn't you mention it to me before?'

'For a long time I didn't know what it was,' I

said. 'I was afraid it might mean there was something wrong with me. Especially after the way my mother reacted.'

'Of course,' said Dr Minta. 'That would make anyone cautious. But why do you think she was so upset when she realised you were seeing sounds? What made her so quick to assume that you were mentally ill?'

'I don't know,' I said.

'Perhaps you should ask her,' Dr Minta said, in a neutral tone that made me suspect he'd already guessed the answer. 'In any case, I think it would be beneficial to arrange some family counselling sessions with you and your parents, so we can share this information with them.'

I would rather have swallowed a live puffer fish and chased it down with broken glass, but I could hardly say no. Not when I'd sworn to myself that I'd do whatever it took to get out of this place.

'OK,' I said. 'But can I ask you something? Now that you know why I reacted the way I did, and that it won't happen again unless I get really stressed out, do you think I might be allowed to…' I stopped just short of saying *go home*, swallowed and went on, '…to leave Pine Hills?'

Dr Minta looked pained. 'Alison, I don't want to mislead you. What you've just told me goes a long way towards helping me to understand your situation and your psychological needs, but I still have reason to be concerned about your mental wellbeing. I believe it would be premature—'

'I don't mean for good,' I said. 'Just for a day or two. After everything that's happened... I think it would help to get away.'

'Ah, yes.' He relaxed. 'Well, I have to say that I'm impressed by how well you've responded to this difficult situation. I'm not sure I can convince your mother to allow you to come home for the weekend, but I think I can arrange for you to join one of our group outings into town, if all else fails.'

A group outing would mean maybe four hours away from the hospital, all of it supervised. It probably wouldn't be enough – but I'd take what I could get. 'Thank you,' I said, and rose to leave.

'Alison – just one more question, if you don't mind.'

'Yes?' I said.

'You mentioned earlier that you'd fought with Tori just before she disappeared. What else do you remember?'

I should have known this was coming. Keeping my back to him I said carefully, 'What I remember… doesn't make any sense. One minute she was there, and the next she was gone.'

'Do you think it's possible,' said Dr Minta, 'that you might have killed her, by accident perhaps, and blocked the memory out?'

You're not insane, whispered Faraday's voice in my mind. *You're not a murderer.*

Even now, part of me believed him. But I'd believed I'd written that poem about the martyred leaves, too.

'It's possible,' I said. 'And if the police find some clear evidence that points to my guilt, then I'll have to accept that. But I never meant to kill Tori. And right now, I don't know how I could have.'

My psychiatrist toyed with his pen, his expression distant. Then he said, 'Thank you, Alison. You may go.'

I was halfway through lunch when Micheline dropped her tray onto the table beside me, dragged out a chair and threw herself into it. She tossed the black flag of hair out of her eyes and said in her throaty crow's voice, 'Hey, stupid.'

I watched her sidelong, not sure what to expect. Her knuckles were swathed in gauze, but apart from that she seemed more comfortable and even happy than I'd ever seen her.

'Tell you something,' she said as she stabbed a forkful of fries. 'First time I saw you, I thought you were a narc. That whole *I'm-so-quiet-and-well-behaved* thing, you know? Like you weren't even trying to fake being schizo, just hanging out in Red Ward so you could spy on us.'

'But you don't think that any more?' I asked.

'Nah. You're as screwed up as the rest of us. Just better at faking sane.'

Not long ago, I would have been horrified by those words. I'd grown up believing that mental illness was one of the worst things that could ever happen to anyone, and when I'd first met Micheline in Red Ward, she'd seemed as sinister and unknowable as one of Sanjay's aliens. But now that I'd actually talked to her – or at least listened a little – I'd realised she wasn't so different from me after all. Just another confused, hurting teenage girl, trying to make sense of the world as best she could.

'Gee, thanks,' I said.

She snorted. 'Watch your smart mouth, princess. You start getting full of yourself again, I'll beat the crap out of you.' But there was no malice in her tone, and she finished the sentence with a flash of her uneven teeth.

Tentatively, I smiled back.

'Alison?' Jennifer stuck her head out the door into the courtyard, where I was sitting with Micheline as she finished her afternoon cigarette. 'Dr Minta wants to see you.'

I got up quickly and came inside. As I walked into the office my psychiatrist rose to greet me, looking pleased with himself. 'I have good news,' he said. 'I've just had a call from your mother.'

'You mean…she called you?' I was startled. 'What about?'

'It appears she's had something of a change of heart,' he said. 'She asked me if there'd be any chance of bringing you home for the weekend. So I've made arrangements for her to pick you up later this afternoon.'

Home? Tonight? Even my wildest hopes hadn't gone this far. I fumbled for a chair and sat down, no longer sure that my legs would hold me.

'However,' said Dr Minta, holding up a cautioning hand, 'this privilege comes with a few conditions. You'll need to stay on your medication schedule, and

I've advised your mother that you should remain in the house and keep visitors to a minimum, to avoid any undue shock or stress. And we'll expect you back here Sunday evening. All right?'

It was more than all right – it was incredible. 'Yes,' I said weakly. 'Yes, that's fine.'

Dr Minta's round face softened. 'I'm glad you decided to confide in me, Alison. This is a big step forward, and I know you won't regret it. If this weekend goes well, and your mother seems happy with the result…well, we can talk about that on Monday. But let's just say I'd consider it a very good sign.' He shook my hand. 'Good luck.'

'You can't go,' said Sanjay fretfully, trailing after me as I carried my suitcase out of the residential wing. 'It's not safe. They'll take you away and put their mark on you, and then you won't be Alison any more.'

Ever since Kirk had been disciplined – all privileges revoked, and an aide assigned to follow him wherever he went – Sanjay had been wandering around like an abandoned puppy. But now he'd latched onto me, not even Micheline's warning glare could discourage him. 'He's going to find you,' he insisted. 'He knows where you live.'

'Get lost, spaceman,' Micheline told him. Then she turned to me and said, 'You gonna be OK?'

'I think so.' But my voice wavered as I said it, because I'd just realised that Sanjay was right: Faraday *did* know where I lived. He'd seen it in my records – the ones I'd given him permission to look over, back when I still believed he was a real neuropsychologist.

Micheline's eyes narrowed. 'Yeah, well, you better not do anything stupid. You know what I mean.'

I did, but I wasn't sure that was a promise I could make. 'I'll be careful,' I said.

Sanjay fumbled in the pocket of his slacks. 'You need this,' he said, thrusting a scrap of paper at me. 'It has the words that will stop them.'

I unfolded the note and looked at it. It read:

KLAATU BARADA NIKTO

A pang went through me – not pity this time, but sympathy. I remembered the poem I thought I'd written, and how hard it had been to accept that I hadn't. And what a scary thing it was to face the possibility that what I perceived as reality might not be real at all. I folded up the page carefully and tucked it into my jeans.

'Thank you, Sanjay,' I said.

*

I thought my mother might be annoyed when I emerged from the hospital lugging my keyboard as well as my suitcase, but I couldn't bear to leave it behind. There were just too many emotions inside me needing to be turned into music, especially now.

Fortunately, she didn't object. She even came around to open the back door of the SUV and help me slide it in. And when I started to get in after it, she put a hand on my arm and said, 'Why don't you sit up front?'

She *wanted* me beside her? That didn't seem like my mother at all. Feeling like I'd just had a glimpse into some alternate universe, I climbed up into the passenger seat and buckled myself in.

All my life I'd lived in the Sudbury Basin, one of the largest meteorite craters in the world; and most of that time I'd wished I'd been born somewhere else. But after being locked up in Pine Hills for nearly two months, those rugged hillsides, scattered lakes, and stands of twisted pine seemed almost unbearably beautiful to me. As we emerged from the forest and turned onto the highway I found myself pressing my hands and face to the window, reaching out with all my senses to hear that landscape, taste its contours, smell its hues.

'Alison?' My mother's voice was tentative, the merest brush of lavender across my mind. She drew a ragged breath, hands clenching around the wheel. 'I...I need to apologise. To you.'

'Mom...'

'Please. Let me finish.' She shot a nervous glance into the mirror at the eighteen-wheeler rumbling up behind us and accelerated a little. 'For a long time now, I've been afraid that...I mean, I've been concerned about you. About your mind. Because of that, I haven't always been there for you when you needed me, and... I realise now that I was wrong.'

Who was this alien inside my mother's skin? I'd never heard her apologise like this in my life. She'd obviously prepared her speech in advance, but her red-rimmed eyes showed that the emotion behind it was real.

'You see,' she went on tremulously, 'when I was young—'

'Mom, the road!'

She gasped and swung the car back over the yellow line, then pulled off onto the shoulder. The truck roared past, rattling us in its wake.

'I'm sorry,' she said to me. 'Are you all right?'

I uncurled my fingers from the armrests and forced

myself to breathe. 'I – yes. I'm fine. Go on.'

My mother folded her hands along the top of the steering wheel, her dark eyes haunted. 'My mother, your *grandmère*...she was not right in her mind. And once your *grandpère* died, and it was only the two of us... I did everything I could to keep her happy, but it was never enough. Whenever I came home from school, or from being out with my friends, she accused me of all kinds of things, terrible things. The angels had spoken to her, she said, and told her my sins...and now I had to be punished, to save my soul. So she would beat me with her hands, or with my father's belt, or with the handle of her broom, until I cried and promised to repent.'

I sat motionless, stunned by her words. I'd known my grandmother had been strict and even harsh at times, but this was worse than I'd ever imagined.

My mother cleared her throat and went on, 'And even when she wasn't hearing voices, she seemed to live in a different world. She talked of shapes and colours in the air that I could never see. She said she could smell food burning, even when there was nothing in the oven or on the stove. She commanded me not to say certain words to her, because they had a bad taste...she especially hated the sound of English, so

I was never allowed to speak it in her presence.

'To me it seemed that all these things were part of her madness, and that if she would only listen to the doctor and take the pills he gave her, the voices and the visions, the bad smells and tastes, would all go away. But she refused to get help, and she became worse and worse, until—'

She broke off with a sob, and covered her face with her hands. For a long, dreadful moment she wept with the messy abandon of a child, while I scrambled for tissues in the glove compartment and thrust them at her, not knowing what else to do. But at last she drew a shuddering breath, wiped her eyes, and sat up again.

'She spent two years in the hospital,' she went on, her voice so soft that I could barely taste it. 'Then the cancer took her, and she passed away. But the doctor told me that her illness – schizophrenia – runs in families, and that if I ever had children, they might have it too...'

I stared out at the darkening sky, feeling cold all over. No wonder all the doctors who treated me had been sure I was mentally ill. Not just because of my violent reaction to Tori's death or the bizarre-sounding things I'd babbled as the police were taking me away, but because they'd talked to my mother and found out her family history. And with such an obvious explanation for my behaviour in front of them, why should they even consider anything else?

'Do you understand now?' she pleaded. 'Why I was so afraid? Why I did…the things I did?'

I understood, all right. For all that I'd prided myself on being nothing like my mother, I'd followed the same pattern of fear and denial and avoidance as she had. 'Yeah,' I said.

'I'm so sorry,' she whispered. 'I know I've hurt you…disappointed you…in so many ways. I don't expect you to forgive me, but…I want you to know that I love you, Alison. And that if I could turn back time, and change everything that's happened between us…I would.'

I snatched up a tissue and crumpled it against my mouth, breathing hard. Then I dropped my head against my mother's shoulder, and she put her arms around me and held me tight.

We stayed like that for a long time.

FOURTEEN (IS SEDUCTIVE)

'There's one thing I don't understand,' I said to my mother, when we were back on the highway again. The sun was low in the sky now, melting towards the horizon like a scoop of orange sherbet, and I flipped the shade down to protect my eyes. 'What made you realise you were wrong about me? I mean, I've done some pretty crazy-seeming things, and Dr Minta still thinks…'

She glanced at me, surprised. 'You mean he didn't tell you?'

'Who didn't tell me what?'

'Dr Faraday. When he called yesterday, I assumed he'd talked it over with you first. He was the one who told us about your…what's it called again?'

'Synesthesia?'

'Yes. He told us that you were tremendously sensitive, even for a…for someone with your condition. He explained why you'd been so upset when you came home that day after school, and – and afterwards, and why you reacted so violently to the fire alarm. He seemed to have an answer for

290

everything… I was sorry to see him go.'

'See him? You mean – he came to the house?'

She nodded distractedly, her eyes fixed on the road. 'Last night. He spent more than an hour sitting in our living room, talking with us. It was such a relief to meet someone who knew so much about what had happened, and thought so highly of you. It's too bad he's going back to South Africa.'

My breath caught in my throat. 'He is? Did he say when?'

'A few days, I think. I suppose that now he's done with his study, he's anxious to get back home.'

I clenched the damp tissue in my hand. If she was right, then I had even less time to carry out my plan than I'd thought.

'Yeah,' I said. 'I'm looking forward to getting home, too.'

'Ali!'

Chris exploded out the door of the basement and hurled himself at me so enthusiastically he nearly knocked me over. Mom made an incoherent noise of protest, but I only laughed and hugged my little brother back. 'Hey there, Puck.'

He dug his elbow into my ribs. I stepped on his toe.

Proper sibling relations re-established, we broke off and he flopped onto the couch. 'So how's the loony bin?'

'Chris!' exclaimed my mother.

'Honestly? It sucks,' I said. 'And the food's no good either. You'd better not have been messing up my room while I was gone.'

He just grinned.

The stairs creaked, shooting grey arrows across my vision, as my father stepped into view. He greeted me with a hesitant smile, but didn't move until I took his bony hands in both of mine, and stretched up on tiptoe to kiss his cheek.

'It's OK, Dad,' I whispered. 'Everything's going to be OK.'

And for the moment, I almost believed it.

'I told Mel you were coming home this weekend,' said Chris, reaching across the table to spear another slice of roast beef. 'She said you should call her.'

Considering that she hadn't come to see me in over six weeks, I was surprised she had the nerve. 'Has she been asking about me a lot?' I asked.

'Right after you left she did, yeah. Not so much lately. Hey, does anybody want more potatoes?'

'Go wild,' I said, handing him the bowl.

'If you'd like to ask Melissa to come over,' said my mother, 'I don't think Dr Minta would mind.'

I nudged a carrot around with my fork. 'OK. Maybe I'll call later.'

But it wasn't Mel I was planning to call.

Dessert was chocolate silk pie, my favourite, but I was too full of roast beef and nervous anticipation to enjoy it. And when the dishes were cleared away, we only stayed around the table a few minutes before the usual gravitational forces pulled my family apart – my father to his study, my mother to the kitchen, and my brother to play road hockey with his friends outside. It was hard not to feel a little wistful about that, but it would have been awkward if they'd all hung around trying to make conversation for my sake. Besides, I'd have plenty of time to spend with them tomorrow.

It felt unreal to be back in this house, after I'd dreamed of coming home so long. As I climbed the stairs to my bedroom, part of me was convinced that any second now I'd wake up and find myself back at Pine Hills, a victim of some drug-induced delusion. But I opened the door and there it was, just as I remembered it – the desk beneath the window, the bookshelf crammed with paperbacks and sheet music, the single bed neatly covered with the same quilt I'd been hiding under when the police came in.

I sat down on the bed and opened the drawer of my night table. My neglected cell phone gazed up at me blank-faced, so I plugged it in and lay back to wait. Soothed by walls the smoky purple of evening, I felt the restless energy that had been driving me all day begin at last to subside. Within minutes I was asleep.

If it hadn't been for my phone beeping to tell me it was charged, I might have slept all night. But that shocking pink ribbon unfurling across my dreams was enough to jolt me awake, and I scrambled upright to find the room dark and my clock reading 11:21 PM.

There was no calm left in me now. I paced from the bed to the closet and back again, chewing fretfully at my pinky nail. What if it was already too late to call? What if I got no answer – or worse, some tapioca-bland voice telling me the number was out of service?

But there were worse things than disappointment, and I'd lived through several of them already. I had to try.

I closed my eyes, reaching back into memory for the number I'd seen on the business card. It had started with purple and black, then shaded into brown... I pressed the keys one by one, translating the colours back into numbers. Then I raised the phone to my ear and forced myself to keep it there.

'Hello?' The voice on the other end sounded preoccupied. I heard the hum of some machine working in the background, a wobbly green noise that tasted vaguely familiar – but then it died away, leaving only the electric silence.

'Faraday, it's me,' I said.

A sharp intake of breath. A long pause. And then, in a tone so warm I thought my spine would melt, 'Alison. Where are you?'

You better not do anything stupid, said Micheline's warning voice in my mind, but I ignored it. 'I'm at home. We need to talk.'

'Yes, of course. As soon as I've finished here —'

'I mean now.'

He hesitated. 'Well, we could, but wouldn't you rather have this conversation in person?'

I backed up to the edge of the mattress and sat down, clutching the phone with both hands. 'What?'

'I was going to say, give me a few minutes to finish what I'm doing, and then I'll come over. Will you still be awake in half an hour?'

He wanted to come. To my house. Tonight. Hysteria surged inside me, and I choked off a laugh.

'Oh, yes,' I said. 'I'll be here.'

As I squirmed out my bedroom window onto the roof, it struck me that this was the most deliberately crazy thing I'd ever done in my life. Yes, I wanted answers, and I was afraid this might be my only chance to get them. But I also wanted to get out of Pine Hills, and if my mother found me missing from my bedroom and called the police, it might be weeks before Dr Minta would even consider releasing me again.

Yet there stood Faraday in the yard below me, his upturned face pale with worry and moonlight, and I couldn't sit on the windowsill forever. 'I have one question,' I whispered down to him. 'If I told you I hate you and don't want to talk to you or see you ever again, would you go away and leave me alone?'

He barely even paused. 'Yes.'

He wasn't lying. He'd allowed me to believe any number of things about him that weren't true, but he'd never directly lied to me.

I crab-walked down the shingles to the edge of the roof, rolled over on my belly and swung my legs out into space. The drop from the porch overhang to the picnic table was only a few feet, but if I didn't land just right...

'I've got you.' Strong hands gripped my thighs, pulling me downwards. My fingers scrabbled wildly at the shingles, and I nearly ripped out the eavestrough before I let go and fell backwards into Faraday's arms.

He caught me so easily I might have been made of cotton. 'All right?' he whispered, breath warming my cheek as he set me down. He smelled like sweat and chemicals, neither one pleasant, and yet for one treacherous second my knees buckled. Part of me wanted to turn around and slap him, to shout my fury and my betrayal, to demand the answers only he could give...and the rest of me wanted to slide my fingers up into his hair and pull his mouth down to mine and not ask any questions at all.

And that really *was* crazy. How could I let myself forget, even for an instant, what he'd done to me? 'You could have warned me,' I snapped, as I twisted away.

'But I did,' he murmured, sounding perplexed. 'Or are we not talking about the roof any more?'

Ignoring the question, I climbed off the picnic table and jumped down onto the patio. He followed, and we soft-footed it out to the street, where a rust-speckled Volkswagen was waiting. 'This is your car?' I asked.

Faraday jingled his keys at me, a shower of tiny gold stars. 'For what it's worth. Where do you want to go?'

I glanced back at my house, with its darkened windows and curtains closed against the night. This was my last chance to change my mind. If I left with Faraday now, anything might happen.

'Just start driving,' I said. 'I'll tell you when we get there.'

The parking lot of the mall wasn't the most interesting place in the city, especially at one in the morning. But it was quiet, and close to home, and lit well enough for us to see each other without anyone else seeing us. Faraday's car smelled even soapier than he did, so I rolled down the window to let in the mellow night air.

'Sorry about the smell,' said Faraday. 'I came straight from work.'

I looked at him – really looked at him, for the first time that night. He was wearing a button-down shirt with the sleeves rolled up to the elbows, and grey uniform trousers that made him look vaguely like…

No, it couldn't be, the idea was ridiculous. And yet as soon as it had crossed my mind, all the clues I'd been missing slotted into place: the scent of industrial-strength cleanser on his hands, the muffled whirring I'd heard when he picked up the phone...

'You're a *janitor*?'

'A night custodian, yes. I don't need much sleep, and it gives me time to work on other things during the day.'

'Like your magazine, I suppose,' I said.

'There is no magazine,' he replied. 'But if you're planning to poke around in odd places and ask questions, it helps to pretend you're a journalist.'

My jaw tightened. 'Or a scientist.'

'No,' he said. 'I really am a scientist.'

He was telling the truth, but it wasn't helping. Irritably I scraped my long hair back from my face and tied it into a knot. 'All right, then. How about you start by telling me exactly what kind of scientist you are and where you really came from and why you fabricated a whole research project just so you could talk to me, and I'll interrupt whenever you lie or stop making sense?'

'I've never lied to you,' he said.

'I know. I would have tasted it if you did.'

'Not just that.' He unbuckled his seat belt and turned to face me. 'I didn't want to. You'd been honest with me, told me things you'd never told anyone else.

It seemed wrong not to be honest with you in return.'

'But not completely honest,' I said with a touch of bitterness. 'When Dr Minta told me what you'd done—'

'I was going to tell you. I was just waiting for the right moment, when I could be sure you were ready to listen. Because...' He blew out a sigh. 'It's not the kind of story that most people would find easy to believe.'

'Faraday...' I began, then was struck by a disquieting thought. 'Is that even your real name?'

'Legally yes, otherwise no. Michael Faraday was a famous physicist, as you probably know, so it seemed like a good choice for an alias. Sebastian is closer to the name I was raised with.'

But I'd *liked* Faraday. And I wasn't ready to start calling him Sebastian, especially if that wasn't his real name either. I felt like I'd been cheated somehow, robbed all over again of the man I'd thought I knew. 'Go on, then,' I said flatly. 'Tell me your story.'

Faraday was silent for a moment. Then he said, 'Once there was a young man – just a boy, really – who was part of a team of scientists, an apprentice to one of their leaders. They lived on a base that was very remote and isolated, a place you wouldn't know even if I told you the name. And they were there to study an extraordinary and very powerful natural phenomenon, which they'd discovered by accident some years ago and were only just beginning to understand.

'So far their experiments were going well, but the boy was impatient. The scientists had some very sophisticated instruments, but they were still making all their observations from a distance. The boy believed that they could learn even more if one of them went and investigated the phenomenon firsthand, and he even volunteered to do it.

'The other scientists said no, it was too dangerous. There were too many things that could go wrong. But the boy was determined to prove himself, and with the help of another apprentice, a boy about four years older than he was, he went ahead with his plan anyway. They borrowed a machine that the scientists used to transport cargo, and the older apprentice set it up to take the boy right into the middle of the phenomenon they'd been studying.

'At first, the plan worked perfectly. The boy arrived safely at his destination, and spent a couple of days exploring and making discoveries without suffering any obvious harm. But when he tried to contact his friend to tell him he was ready to come home, there was no answer. And when he looked for the machine he'd used to get there, he could no longer find it. He was stranded.'

A group of scientists in a secret base, studying some weird phenomenon – this was almost as bizarre as one of Sanjay's delusions. If Faraday hadn't sounded so serious about it, I'd have thought he was mocking me. 'The boy was you?' I asked.

He nodded. 'I was barely a teenager when I arrived here. I had no home, no friends, no money, and I didn't know a word of English – or French, for that matter. I'd only planned to be here for a couple of days, not the rest of my life.'

'Here?' I said. 'You mean Sudbury? But what kind of—'

'Let me finish,' said Faraday. 'Please.' I fell silent and he went on, 'For the first year or so, it took all my wits and determination just to survive. But once I'd discovered the library and taught myself to read English, I was able to start learning the things I needed to know.'

I could sense a hundred stories between every sentence: tales of homeless shelters and foster care, of frustrated police and bewildered teachers. But I swallowed my curiosity, and let him keep talking.

'It didn't take me long to realise that computers

were the key to everything I needed – or at least, they were fast becoming so. I read every book on the subject I could find and took every course I could afford, until I'd learned how to hack into just about anywhere. Once I'd created a legal identity for myself, life became easier. But I needed to do more than just live. I needed to find the machine that had brought me here and get it working properly again, so I could go home.'

He paused, waiting for my reaction. At last I said, 'So where's home? Not South Africa, I take it.'

A sad smile touched one corner of his mouth. 'No.'

'Russia?' They were just the other side of the pole, after all.

'No.'

I made a frustrated noise. 'Faraday, I don't want to play guessing games with you. Just tell me.'

'I can't. Not like that. I need you to figure it out for yourself.' He reached across and took my hand between his warm, calloused ones. 'Think about it, Alison. I told you I was a real scientist, and I am. Yet I've spent nearly my whole time in this city investigating every bizarre newspaper story, urban legend, and coffee-shop rumour that crossed my path. Strange lights, odd noises, people disappearing without trace—'

Shock jolted through me, and I snatched my hand away. 'Tori,' I breathed. 'That's what all this is about. You chased me down, studied me like a lab animal, manipulated me into trusting you – just so you could find out what happened to *her*.'

'I already know what happened to her,' he said patiently. 'She disintegrated. You told me that a long time ago. If that was all I cared about, I would have ended our sessions right then, and left you on your own.'

'Then what do you want from me?' My voice cracked with frustration. 'I don't see what I have to do with you being stuck here, or with this 'machine' you've been looking for, or—'

'You have everything to do with it,' said Faraday. 'You're the only person I've ever met who could actually help me. Because you were there when Tori disintegrated, and you saw it all. I found that out from talking to one of your neighbours – she'd heard you shouting about it as the police took you away.'

Mel. He'd been talking to Mel. My head began to throb, and I pushed the heels of my hands against my eyes. Was that why she'd come to visit me, that one time? Because *he* needed more information?

'I had to find a way to talk to you,' Faraday went

on. 'So I hacked into your patient files at St Luke's. And when I read about some of the things you'd said and done after Tori died, it dawned on me that you might have synesthesia.'

'So that's when you...' I couldn't finish the sentence. It hurt too much. To think that all along Faraday had been using me, that all his seeming generosity and kindness had been tainted with self-interest, made me want to smash the window and cut my wrists with it. To think that I had trusted the wrong person yet *again*—

'I came up with the study as a way of getting close to you, yes,' he said. 'And to see if I could persuade you to help me. But once I'd met you, and realised what you'd been going through, my priorities began to change.'

'You felt sorry for me.' My voice was flat.

'More than that. I felt a connection to you. A sense of...kinship.' He shifted closer, the musk-and-soap of his skin filling the space between us. 'Yes, I was hoping you could help me find my way home. But I wanted you to be able to go home, too. And I believed – I still believe – that the solution to my problem and the solution to yours is the same.'

'Is that so,' I said. I was hardly even paying

attention now. All I could think was that I wanted this conversation to be over, so I could go home.

'Let me put it this way. When you told me you'd disintegrated Tori, I told you there was no way you could have done such a thing. But didn't you ever stop to wonder what could?'

Of course I had. But the only explanation I'd been able to think of was that I'd killed her some other way, and then deluded myself into thinking she'd disintegrated. How was that any better?

'The truth is,' said Faraday, 'that if anyone's to blame for Tori's death, I am. Because the machine that brought me here, the one I've been looking for all these years…is the same one that tore her apart.'

'*What?*'

Faraday pushed a hand through his hair, making it more rumpled than ever. 'Alison, before I tell you anything more, I need you to know that the last thing I want is to hurt you or frighten you or make your life any harder than it already is. What I'm about to say is going to sound bizarre, maybe even impossible – and yet, I swear to you, it is the truth. If you…' His beautiful voice roughened. 'If you can't trust me, can you at least trust your senses? Shouldn't you be able to taste it, if I'm lying?'

I'd thought so when I came out here, but after hearing Faraday's story, I wasn't sure any more. Maybe the sheer pleasure of listening to him talk had messed up my synesthesia. Maybe he'd been lying to me all along, and I'd missed the bitter aftertaste because his words had been so sweet in other ways, because I'd *wanted* to believe.

There was only one way I could think of to be sure.

'Lie to me, then,' I demanded. 'Tell me something that you know isn't true.'

Faraday reached out and cupped a hand under my chin, his fathomless violet eyes holding mine. 'I don't care about you,' he said quietly. 'And I'm not from another world.'

FIFTEEN (IS AMBIVALENT)

The taste of Faraday's words was like cocoa powder, dry and bitter. There was nothing wrong with my ability to tell when he was lying. Which meant—

My chest felt heavy, as though my lungs had turned to lead. A mosquito whined around my ear, a distant cousin of Tori's Noise, as I fumbled off my seat belt and shoved the door open.

'Where are you going?' Faraday's voice was a zigzag of alarm. 'Alison—'

But by then I'd already stepped out onto the asphalt and was walking away as fast as my shaky legs would carry me. I understood now, with nauseating clarity, how cruelly I'd been deceived. What difference did it make that Faraday thought he was telling the truth when the truth was nothing more than a delusion? Why should it matter if Faraday believed in my sanity now that I knew Faraday himself was insane?

'Alison.' Faraday sprinted up to me and caught my arm. 'Don't. Let me explain.'

'I've heard enough,' I said. If I wanted stories

about aliens spying on the people of Earth and using them for their secret experiments, I could get better ones from Sanjay. I wrenched free of his grasp and kept walking.

'You saw Tori disintegrate,' Faraday called after me. 'You knew nothing on this world could do that to a person, and yet you convinced yourself you'd made it happen. If you could believe that, why not this?'

I stopped.

'Don't think of me as an alien,' said Faraday. 'Think of me as a long-lost relative, who just happens to live on the other side of the universe.' He caught up to me and put a hand on my shoulder. 'I'm not asking you to believe in little green men, Alison. More like… accidental colonists.'

I shook him off. 'I can't do this. Don't you understand? I *can't.*'

'Why not?'

'Because,' I shouted at him, 'the whole idea is crazy!'

There was an uncomfortable silence. Then Faraday said, 'Well. You've spent enough time doubting your own sanity. I suppose it was about time you started questioning mine.'

I looked away, unable to bear his level, faintly

reproachful gaze. The worst of it was, Faraday didn't *seem* crazy. There was nothing excitable about his manner, no hint of paranoia. He hadn't assumed I'd buy his story, in fact just the opposite; he'd tried to ease me into it, because he knew it would be hard for me to believe. That was a lot more self-awareness than I'd ever seen from Sanjay – or any of the other patients at Pine Hills who suffered from delusions.

And yet if I accepted what Faraday was telling me, it would cast doubt on everything I'd believed was – and even more importantly, *wasn't* – real.

'The phenomenon that my team was studying,' said Faraday, 'is a dimensional rift, a spacial and temporal anomaly that links our part of the universe to yours. One of my colleagues measured the rate at which the rift was moving through space, and calculated that a few thousand years ago, it would have passed directly through our planet. So for a while, it might have been possible to step out of our world and end up in yours, or vice versa…and that means your people and mine might have come from the same ancestors.'

'Which explains why you look exactly like an ordinary human, except for the eyes,' I said dryly. 'That's convenient.'

'Not exactly.' He leaned forward and parted his hair with his fingers. 'Look. Feel.'

Against my better judgment I reached up, sliding my fingers into the shaggy strands and lifting them away from his temples. Even in the dim light of the parking lot, the roots of his hair glittered – and it wasn't just premature grey, no matter how much I tried to tell myself otherwise. It had a metallic sheen to it, like pewter.

'It doesn't take dye very well,' he said. 'That's why I keep it a bit messy, so the grey parts aren't as obvious.' He straightened up again. 'What about my eyes?'

'They're violet?'

'Really? I thought they were just sort of bluish.'

So even he couldn't see it. Wonderful. I pinched the bridge of my nose, exhausted by my own uncertainty.

'Come back to the car,' said Faraday. 'Let me tell you more about how I got here and what I think happened to Tori. If you're willing to come back to the school with me, we might even be able to prove it. And then you can decide what you want to believe.'

He ran a hand gently down my arm as he spoke, and I struggled against the temptation to give in. Not because he'd convinced me, but because part of me wanted to pretend it didn't matter. So what if Faraday thought he was an alien? There were worse ways to be crazy. Yes, he'd tricked me into believing he was a neuropsychologist, but only because he'd thought I wouldn't listen to him otherwise. Apart from that he'd been nothing but kind and patient and charming, and when he'd told me he didn't care for me, he'd been lying...

'This proof of yours,' I said. 'You mean the machine, don't you? The one that killed Tori. You think it's still at the school somewhere.'

He nodded.

'So what is this thing, then? A killer spaceship?'

Which sounded so incredibly dumb that as soon as I'd said it, I wanted to smack myself. Fortunately, Faraday was gracious enough not to call me on it.

'No, just a relay,' he said. 'A device that transmits and receives information. Roundish, about the size of my fist, with built-in camouflage and protective mechanisms. There's a relay unit here and another back on the base, and they send signals to each other. Or at least they did, before the one on this end malfunctioned.'

If it was camouflaged, that would explain why he

hadn't been able to find it. Not that I was buying in to his story yet. 'So what was this relay thing doing outside Champlain Secondary? And why did it kill Tori?'

'I don't know,' said Faraday. 'Until I've had a chance to inspect it, I won't be able to tell what went wrong. That's why I'm hoping you can help me find it, and get it working properly again.' He took my hand in both of his. 'Just come with me, Alison. Just for a few minutes. That's all I ask.'

I'd always known I'd have to go back to the school one day, but I hadn't expected it to be tonight. I wasn't sure it was even a good idea, when I was under so much stress already. And yet, if there was even a chance that this relay actually existed, and that finding it could explain what had happened to Tori...

'Please,' Faraday said, his voice so low I could feel it at the base of my spine.

I closed my eyes. 'All right,' I said. 'I'll come.'

A few minutes later Faraday and I stood facing the north-west door of Champlain Secondary, bathed in the exterior lights' jaundiced glow. The moon was muffled with cloud, but I could hear the stars keening as I pointed to the spot on the concrete where Tori had fallen.

'There,' I said.

And that was all. No blazing epiphany or sea-green wave of sorrow. There was no trace of Tori here, only a patch of empty concrete, and the darkness made everything so remote it might have been a dream. The only thing I felt, standing there, was tired.

Faraday glanced back at the shadowy line of trees behind us. 'I've been here before,' he said. 'I went over this area even more carefully than the police did. But if the relay's still here, it's too well hidden for me to find it.' He turned slowly, his gaze sweeping over the parking lot. 'What I don't understand is why it would have ended up here in the first place, or why it malfunctioned the way it did. Why disintegrate Tori, and not you as well? And why hasn't it activated for anyone else, before or since?'

The disturbing thing about Faraday spouting technobabble was that he sounded so matter-of-fact about it. 'I thought this thing was for transmitting information,' I said. 'Why would it be capable of disintegrating a person in the first place?'

'Because,' Faraday replied, 'matter is information, too. And when it's working properly, the relay can record every detail of an object down to the subatomic level, and then transmit that information to the relay on the other side of the rift for reassembly.'

'You mean…the relay isn't supposed to kill people? It's supposed to *transport* them?'

'It does transport them,' said Faraday. 'Mind you, anyone who's tried it agrees that it's an extremely painful experience, so it's not often used for anything but moving cargo. But it works. That's how I got here.'

Extremely painful… I felt like the ground was sliding out from beneath me. 'Why?' I asked in a strangled voice. 'Why would it hurt, if it's just…'

'No one knows,' he replied. 'The process is virtually instantaneous, even if it doesn't seem like it, and scientifically there's no reason that anyone should be conscious of feeling anything after their brain and nerves have disintegrated. It's almost enough to make one believe in the soul.'

I sat down hard on the kerb, my eyes glazed with disbelief. In the back of my mind I could hear Tori screaming, fluorescent shrieks of agony that rang in my ears long after there was nothing left of her—

'I didn't want to say it until I was certain,' said Faraday. 'But I think you've already guessed. If the relay wasn't seriously damaged…then Tori might still be alive.'

Alive. All at once, I wanted to believe. If Tori

wasn't dead, she could be rescued. By bringing her home, I could clear my name and lift my burden of guilt all at once. But my heart felt too small to hold so much hope. I covered my face with my hands.

Faraday crouched beside me. I could hear the mosquitoes buzzing, but for once they didn't bite. 'Are you all right?' he asked.

'I'm fine. Just…a little overwhelmed.'

'Do you want me to take you home?'

I lifted my head, disbelieving. How hard must it be for him to ask me that, after he'd worked so long and risked so much just to bring me here? 'I thought you needed me to help you find the relay,' I said.

'I do. But I've waited years for this, Alison. I can wait a little longer.'

I wanted to kiss him so badly just then, it was all I could do to hold back. But even though I knew he cared, I wasn't sure exactly what *kind* of caring he'd been talking about. And I didn't want to do to him what Kirk had done to me. 'No, it's all right,' I said unevenly. 'What do you need me to do?'

'The relay can't be detected by ordinary vision or hearing,' said Faraday. 'But you're capable of sensing far more than the average person. If you felt anything when the relay activated, any unusual sound or taste that you'd recognise if you came across it again...'

So that was why he'd been so interested in my synesthesia. I was his human metal detector.

'I felt *everything* when it happened,' I said. 'It was like all my senses got turned up to full blast at once. I can barely remember how I got back on my feet after that, let alone whether I noticed anything that could have been the relay.'

'I understand,' said Faraday. 'But you're the only hope I've got. If you could just walk around a little bit, and...' He made a vague gesture. 'Look. Listen. See what you feel.'

I'd never really tried to *use* my synesthesia before. It had always just been there, as natural and inevitable as breathing. What would happen if I opened myself up to it, as Faraday was suggesting? Threw down all my defences, and abandoned myself completely to sensation?

The idea was tempting – and terrifying. I'd spent so much of my life trying *not* to show my feelings, or let myself be ruled by them. If I dropped my shields of self-restraint, would I be the same Alison any more?

I wasn't ready to take that risk. But I didn't want to say no to Faraday either, at least not yet. 'I'll try,' I said, and got up.

Faraday didn't follow. He just sat back on his heels and watched me as I headed for the edge of the woodlot – my best guess for where the relay had to be – and stopped, listening with all my senses.

A feather-brush of maroon as the wind rustled the trees. A crow's call plucked at my elbow like an impatient child. The sound of crickets tasted like Rice Krispies. Gasoline and exhaust fumes wafted from the parking lot behind me, while the wood smelled of mulch and discarded beer bottles. And loudest of all, the mosquitoes droned...

But that was all.

When I looked back Faraday was on his feet, tensed like a sprinter waiting for the shot. He believed I could do this. He *needed* me to do it. If I gave up now, would he believe I'd done my best to help him?

I had to try again, and harder. I walked a little way into the trees and turned my senses loose for a second time. Then I backed out and tried a little further down the drive. Each time I dared myself to stretch my perceptions further, until panic scrabbled around the edges of my mind and I had to stop – but even then I sensed nothing. Or at least, nothing out of the ordinary.

'I'm sorry,' I said, when I came back to Faraday. 'If it's here, I can't find it.'

Faraday let out a long breath, and his shoulders bowed. 'Well,' he said quietly. 'That's the end of it, then.'

By the time Faraday and I walked back to his car, the clouds had parted and the moon hung clear and luminous in the sky. The night was so beautiful it seemed almost cruel. 'So what will you do now?' I asked.

'I promised to help you get out of Pine Hills and clear your name,' said Faraday distractedly, turning over the keys in his hand as though he'd forgotten what they were for. 'I intend to keep that promise. Unless you don't want me to.'

He'd performed one miracle for me already, by convincing my mother to let me come home. What other wonders did he have in mind? 'I do,' I said, 'but that wasn't what I meant. You're really giving up? After everything?'

Faraday lifted his head, gazing out across the parking lot to the softly lit neighbourhood beyond. 'You know,' he said, 'It doesn't feel like giving up, not as much as I'd thought it would. Coming here alone as I did, knowing nothing of your language or your culture, forced me to notice other people in a way I'd never done before. I learned to watch them with all my attention, and listen closely to whatever they had to say – because I never knew when I might learn something important. And after a while I came to see that not just as a necessity, but as a privilege.'

'It shows,' I said.

'And yet there was a selfish aspect to it, too. Because the more I encouraged other people to talk about their lives, the less likely it was that they'd ask me about mine. I made plenty of useful contacts, a few good acquaintances, but no real friends.' He turned his head, violet eyes focusing on mine. 'Until I met you.'

I held my breath.

'Talking to you day after day, getting to know you just a little more each time…' One corner of his mouth turned up in a rueful smile. 'You have no idea what a revelation that was for me. Partly because I was learning about your synesthesia, which gave me the chance to use my scientific background in a way I hadn't done for years. The things you could do with your senses were so fascinating to me, there were times when I forgot the study we were working on wasn't real.'

I could spend the rest of my life studying you, he had told me, *and there wouldn't be a moment wasted.* Part of me wouldn't mind if that was what he wanted to do – but was that really how he saw me? Like a rare orchid or a new species of butterfly, something to be preserved for the advancement of science?

'But what struck me even more, as time went on,' Faraday went on in the same thoughtful tone, 'was how much the two of us had in common. We both had secrets we were afraid to share, in case people thought we were insane. Both of us were trapped in a place we never would have chosen, longing to go home. It was easy to talk to you, and the more time we spent together, the more I started to think about what was really important to me – and what made my life worth living.'

He turned to face me, a lean shadow in the darkness, so near I could feel his warmth. He smelled like buttered toast and electricity, comforting and dangerous at once, and I didn't know whether to reach out to him or back away.

'When you played for me on your birthday,' he continued, 'I realised what a precious gift you'd given me. Something so personal, and so beautiful – it made me wonder how many other good things I'd missed or ignored over the years, because I was so obsessed with getting back to my old life. And that night, I decided that one way or another, this attempt was going to be my last. If you couldn't or wouldn't help me, then I'd give up and try to move on.

'So when Dr Minta banned me from Pine Hills, I thought, well, there's my answer. I went and talked to your parents – it seemed like the least I could do – but I knew I'd probably never see you again. And that was...hard.' His gaze turned distant. 'But then you called me, and told me you wanted to talk. And suddenly I felt that things were going to work out after all. That it was somehow...meant.'

'I'm sorry—' I started to say, but he shook his head.

'No, Alison.' He tucked a loose strand of hair behind my ear, let his hand drop to my shoulder. 'You have nothing to apologise for. You're the best thing that's come into my life in a very long time.'

I gazed up into his face with its slow eyes and long mouth and gently angled bones, and my heart felt like it was falling. 'This... This can't be right, can it? Dr Minta warned me about patients and therapists—'

Faraday breathed a laugh. 'I wasn't your therapist, Alison. If anything, you were mine. You don't know how many days I woke up alone in my miserable little apartment, after a night of mopping floors and scrubbing toilets, and the prospect of seeing you again felt like the only thing keeping me sane.'

Daring, I reached up and touched his face for the first time. His skin was warm, his jaw rough with stubble, and when he turned his head and kissed the palm of my hand, I felt as though I were dissolving. 'Sebastian,' I whispered, not caring any more whether he was crazy or not. I didn't need proof of his story now, didn't even want it. All I wanted was him.

Faraday's fingers laced into the knot of my hair, gently working it loose and stroking his fingers through it. Then he drew me into his arms.

As our bodies pressed together, every inch of my skin came awake, every sense alight. I heard Faraday's breath quicken, saw the colour of his heartbeat pulse and fade behind my eyes. Music blossomed inside my head, a cascade of deep, shivering notes like the voice of a bassoon, and suddenly I wanted to feel everything. I slid my hands up the muscles of his back, over the broad line of his shoulders, down his arms—

Something buzzed against my palm, like a cell phone set to vibrate. Startled, I jerked away.

'What is it?' Faraday asked.

My heart was pounding fast, but for all the wrong

reasons. 'I felt something.' Hesitantly I touched his arm just above the elbow. 'There.'

Faraday gave me a puzzled look. 'You mean my transmitter?' he said, and pushed his sleeve up to reveal a faint, sun-shaped mark beneath his skin.

For a moment I was too appalled to do anything but stare. Then I clapped my hands over my ears and spun away, but it was too late. Rust speckled my vision, and my head filled with a piercing, hateful drone – the Noise I'd hoped never to hear again.

No.

No.

How could this happen? Why this—why *him*?

But the Noise kept shrilling, despite all my efforts to deny it. And now I could hear something else besides – sirens in the distance, coming closer. Police, on the hunt for someone… For me? Had my mother found my bed empty, my medication ignored, and called for help?

'Alison?' Faraday reached for my hand, but I jerked away. The Noise he made was so loud now, it was worse than Tori's had ever been—

This was it. This was the end. Whatever Faraday and I might have had together, it was over now. Tear-blinded, I stumbled back towards the school, leaving him behind – but even then I couldn't get away from the Noise. Worse, it was coming at me from all directions now, as though I were being swarmed by a cloud of—

'Mosquitoes!' I spun around and shrieked at Faraday, not caring if I made any sense. 'All night I thought I was hearing mosquitoes but it wasn't, it was you, and that – *thing*!'

The sirens were louder now, but I barely noticed them. My head was thrumming with another resonance entirely. In the churning darkness before my eyes, Faraday's Noise and the fake-mosquito buzz from the edge of the woodlot connected in a blazing orange line. I rushed up to one of the pine trees, ripped the relay off the trunk where it had been clinging invisible all this time, and hurled it straight at Faraday.

He leaped to meet it, and caught it just before it hit the ground. He gave me an incredulous look, but I shook my head wildly and backed away.

'What is it?' he asked, cradling the metal sphere against his chest. 'What's wrong?'

It hurt. It hurt so much. The two Noises together, so close, so hotly shrill – it was like a sword driven through the top of my head and into my spine. It wouldn't stop. I had to make it stop. I dived at Faraday, snatched the relay out of his hands and started fumbling with it.

'Alison, no!'

He grabbed my arm, just as my thumb found the depression on the relay's side. Its whine cycled up into an ear-bleeding pitch as the device slipped out of my fingers, hit the ground—

And exploded, with a sound like the end of the world.

PART THREE:

TOUCHING TOMORROW

SIXTEEN (IS OVERWHELMED)

I'd felt pain before, but nothing like this. It felt like I was being eaten alive by horseflies and regurgitated one chunk at a time through a glass tube the diameter of a baby's hair – only the tube seemed to go on forever and the horseflies never stopped biting. Long after I should have lost consciousness, the agony went on and on, my soundless shrieks ringing in my nonexistent ears. Then the tube vomited me out on the other side, and I landed in a messy heap.

For three skipped heartbeats, I thought I was dead. Then, as air shuddered into my lungs and a world of unfamiliar colours, scents and sounds crashed in upon me, I wanted to be.

'Alison! Are you all right?'

Even whispering, Faraday's voice scalded my mouth like hot cocoa. His every breath was a tidal roar, and my head ached with the slamming of his heart. I felt the texture of his clothing as surely as though I were wearing it myself – but worse, I could sense the shape/taste/smell of every other surface, every object, in the entire room. The brushed metal walls. The stacks of grey foam packing crates. The relay fixed to the ceiling above our heads, still blaring its tangerine scream...

And I could feel energy. Pulsing inside the walls, vibrating through the floor. An intricate web of connections stretching out as far as my senses could reach, like the biggest computer network on Earth.

This could not be happening. It wasn't real. I was having a complete mental breakdown somewhere in Red Ward, and everything that had happened to me in the past twenty-four hours was a schizophrenic delusion. I let out a little sob and covered my face with my hands.

Faraday reached for me, but I rolled away, curling in on myself like a withered leaf. The lightest touch was more than I could endure right now. All I could do was block my ears, hide my eyes, and pray for the agony to stop.

Fortunately, Faraday seemed to understand. He slid away from me and sat with his back against one of the crates, giving me the space I needed. I huddled on the floor, breathing shallowly, terrified that I'd be stuck this way forever, that this unbearable *awareness* would never end—

But just before the panic could engulf me

330

completely, the Noise from Faraday's transmitter stopped. The relay went quiet. And little by little the chaos of my senses began to subside. My limbs felt weak and shaky, as though I had just wakened from a long illness, but in another few minutes I was able to sit up again. And when Faraday touched my shoulder I felt no pain, no overpowering impulse to fight or flee. I turned to him and buried my face against his chest.

He stroked my hair, murmuring words I didn't recognise, and then pulled back to look at me. 'What happened?' he asked.

'It was...like it was after Tori died. Disintegrated. Only worse.' I drew a slow breath and let it out again. 'But I'm all right now.'

And I was, but it was the strangest feeling. I could still sense everything around me, a consciousness broader and deeper than I'd ever experienced before. I could have walked through the storage room blindfolded without hitting a single crate and then described the contents of every one. I could tell that Faraday was frowning even though my eyes were shut; I could smell his worry, his guilt, his uncertainty. But the constant stream of information didn't overwhelm me any more. Instead of struggling against the current,

I felt like I was flowing with it.

But what had made the difference? Had something changed inside me, or was it some other factor beyond my control?

'I need to get you home,' said Faraday. 'You can't stay here.' He let me go and climbed to his feet, looking up at the relay above us. 'The question is, can we reverse the process from here, or…?'

I knew he was only trying to help me. But the prospect of taking that agonising journey again, especially so soon, was unbearable. 'Wait,' I said, but he didn't hear me. He'd already started dragging crates across the floor, stacking them into a makeshift ladder.

I got up awkwardly, nerves still buzzing with remembered pain, and looked around. Apart from us, there was nothing to see but the boxes and the relay. No windows, no portholes, no obvious way to prove that we weren't just in some bunker or storage shed back on Earth. Yet if Faraday's story was true, we'd just been reduced to a stream of information and transmitted through a dimensional rift to rematerialise in some far-off region of the universe. And after what I'd just experienced, it was hard to disbelieve him.

'Someone's cut off the connection to the central computer,' said Faraday, climbing back down. 'I'll need to re-establish the link. Stay here.' He jumped off the last crate and headed for the exit.

'Wait,' I said, louder this time.

He stopped. 'What is it?'

'I know I shouldn't be here,' I said. 'I know this is all a gigantic mess, and you'd like to fix it as soon as you can. But this is your chance to prove everything you've told me about yourself. Aren't you going to at least show me around?'

Faraday looked pained. 'For someone with paranormal abilities,' he said, 'you're the most sceptical person I've ever met.' He came back to me and took my hand. 'As it happens, I would love to show you around. But I'm not sure that would be a good idea. It's going to be enough of a shock for my fellow scientists to see me again, without introducing them to you as well. And if they find out I've brought you here, there could be…difficulties.'

'You mean,' I said, 'they might dissect me in the interests of science?'

I'd been joking, however feebly, but Faraday's grip on my fingers tightened. 'No,' he said. 'Believe me, Alison, I won't let them do that to you.'

The implication that they might try was enough to send eels down my spine. Suddenly the idea of staying here in the storage room, or whatever it was, didn't sound so bad after all. 'OK,' I said.

Faraday bent and kissed my forehead. Then he tugged the door, and with a metallic crack it popped open. I caught only the briefest glimpse of the corridor beyond – narrow and dimly lit, lined with doors on either side – before he slipped through and shut it again, leaving me alone.

I sat down on one of the crates and tried to be patient, but after a few minutes I was up and pacing. What if something happened to Faraday, and he couldn't get back to me? What if the other scientists decided they didn't trust him, and shut him up in a cell somewhere? I could be stuck here for days, and nobody would know. I could die of thirst before anyone found me…

And that was the paranoia talking, which was a bad sign. I'd already missed my evening pill, and my medication was still sitting on my night table at home. In another few hours, I'd be shaking and nauseated if Faraday didn't get me back to Sudbury in time.

But if he did manage to get the relay to work, I'd have to suffer through that horrible journey all over again…and compared to that, withdrawal didn't seem so bad after all.

I sat down and got up again several times before I couldn't bear the silence any more. I went to the door and pressed my ear against it, listening with all my senses. All seemed quiet. I grabbed the door handle and pulled.

The *clunk* of the mechanism made me cringe, but it opened easily enough. Before me stretched the same door-lined hallway I'd seen when Faraday left – still silent, still empty, still bland as porridge. But now I could see there was also a second corridor running perpendicular to the first, curving gently away in both directions. I stepped over the threshold, the door of the storage room swinging closed behind me...

And naturally, locking me out. I spent a futile moment pushing and pulling at the handle, then rested my forehead against the wall and let out a little moan of despair at my own idiocy.

I was still cursing myself and wondering where else I could hide when something shifted in my awareness. About ten metres to my left, just around the curve, another door had cracked open, sending air currents swirling along the corridor in ribbons of peach-tinted warmth and periwinkle cool.

Faraday coming back? But no, the smell was all wrong for that, and the shape in my mind wasn't right either. It smelled like blood and sweat and the burnt-coffee stench of anger, with an undertone of something metallic. Like a weapon.

And it was heading towards me.

I backed away down the right-hand corridor, too distracted to watch where I was going. Which was how I tripped over something large and warm lying across my path, and then fell on top of it.

Not it. Him.

'Faraday!' I gasped, turning him over. His eyes were shut, his chest rising and falling slowly. He didn't seem to be injured, but he was definitely unconscious. I ran my fingers along his neck and found a swelling just beneath his jaw, as though something had stung him. 'Faraday, wake—'

Someone grabbed me by the shoulder, twisting me off balance and slamming me down. I fell hard, breath whooshing out of my lungs, as my attacker shoved my face into the floor and dropped a knee onto my spine. I was still struggling to get away when something bit into my neck with a serpentine hiss, and I blacked out.

I woke to the taste of stale marshmallows, feeling like a moose had kicked me in the head. My mouth was a drought, and my stomach churned. For a moment, I could hardly bear to open my eyes in case I found myself back at Pine Hills.

But I wasn't in Red Ward, or at least it didn't look like it. I was lying on a spongy sort of mattress in a room with dust-grey walls, facing a rectangular alcove that might have once been a window but was now opaquely black. Fighting dizziness, I turned over…

And there she was, sitting cross-legged in front of the door, looking like a rebellious angel. She was wearing the same lacy sweater and blue jeans in which I'd last seen her, but her nose had a crook in it that hadn't been there before, and the hollows beneath her eyes were dark with bruises.

'You broke my nose, you know,' said Tori Beaugrand.

'I'm…sorry,' I said, so hoarse that I could hardly get out the words. The relief of seeing Tori alive, of knowing without a doubt that I hadn't killed her, was incredible. And yet to find her here like this, when I'd only just begun to consider the possibility that she might not be dead after all…it was hard to believe she wasn't just part of some elaborate hallucination. Especially since she wasn't making the Noise.

'Apology not accepted,' Tori said. 'Because as it

turns out, you popped an artery and I just about bled to death. But I'll give you the chance to make it up to me.' She unfolded herself and got to her feet. 'Getting me back home would be a good start.'

Home. I sucked in my breath. 'Faraday. Is he all right? Where is he?'

'Your boyfriend?' The last word was lemon-iced with sarcasm. 'Don't worry, he's fine. After he finished tearing me a new one for using sedatives without a licence, he got tired of waiting for you to wake up and went off to look for an antidote.'

Faraday, losing his temper? I was sorry to have missed that. But if he'd felt comfortable enough to leave me alone with Tori, the two of them must have come to an understanding. 'So...you talked to him, then?' I said. 'How much did he tell you?'

'Pretty much everything,' Tori replied, her tone casual although the taut line of her shoulders was anything but. 'He kind of had to, because I was threatening to smash his head in with my toolkit if he didn't.'

This conversation was not going anything like I expected. 'Your...what?'

She nodded at a grey mesh bag lying beside the door. 'I got so bored after the first couple of hours,

I was going to start climbing the walls if I didn't do something. So I've been collecting whatever tools I could find lying around. I figured if I could learn how to use them, I might be able to break into the rest of this place.'

'You mean you haven't talked to anyone, or seen anyone, all this time? You've been alone until now?'

'Yeah,' she said. 'I'm not sure if I'm a prisoner or a lab rat or just stuck in quarantine, but anyway I've had enough of it. I've been here about eighteen hours, and—'

'*What?*'

Tori's expression was almost sympathetic. 'I forgot to tell you that part,' she said. 'For you, it's been months since we saw each other. But for me, it's been less than a day.'

Until that moment, the idea that time might be moving differently here than it did on the other side of the rift had never occurred to me. My first impulse was to deny it – but how could I? The bruises under Tori's eyes were still fresh, and so was the ugly scratch across her cheek where my ring had cut her, even though we'd had our fight nearly ten weeks ago.

But if the time difference between here and Earth was that great, then there was no way I could get back to Sudbury before anyone noticed I was gone. Already I'd been missing for hours, or even days. So if the police hadn't been looking for me before, they definitely would be now...

'Anyway,' Tori said, 'let me tell you the rest of the story.'

Unlike myself and Faraday, who had come through the relay to an empty storeroom, Tori had been confronted by a suited and helmeted figure, who'd injected her with the same sedative she'd used on Faraday and me. When she regained consciousness some time later, she'd found herself lying on the same bunk I was using now – broken nose fixed, bleeding stopped, and the pain and swelling in her face mostly gone.

'I waited for a while, thinking a nurse would show up, but nobody came,' she said. 'And when I got up I found the place just like it is now – all quiet, with most of the doors shut, and no obvious way out. I ran around yelling for help, but nobody answered, and the only rooms I could get into were empty. I mean *empty*, as in bare walls, nothing in the closets. Like they'd all moved out days ago.'

Once Tori had calmed down enough to explore her surroundings more carefully, she'd found a box stocked with food, drinks and medical supplies – so whoever had taken care of her injuries had taken her other needs into account as well. 'But the outer corridor's sealed off on both ends,' she said, 'and the inner one, the straight one, doesn't seem to connect to anything. So I'm still trying to figure out how to get out of here and find whoever did this to me.'

'You don't have any idea what they want with you?' I asked.

'No, but I'm pretty sure I know why they brought me here,' she said. 'After you broke my nose, they realised I was going to bleed to death if they didn't do something fast, so they zapped me back here to fix it.'

She spoke so casually, as though it made perfect sense that her vital signs were being broadcast across time and space to a group of alien scientists. I stared at her, baffled and more than a little disturbed—

And then the mystery started to solve itself, one clue at a time.

That golden hair, with its faintly metallic gleam. The peachy glow of her skin, so different from the skin tones of her parents, or anyone else I knew. Those amazing eyes, a turquoise almost as unusual as Faraday's violet...

And the transmitter in her upper arm, just like his.

'So,' I said, clearing my throat, 'you know you came from another planet?'

'Of course,' Tori replied. 'I've known it for thirteen years.'

'Why do you think I freaked out when you started telling people I was adopted?' Tori continued as she led me down the corridor, her toolkit slung over one shoulder. 'The last thing I wanted was anybody wondering where I came from. But what I don't get is how you knew.'

'About you being...from this place?' I said. 'I didn't. I only just figured it out.'

Tori scowled at me. 'Oh, right. So ever since seventh grade you've been staring at me in class like I was some kind of monster, avoiding me in the halls, getting all jumpy and hostile whenever I talked to you, and all of that meant *nothing*?'

Her accusations left me flabbergasted. I knew we'd misjudged each other, but I'd had no idea how much.

'You scared the crap out of me,' Tori said. She quickened her stride, moving so briskly that I had to scramble to keep up with her. 'The way you acted whenever I was around, I was sure you knew I wasn't human. My parents had a fit when I told them. My mom wanted to pull me out of school—'

'Your parents knew? About you?'

'Of course! They were the ones who took me to the doctor when I was a kid, and then paid him off to keep quiet about all the weird stuff he found. They thought I'd been part of some twisted medical experiment...until they found the chip in my arm. Then they got *really* scared, because it was made of this liquid metal stuff that had grown right into the muscle, and no technology on Earth could make something like that.'

She stopped at the formidable-looking barrier that blocked the end of the hallway, and dropped her toolkit in front of it. 'For a while my parents wanted to move away, thinking it might keep whoever had abandoned me as a baby from finding me again. But as soon as they drove out of the Sudbury Basin, I started having seizures – big, scary, life-threatening seizures. So once they realised they couldn't move without killing me, they decided the only solution was to hide in plain sight. We'd all act like I was an ordinary kid, and then maybe everybody else would believe that I was ordinary, too. It wasn't much of a plan, but it seemed to be working...until you came along.'

For years I'd envied Tori her popularity, her

343

accomplishments, her seemingly unassailable self-confidence. Only now was I beginning to realise how fragile all those things had been – and how hard she'd worked to keep them. 'OK,' I said. 'But if you were that afraid of me, why go out of your way to make me your enemy?'

'Me? What did I ever do to—'

'The poetry contest? When you got me disqualified by telling Mrs Mailloux I'd copied my entry out of a magazine?' Which I really had done, to my lasting shame – but I hadn't known that at the time, and neither had the judges. I'd been disqualified on a suspicion, nothing more.

'I didn't say anything to Mrs Mailloux.'

'What do you mean? Of course you did. You even warned me you were going to do it.'

'I told you *somebody* was going to do it,' she retorted. 'I never said it would be me. Lara was so upset that her poem didn't get picked for the contest, she kept saying you must have cheated, and finally I told her I'd talk to you and try to get you to admit it. But you wouldn't, so I told her to leave you alone.' She crouched and began pulling tools out of the bag, lining them up like surgical instruments. 'So you really got disqualified?'

'You don't remember?'

'Don't *you* remember? That was right around the time my dad had a heart attack and spent three weeks in hospital. You really think I'd be paying attention to some stupid poetry contest I didn't even enter, with that on my mind?'

She spoke with fierce conviction, a truth so raw I could taste it. Which meant...Tori really *hadn't* accused me after all. All this time, I'd been blaming the wrong person.

'And what about you?' Tori demanded. 'Accusing me of trashing the sound equipment at the Spring Cabaret? Why on earth would I do something like that? I wasn't wrecking that stuff, I was trying to *fix* it.' She dumped the last of her tools on the floor and tossed the empty bag aside. 'Why would I want to ruin an event I'd been helping plan for weeks? Why would I humiliate my best friend in front of everybody? When you came in, I'd just broken up with Brendan because he kept pressuring me to have sex with him. It wasn't my fault he threw a tantrum like a freaking two-year-old—'

Shame scorched my cheeks. No wonder Tori had been furious with me after the Cabaret, determined to hunt me down and set the matter straight. Still, it must have taken all her courage to face me down in the cafeteria and demand to know what my issue was, especially when she had good reason to be afraid of the answer.

But hearing the Noise from her transmitter, so close and so loud, had pushed me to the edge of panic – and when Tori insisted that I stay and listen to what she had to say, I'd ended up struggling with her. Which was how I'd wound up in after-school detention with her for forty minutes, with the Noise needling at me all the while. Then just as I grabbed my knapsack and hurried out the side door, thinking my torment was over, Tori had caught up with me again. That was when she told me the last thing I wanted to hear – that Mel had been spreading nasty rumours about Tori all over the school, and when Tori's friends confronted her she'd blamed it all on me.

I wasn't the one who had torn Tori to atoms. But at that moment, I'd been so hurt and angry that I would have, if I could. That was why I'd always felt responsible for what happened next – why I *was* responsible. Because if I hadn't lost control and lashed out at her, she wouldn't be here.

'You were right,' I said.

'About what?'

'About Mel. You told me she was using me, that she wasn't really my friend.' Maybe once she had been, but over the past couple of years she'd changed, and I'd been too wilfully blind to see it. 'You were right.'

Slowly Tori straightened up from her crouch until we stood face to face. 'OK,' she said. 'Good to know. But couldn't you have figured that out *before* you hit me?'

Embarrassed, I looked away. 'I already had. I just didn't want to admit it. She was my best friend. Pretty much my only friend.'

'You could have had a lot more friends,' said Tori, 'if you hadn't acted so…'

'Full of myself?'

'Well, yeah, that was how it looked. Like you knew some big important secret about life, the universe and everything, and you were keeping it all to yourself because the rest of us weren't good enough.'

'I wish,' I said, and then with sudden daring, 'You want to know the big important secret? Your name tastes like cough medicine.'

Tori's nose wrinkled in confusion. 'What?'

'Well, *Victoria* does, anyway.' And more than once, when I was sick of hearing how perfect and talented and beautiful she was, I'd consoled myself with that thought. 'Though *Tori* isn't so bad. It's more like black liquorice.'

'Wait a minute.' A suspicious look came over her face. 'You're telling me you have – what's it called – synesthesia?'

I was surprised. 'You've heard of it?'

'Well, yeah. I read an article on it in a science magazine, just a few months ago. About a guy who could taste words and a woman who could see music… Can you do that?'

I nodded.

'Oh, that's *prime*. I am so jealous. What colour is my name, then? Does it look like cough medicine, too?'

Without the Noise poisoning my senses, without the cloud of suspicion and hostility between us, it was easy now to see what I should have realised a long time ago – that, like Micheline, Tori was a better person than I'd given her credit for. 'No, it's kind of bluish-brown,' I said. 'But, Tori…'

I'd meant to apologise, but as usual, she was quicker than I was. 'Truce,' she said, sticking out her hand. 'We've got other things to worry about right now. You know?'

'I know,' I said, and shook it.

*

A few minutes later Faraday rejoined us, empty-handed but visibly relieved to find me awake.

'How do you feel?' he asked, as his fingers probed the swollen place on my neck and the bump on the back of my head to make sure neither was serious. 'You're not having any withdrawal symptoms, are you?' He glanced at Tori and added in a lower tone, 'Or any…other difficulties?'

'I'm fine,' I said. 'We're fine. We're just trying to find a way out of here.'

By now Tori had pried the front panel off the door and was studying the mechanism inside, a bewildering array of silvery globules trapped between two transparent plates. 'If this is the sequence when it's locked,' she murmured, 'then maybe if I altered the pattern *here* and *here*—' She picked up a tool that looked like a tyre gauge with delusions of grandeur, and set to work coaxing the beads in different directions.

I edged closer to Faraday and whispered, 'How does she know all this?'

'Bred into her, I expect.' He raised his voice. 'Have you always liked fixing things, Tori?'

'Yeah,' answered Tori over her shoulder. 'Even as a little kid, I could see at a glance how stuff worked and how to make it work better. It drove my mother up the wall. She kept trying to get me interested in dance and gymnastics and modelling, and I kept collecting old electronics junk and tinkering with it. The only way to settle her down was to tell her I was going into engineering.'

Faraday nodded. 'So one of your biological parents must have been a technician.'

'Not both?' I asked.

'If they had been, she wouldn't be here right now. I'm guessing she was an unlicensed conception, sold as a foetus for experimental purposes.' He spoke evenly, but with an acrid undertone that assured me he didn't like that idea any more than I did. 'After I left, someone must have got the idea to send her through the rift and see how growing up on Earth would affect her.'

I choked. 'They did that to a *baby*?'

'It's OK,' said Tori, still poking at the door, 'I got over it. I'm more ticked off about the transmitter thing, especially since it wouldn't let me go anywhere but Sudbury.'

'Why would that be?' I asked Faraday.

'I don't know,' he said. 'When we sent the first relay through the rift to your world, we suspected that it had been drawn to the Sudbury Basin because of the large amount of nickel in the rock. But that shouldn't have kept it, or Tori, from going elsewhere.'

'Well, you have a transmitter in your arm, too, right?' said Tori to Faraday. 'So maybe the relay was trying to stay close to both of us, and it couldn't do that unless we were in the same place.'

'Yes, but my transmitter was broken,' Faraday said. 'If it had been communicating properly, I wouldn't have had to search for the relay at all. I should have just been able to talk to Mathis – the older apprentice who'd sent me through the relay – and get him to bring me home.'

'But you were still transmitting *something*,' I said. 'I could hear it, and even see it, once I'd touched the mark on your arm. And the relay was receiving the signal, too. How else do you think I found it?'

Faraday's eyes darkened, and I could see I'd troubled him. But then Tori interrupted, 'Hey, Sebastian or Faraday or whatever, does this pattern look right to you?'

'I have no idea,' he replied. 'Not my genetic expertise. However, if you don't mind shutting that panel for a moment, we could try this.' He pressed his palm against the door, and it opened.

Tori threw me an exasperated look. 'Can I hit him? Please?'

'Sorry,' said Faraday, though he wasn't. 'It seemed worth a try, since I doubted they'd bother to erase my security clearance once they thought I was dead. *If* they thought I was dead.'

The last phrase was telling, and I knew we must be thinking the same thing. What if his fellow scientists had decided to make Faraday part of their experiment, and left him stranded on Earth on purpose?

'You should go back to the cargo hold,' he said, looking at me. 'They know Tori's here, but there's no reason they need to find out about you.'

'I don't know why not,' said Tori. 'If they've been keeping an eye on me, they must have seen Alison by now, unless they're all asleep or something. What about safety in numbers?' She pulled one of the tools out of her bag, hefted it, and handed it to me. 'If anybody tries to grab you, hit him with that.'

I took the makeshift club gladly, though I was sure Faraday would tell Tori she was being ridiculous. After all, if this science base belonged to a technologically advanced alien society, shouldn't they have guns?

But he only looked resigned. 'Fine,' he said. 'But let me go first. And stay back a bit, just in case.'

SEVENTEEN (IS DEVIOUS)

Compared to the dim quietness on the other side of the door, I'd expected to find this part of the science base buzzing with light and activity. But the curving hallway ahead of us looked no different than the one we'd left behind. We moved slowly at first, Faraday pausing now and then to listen at one of the closed doors, then to open it and stick his head inside. But they were all just as empty as the other rooms we'd seen, bare but for the occasional abandoned workstation or dusty bit of equipment. And there was no sound except the low, omnipresent thrum of energy I'd felt since we first arrived.

'I don't understand,' Faraday said. 'The project was fully staffed when I left. Where is everyone?'

'Well, we know there's at least one person here,' said Tori. 'The guy who knocked me out and fixed my nose. So all we need to do is find him, and he can tell us what happened to everybody else.' She paused. 'Unless he went crazy and murdered them all. Then maybe finding him wouldn't be such a good idea.'

I'd met a lot of crazy people in the last few weeks,

and most of them hadn't been a danger to anyone but themselves. And yet her words gave me an uneasy feeling, just the same. What if Tori was right about the outcome, even if she wasn't right about the cause? What if the other scientists were all dead, or dying, because of some plague or environmental disaster – and they'd blocked off half the station not to protect themselves from us, but to protect us from them?

'Faraday,' I said, catching his arm. 'The room I woke up in – the window was black. What does that mean?'

'Nothing,' he said. 'It was turned off, that's all.'

'So there aren't any real windows here? They're all just…screens?'

He nodded. 'That way they can serve a variety of functions: communication, work, entertainment. And when you're done, you can switch it back to show whatever view you prefer.'

'How about the real one?' I said.

'That, too – but when they're off-duty, most people prefer to look at something else.' Faraday stopped at a junction almost identical to the one I'd first encountered outside the storage room, where a straight corridor ran perpendicular to the curved hallway in which we stood. 'There's nobody in the outer ring,' he said. 'They must all be in the observatory.' He headed up the new corridor, and Tori and I followed.

Unlike its dead-end twin on the other side of the base, this particular hallway ended in a door. Solid metal, like all the others we'd seen, but this one had a porthole. Faraday paused briefly to look through it, then turned back to us with a frown. 'There's only one person in there,' he said.

'Then we can take him,' said Tori, slapping a tool against her palm. 'Let's go.'

Faraday touched the door open, and one by one we stepped through. We emerged into an enormous circular room, whose domed ceiling looked out on a dazzling expanse of night sky.

I'd never seen so many stars, all of them unfamiliar. More than half of them were colours I had no names for, and the music they made inside my head was strange as experimental jazz. But as my gaze travelled slowly from one edge of the dome to the other, what struck me even more was the sheer breadth of the view. No matter where I looked, there was nothing but stars – not a hint of surrounding landscape or civilization in sight.

A shiver ran through me as I realised, in that

moment, something I should have guessed long ago: this observatory hadn't been built on some remote mountaintop of Faraday's world, as I'd vaguely supposed.

It was a space station.

I was still gazing up at the window – or was it a screen? – when Tori nudged my arm. Across the room stood a young man in a crisp grey tunic and slacks, one hand poised over the console in front of him. He looked not much older than twenty, with bronze hair sleeked back from a long narrow face, and as the three of us walked towards him, he blanched.

'If the viruses and bacteria on Earth didn't kill me,' said Faraday, 'I doubt you have anything to worry about.' He put his hand over his heart and made that odd little bow I'd seen him give before. 'Hello, Mathis. It's been a long time. For one of us, anyway.'

Mathis? I was startled. *This* was Faraday's fellow apprentice, the boy who'd helped send him to Earth all those years ago? But back then he had been older, and now...

For a moment the young scientist remained frozen. Then an incredulous look came over his face. 'Sav Astin!' he breathed, then rushed forward and seized Faraday by both arms, gabbling out a torrent of words in a language I'd never heard before. They tugged at my shoulder and raised the fine hairs at the back of my neck, but they were all the same hazy green colour, and they refused to tell me what they meant.

'I'm glad to see you alive, too,' Faraday told him, half-smiling. 'Though you can leave off the *Sav* part. I'm too old to be anyone's apprentice now.'

Mathis rattled off another string of syllables that sounded like a question.

'Because,' Faraday said, 'Tori and Alison deserve to know what's going on. And I'm sure you've studied enough English by now to understand most of what I'm saying, even if you can't speak it.'

'He understands English?' asked Tori. 'Does that include insults and swear words? Because if he's the one who locked me up—'

'Wait,' said Faraday. 'Give him a chance to explain. That's only fair, isn't it?' He raised his eyebrows at Mathis, who seemed to understand. He led us to a circle of chairs on the other side of the observatory, and we all sat down while he launched into his story.

He talked for a long time. I struggled with the unfamiliar words, trying to wring shapes and tastes out of them, but nothing made sense until Faraday spoke up again.

'That's not your decision,' he said flatly. 'Whatever her scientific value, Alison is here as a visitor, not a specimen. As for Tori, I understand that the data you've collected from her is extremely important to your research. But whether you paid for her or not, she has a right—'

'*Paid?*' exploded Tori. 'You mean this is the guy who's been experimenting on me?' She lunged forward, but Faraday flung out an arm to hold her back.

'Sit down,' he told her, in an authoritative tone I'd never heard him use before. 'We'll deal with that later.' He held her furious gaze with his own level one until she subsided, then returned his attention to Mathis. 'I understand about the war back home,' he said, 'and the government's decision to strip this station down and repurpose it for military use. It's stupid and infuriating, but it's the kind of thing I'd expect the Meritocracy to do. And yes, I realise you've invested years in studying Tori, and that you didn't want to leave without finishing the experiment—'

Mathis tried to interrupt, but Faraday cut him off. 'I'm explaining it to them, not to you. Be patient.' He turned to Tori and I and went on, 'Our homeland is going through a civil war. The State's running out of money and resources to fight the uprising, so they're scavenging all the technology and personnel they can get their hands on. That's why this base is empty, because the scientists have all gone back home and taken a lot of our best equipment with them. Mathis had to fight for the chance to stay behind, and he's only got a few days until the troops arrive, so he's been trying to collect as much data as he can before closing the wormhole.'

'Wormhole?' I asked.

'The dimensional rift is enormous,' said Faraday. 'And it's constantly fluctuating, so if you go through it, there's no telling what part of the universe you'll end up in. The wormhole is an artificially generated vortex that keeps the rift, or at least one tiny part of it, pointing to a single location – in this case, Earth. But it takes a tremendous amount of energy to keep that connection open, and the government wants to use that power for…other things.'

I'd read enough military sci-fi novels to imagine just how ugly those 'other things' might be. 'So once the wormhole's gone, the rift won't be stable any more.'

He gave a sober nod. 'And then we'll have lost all contact with your world.'

'But we still have time, right?' I said. 'As long as you send us back right away, then…'

The rest of the sentence died on my tongue, obliterated by a new and painful thought. If Tori and I returned to Sudbury together, that would prove to everyone that I hadn't killed her. It might even be enough to prove I wasn't crazy. I'd be able to go home to my family, my music, my life…

But I'd never see Faraday again.

'That's what Mathis and I were discussing—' Faraday began, but the younger man interrupted.

'There is nothing to discuss,' he said in English, his accent so heavy it made my knees ache. 'All of you will remain here.'

'Oh, really?' said Tori, hefting her toolkit, but Mathis was unmoved.

'There is no point in threatening me,' he said. 'There is nothing I can do.'

'What do you mean?' Tori demanded.

'I mean,' Mathis said, 'that the wormhole is already closed.'

My heart thudded into my diaphragm. 'What? But we just came through it—'

Then it hit me. The flood of sensations that had overwhelmed me when the relay disintegrated Tori, and again right after Faraday and I came to this place...they hadn't happened by accident. The first time it had taken me weeks to recover, but this time I'd felt better almost immediately, and now I knew why.

Because it was exposure to the wormhole that had been affecting my synesthesia. And right after Faraday and I arrived, Mathis had shut the wormhole down.

'But you can open it again, right?' Tori asked Mathis. She looked at Faraday, then at me. 'Can't he?'

I remembered what Faraday had just told us about the rift, and how it kept fluctuating. I remembered the empty rooms and neglected workstations we'd passed on the way here. And most of all, I remembered the flavour of Mathis's voice as he'd told us, in English, that nothing we could do to him would make any difference.

'No,' I said slowly. 'I don't think he can.'

First Tori had paced around and raged; then she'd dropped back into her chair and burst into tears. I'd tried to comfort her, but she'd pushed me away. Then she'd grabbed her toolkit and fled, the grey bubbles of her sobs trailing behind her. There'd been an awful moment of silence while Faraday, Mathis and I looked at each other, and then the young scientist had got up and walked back to his console.

I knew I ought to cry too, but right now I was too numb to feel anything. I just sat there, staring at the floor, until Faraday edged closer and took my hand. 'I'm so sorry, Alison,' he said, his voice pitched low so Mathis couldn't hear. 'This must be a terrible shock for you.'

I gave a shaky laugh. 'You mean being trapped in a place I never wanted to be, unable to go home, at the mercy of someone who wants to analyse every detail of my existence but has no interest in me as a person? Actually no, it feels pretty familiar.'

Faraday was silent. Then he said, 'I can't speak for Mathis, but you're wrong about Dr Minta. He may be a little clumsy at showing it, but he does care. Did you know that his first wife was diagnosed with schizophrenia, and committed suicide after going off her medication?'

I was taken aback. 'No.'

'Then let me tell you something else you probably don't know,' said Faraday. 'When he was eight years old, Kirk set a fire in the basement of his mother's house, while she and her boyfriend – a drug runner for a motorcycle gang, who had been abusing Kirk physically and sexually for months – were sleeping

362

upstairs. They both died of smoke inhalation, but Kirk doesn't remember it. Sometimes he still talks as though they're alive.'

His words stabbed me with an empathy I'd never expected to feel. Had the fire been an accident, or had Kirk set it on purpose? Did even he know the answer any more? 'Why are you telling me all this?' I asked.

'Everybody has a story, Alison,' he said. 'Everybody has things they need to hide – sometimes even from themselves. Mathis and I were friends once, but he's changed, and I need to know what happened to make him this way. Maybe then I'll be able to get through to him, convince him to let you and Tori go free. If we all work together, we might find a way to open the wormhole again.'

So there was still a chance of getting home? I wanted to believe it, but I was afraid to let myself hope. 'And if you can't get through to him?'

'Then we'll have to try something else. But I have to put Mathis at ease if I want him to open up to me. That's why I'm asking you to let me talk to him alone, and not interrupt us. Will you do that?' Reluctantly, I nodded, and Faraday's eyes softened. 'Thank you, Alison.'

I clutched his hand. 'Be careful. I don't trust him.'

'You don't have to,' said Faraday. 'Just try to trust me.' He squeezed my fingers, then let me go and walked over to Mathis. The younger scientist looked apprehensive at first, but when Faraday spoke to him in their own language, he relaxed and answered in kind. They exchanged a few sentences, and then Mathis motioned to the console beside him, and Faraday sat down.

It seemed like a natural time for me to leave, so I got up from my chair and walked towards the exit. All the while Mathis's eyes followed me, but Faraday kept talking to him, in that rich, mellifluous voice that made even the harshest syllables beautiful. And then something he said made Mathis smile.

As soon as I saw that, it was like a key had turned in my head, unlocking a box of knowledge I hadn't even known I possessed. Suddenly I could smell triumph all over Mathis, the satisfied air of a man who had finally persuaded a fool to see reason. 'I'm glad you've decided to be sensible about this,' he said.

Only he wasn't speaking English. And yet the message came through to me just the same: *pleasure – confidence – trust*, with subtle undertones of other emotions that left me in no doubt of what his words meant. I nearly tripped over my own feet, but

I managed to catch myself in time. Stepping carefully out of the observatory, I eased the door mostly shut behind me, then crouched and listened through the crack as Mathis went on:

'After all that nonsense about sending them back through the wormhole, I was beginning to wonder if I could rely on you. That Earth girl's quite devoted to you, isn't she? What are you going to do with her? Keep her as a pet?'

'Don't be vulgar,' said Faraday, but the reproach was mild. 'I owe her a great deal for helping me find the relay again. I'd like to see her treated well.'

'Ah, yes. The relay.' The amusement in Mathis's voice faded. 'When your transmitter stopped working, I thought you were dead. I scanned for days, trying to find the signal again, but there was no trace of you. If I'd known it was just a malfunction...'

He was lying, and for a moment I wondered why. Then realisation inched up my brain stem, and my skin began to crawl with horror.

'No need to explain,' said Faraday. 'It's all in the past. I'm more interested in what you were doing with Tori. It can't have been easy convincing the others to go along with your idea of sending her to Earth, after what had happened to me.'

But the other scientists hadn't known what had happened to Faraday. He had just disappeared, and Mathis had pretended he knew nothing about it. I wanted to fling the door open and shout at Faraday to get out of there, but I'd promised not to interrupt, and he'd asked me to trust him. I could only hope that Mathis wasn't carrying a weapon underneath that tailored uniform.

'It wasn't easy,' Mathis said. 'But eventually they came around. Still, we'd only been observing her progress for a few years when we got the order to suspend the Earth project. The other scientists were prepared to give up on Tori's part of the experiment, since she was still a child and we didn't know if she'd survive to maturity. If I hadn't come up with the idea of accelerating the mouth of the wormhole...'

Faraday drew in a sharp breath. 'So *that's* what happened. You increased the time differential between the two relays, and collected years' worth of information in – what? A matter of weeks?'

'Exactly. I'd meant to continue my observations until she reached adulthood. But when the readings spiked and I realised she'd been injured, I had to activate the relay and retrieve her a little earlier than planned. Still, she's close enough to maturity that it hardly matters. I think it's safe to declare the experiment a success.'

'I should think so,' said Faraday, with a dryness so subtle that even I nearly missed it. 'So now you've got Tori, what's going to happen to her?'

'Well, the war's going to make it difficult to do much with her right away,' said Mathis. 'But obviously we'll want to examine her and do a few interviews, and put her through a number of medical and psychological tests.'

'And after that?'

'Who knows? It's not my decision. But her conception was unlicensed, she's mixed-class, and she's had no proper education. And with that feisty attitude of hers, I doubt the Meritocracy will think it's a good idea to release her – she's likely to go off and join the uprising. So once we've got all the information we need from her, I imagine she'll just be terminated.'

My stomach knotted. I clutched the edge of the door, clenching my teeth against the impulse to cry out. If Mathis realised that I'd not only been eavesdropping, but that I'd actually understood what he said, Tori and I would be in even more danger than we were already.

'That seems a little excessive, doesn't it?' asked Faraday.

'Maybe,' said Mathis. 'But why waste time fretting over things that can't be changed, especially when you have such a great future ahead of you? Think of it, Astin – you're the first scientist ever to visit another planet. Not only did you make contact with the natives and live among them for years, you brought one back for us to study. If I didn't have Tori, I might envy you.' He chuckled, and for a moment he reminded me of Kirk. 'We're both about to become very famous men, my friend. So why don't we forget these unnecessary details, and go and have a drink to celebrate?'

The taste his words left in my mouth was so thick and foul I wanted to vomit. *Don't go*, I pleaded silently with Faraday. *Don't trust him...*

'I should probably see how Alison and Tori are doing first,' said Faraday.

'Why?' asked Mathis. 'It's not as though they can go anywhere.'

'True,' Faraday replied. 'All right, then.'

My legs felt shaky, and my head swam with nausea. I was afraid to let go of the door, in case it made a sound when it closed. But when I risked a glance through the porthole the two of them were already rising from their seats, and I had no more time for caution.

I held my breath, slipped my fingers out of the crack, and ran.

I found Tori in the storage hold, standing on top of Faraday's pile of crates and looking up at the relay with appraising eyes. She seemed to have calmed down, but when she picked up one of her tools and started poking at the relay, I gasped.

'Don't worry,' she said without looking at me, 'I won't break it.'

'I was more afraid you'd beam yourself into space.'

Tori snorted derisively. 'Accidentally on purpose? Thanks, but I can think of better ways to go.'

I watched her tease the relay open, prying apart its outer shell to reveal the workings within. 'That's what I thought,' she murmured, and then with a deft twist she detached the silvery ball from the ceiling and climbed back down with it in her hand.

'What are you trying to do?' I asked.

She looked at me bleakly. 'I'm not sure. I guess I'm just not ready to give up yet. Everyone and everything that matters to me is back on Earth. There has to be a way to get the wormhole open again, no matter what Mathis says.'

I wanted to tell her what else Mathis had said, but the words stuck in my throat. What good would it do for her to know that she was probably going to die? It couldn't make her any more determined than she already was, and if we couldn't open the wormhole again she'd find out soon enough. 'I hope you're right,' I said. 'This place...we don't belong here.'

'You're really pale,' said Tori. 'Even for you, I mean. Are you OK? Where's Sebastian?'

That name still felt so intimate to me, I could hardly speak it without blushing. Even knowing it wasn't really his, it summed up everything I felt about him, all the things I wanted when he touched me but was afraid we'd never have the chance to share. How could she just throw it out like that, as though it had no significance at all? 'He's with Mathis,' I said. 'They're...talking.'

'Then why do you look so scared?'

I rubbed the back of my hand across my eyes. 'It's probably nothing. Faraday knows what he's doing. But I don't trust Mathis.'

'I don't either,' said Tori. 'Anybody who thinks it's a good idea to stick a chip in a baby's arm and beam her off to an alien planet, just to see if she survives? Not a nice person.' She peered into the relay for a few more seconds, then closed it up and dropped it into her bag. 'Let's go for a walk.'

'What for?' I asked.

'Inventory,' she said cryptically, and off we went.

We spent the next half hour or so exploring the station, particularly the side that had been closed off to us before. Tori stopped to open every box and inspect every piece of equipment we came across, muttering to herself all the while. What this was supposed to achieve was a mystery to me, but at least it gave me something to do other than worry, and by the time we'd completed our circuit of the outer corridor and headed back up to the observatory, Tori was in better spirits.

'There's still some good stuff left around here,' she said. 'We should be able to do *something* with it. I just don't know...' She stopped, frowning at my stiff body and unfocused eyes. 'What?'

I could feel him coming up the passageway behind us, the air around him seething with bitterness and barely restrained anger. There was blood on his knuckles, sweat on his skin, and something metal in his hand.

'Something just happened.' My voice was tight. 'Something very bad.'

'To who?'

'Faraday,' I whispered, and then he walked in.

'There you are.' Faraday sounded as affable as ever, but his eyes were dark. 'Tori, may I borrow you for a moment? I need you to lock a door.'

'Which door?'

'The one Mathis is currently sleeping behind. You can have this back now,' he said, and tossed her the injector he'd been holding. The capsule plugged into its base was nearly empty.

'You drugged him?' I said.

'Seriously?' said Tori.

Faraday didn't answer. He led us back to the outer corridor, where an open door led into a set of living quarters twice the size of any we'd seen before. Inside, Mathis sprawled unconscious on the matting, his bronze hair in disarray and blood seeping out of his nose.

'I'm afraid I had to hit him first,' said Faraday.

Tori's face lit up. She tugged the door shut, dumped out her toolkit and set to work, prying open the mechanism and shifting the beads into the locking pattern. 'He's not going to get out of there any time soon,' she said as she snapped the panel closed.

Faraday looked at me. 'Aren't you going to ask me why?'

'I know why,' I said. 'Because he's a liar. He never really lost the signal from your transmitter. He left you on Earth on purpose, because you were smarter than he was and he was sick of working in your shadow. He tricked you into thinking he was your friend, and then he betrayed you, to serve his own ambition. And if you hadn't stopped him, he would have done it again.'

We were all silent, looking at the closed door. 'So,' said Tori at last, 'now what?'

Faraday straightened up with a visible effort. 'Now,' he said, 'we go to the infirmary so I can get the transmitter out of your arm, and give Alison something to help with her withdrawal. Then we'll see if we can't find a way to open that wormhole again, and get the two of you back home.'

EIGHTEEN (IS DETERMINED)

'I got the docking bay open,' said Tori proudly, carrying a large container into the observatory and dropping it onto the floor. 'There was a bunch more equipment in there. I guess Mathis had been planning to bring it back to the planet with him.'

As she wiped the back of her hand across her brow, I could still see the mark on her arm; according to Faraday, it would take a few months before the transmitter dissolved completely. But it was deactivated now, as was his, and I'd never have to hear either of them make the Noise again.

'Excellent,' said Faraday, not turning around. He'd called up a blueprint of the station on the overhead screen – it looked like a wheel with two spokes and a bubble in the middle – and was studying it intently. 'Fortunately, he hadn't yet got around to dismantling the wormhole stabilizer, and I think we might be able to put together a quantum impulse generator from the components we have left.'

'So you can do it?' I asked, hope and dread warring inside me. 'You really think that you can open the wormhole again?'

'We may be able to open *a* wormhole,' corrected Faraday. 'But the likelihood of getting the right one on the first try, or even the second or third, is infinitesimally small. I can calculate the right coordinates for the rift, but when it comes to finding Earth again – that's going to be the tricky part.'

'I don't care,' said Tori. 'At least we can try. You tell me what you need, and I'll figure out how to make it happen.'

Faraday smiled at her. 'I know you will.'

'What about me?' I asked. 'How can I help?'

The glance that Tori and Faraday shared was a conversation in itself, and it didn't take me long to realise what it meant. 'Never mind,' I told them, backing away. 'I'll just watch.'

The two of them lost no time in getting to work, Faraday checking readings and making adjustments to the controls while Tori dashed around setting up equipment. From the determined way they both went about their tasks, they seemed to have rejected even the possibility of failure.

I wished I could do the same. But as I sat there and watched them, all I could think about was what would happen if this didn't work. As long as Faraday had at least pretended to be on the same side as Mathis, there'd been a chance that he'd be welcomed back by his fellow scientists, and that he could protect Tori and myself with his influence. But now that he'd turned against his former ally and staked everything on getting the two of us back home, there was no telling what the future would hold for any of us.

Faraday must have sensed my worried gaze on his back, because he turned and looked at me. 'How do you feel?' he asked.

I rubbed the tender spot on my shoulder where the injection had gone in. Faraday had said it would help my withdrawal symptoms, but I still felt tired and a little queasy. Maybe it was just the stress. 'I'm all right.'

'No, you're not,' he said. 'Go and lie down. I'll wake you if anything happens.'

I didn't want to leave him. But I didn't want to be a distraction, either – not when what he and Tori were doing was so important. Reluctantly I got up and headed for the door.

'Alison.'

I stirred, blinking, as Faraday's voice warmed my spine. When I lay down, I hadn't expected to sleep at all, let alone so deeply. But now I sensed that I'd been out for at least—

I sat up. 'How long have I been asleep?' Faraday turned his wrist over to look at his watch, but I spoke first: 'Three hours and forty-six minutes.'

'How did you know that?' asked Faraday, and I tasted the ripe-tomato burst of his surprise.

'I've started to see time as a spectrum,' I said. 'When I went to sleep the time was sage green, and now it's lavender.'

'Your synesthesia's changed again?'

I nodded. 'And it's not just the time thing. I can smell emotions now. I can sense the shape of things, feel their texture, even tell you what colour they are, without looking at them. And when you sent me out of the observatory, so you could talk to Mathis in your own language...I didn't recognise any of the words, but I understood what you were saying.'

Faraday exhaled slowly and sat down next to me. 'I wondered,' he said. 'The way you looked at me, when I told you I'd knocked him out... It was a little too knowing. And a little too relieved, as well.'

'I was so afraid for you,' I whispered, leaning against his shoulder. 'After what he said about Tori, how he didn't even seem to care if she lived or died...

I couldn't believe you'd go off with him like that. Especially when he'd already tried to kill you once.'

'He's not a murderer, Alison. He's just like I was before I came to your world, too full of his own ideas and ambitions to think about anything else. He didn't want me dead, only out of the way.'

'Are you sure about that?'

Faraday didn't answer. He just sat there, smelling of soap and sorrow – and that was when I knew what he'd come to tell me.

'You couldn't open the wormhole,' I said.

'Actually, we did. We tested the impulse generator, and it worked perfectly. But…' He looked down at his lean, chemical-stained hands. 'We have no way of detecting what's on the other side, no way to tell whether we've found Earth's solar system or some lifeless region of space. The most crucial component of the long-range scanner is missing, and even if we could rig up a replacement, it would take days to calibrate.' He slid an arm around my waist, dropping his cheek against my hair. 'Days we don't have. I'm sorry.'

The fragrance around him was duskier than regret or melancholy. It was despair. Which meant that we couldn't just transmit ourselves to some far-off hideaway or join the uprising against the Meritocracy.

Faraday had already considered all the alternatives he could think of, and saw no way out of this situation for any of us.

So Tori would be handed over to the scientists for testing. Faraday would have to answer for what he'd done to Mathis – assaulting a fellow scientist, attempting to sabotage his work. And I'd be trapped on an alien world, a prisoner for the rest of my life. I knew I should feel something – scared, upset, maybe even angry – but I couldn't. There was just this empty space in the middle of my chest, like a black hole, swallowing everything.

'I'm sorry,' Faraday said again, his arms tightening around me. I buried my face against his collarbone and clung to him, tears pricking behind my closed eyelids. We held each other for the space of several heartbeats, and then he crooked a finger under my chin and tilted my head up.

A feverish warmth flooded my body as I realised what was about to happen. I'd dreamed of this moment, but I hadn't wanted it to be like this, all tangled up in grief and the desperate need for comfort. Yet as Faraday's lips whispered along my hairline, grazed the curve of my cheek, and brushed across my lashes, all my resistance melted. I couldn't pull away.

His mouth hovered over mine, an unspoken question. I breathed a silent *yes,* and as we kissed his hand spread warm across the small of my back, right where his voice touched me.

Comet trails of indigo and violet streaked through my inner vision, and electricity sparked all over my skin. Our breath mingled, quick and shallow, while my lips melted open and the blood pounded through me in a pleasure so intense it was only a shade away from pain. I had never been this close to another human being, yet I ached to pull him even closer, to merge into him like one drop of water into another and lose myself, even if only for a little while.

It was so tempting to give in. To lie down and pull him over me like a blanket, to bury myself in the weight of his body and the touch of his lips and hands. To shut out the rest of the universe and abandon myself completely to sensation, for as long as I could make this moment last.

But I couldn't, because this wasn't just about me. It was my fault Tori was trapped on this station right now, and it was my responsibility to do everything I could to help her. And the words Faraday had spoken just a few moments before he kissed me – *we have no way to detect what's on the other side* – kept rewriting themselves more and more insistently in my mind.

I caught Faraday's face between my hands and broke off the kiss, breathless. 'I've just thought of something,' I said. 'Something we haven't tried.'

'There's a lot of things we haven't tried,' he said, 'but I'm going to refrain from the obvious, and assume you're talking about the wormhole. What is it?'

'My synesthesia,' I said. 'I know it's probably impossible, but – when I was at Pine Hills, every time I looked at the night sky, I heard music. Always the same music, but totally different from the song that the stars sing out here. I'd know that song again. And there's the relay, too – it's still sending out a signal, isn't it?'

'Yes, but it's incredibly unlikely that you'd be able to sense Earth at such a distance,' Faraday said. 'Even with all the help I can give you. And yet—' His voice brightened with excitement. 'You've never really tested the limits of your abilities, have you?'

'No. I've always been afraid of opening myself up too far, in case...'

In case I lose my mind. The thought scared me so much, I couldn't even bring myself to finish the sentence. And yet if I couldn't do this now, with my senses fully at my command for the first time ever, and all our lives at stake...

I took a deep breath. 'It doesn't matter,' I said. 'I want to try.'

'Once I activate the screen inside this helmet,' said Faraday as he handed it to me, 'you'll be looking at a direct feed from the station's long-range sensors, and nothing else. Try it on.'

As I lowered it over my head I braced myself for discomfort, but it felt surprisingly light, more like a motorcycle helmet than the heavy fishbowl I'd expected.

'You're not claustrophobic, are you?' asked Tori.

I looked down at the crate I was sitting in – seven feet long, three feet wide, and lined with spongy foam. 'No, but I do have a fear of being buried alive.'

'We're not going to bury you,' she assured me. 'There's plenty of oxygen in there, and you can take the lid off yourself if you want to. It's just to keep you from getting distracted.'

I lay down gingerly, lowering my arms to my sides. 'OK,' I said.

'I can close it up now?'

I licked my dry lips. 'Yeah.'

'Good luck,' said Tori, and she fitted the lid into place.

It was dark. It was silent. The box cradled me gently as God's own hand, its soft interior moulding itself to the shape of my body.

'Alison?' said Faraday's voice in my helmet, warm and chocolaty as ever. 'I'm going to switch on the helmet now. Are you ready?'

'Ready,' I said, and when I opened my eyes I was looking at a field of stars, bright and shallow as glitter on black paper. 'This is it?' I asked.

'It should be. Is there a problem?'

'No, but it's sort of…' I squinted. 'Flat.'

'Oh, of course, I forgot your tetrachromacy. My apologies.' My visor flickered and the star-field shifted into three dimensions, all its missing hues and subtle mid-tones sparking to life. 'I just added in the ultraviolet range. Is that better?'

I didn't answer. I was speechless with awe. A tapestry of iridescent light unfurled before me, star-jewelled and shimmering with all the colours of the spectrum and beyond. I'd seen the aurora borealis once and been entranced by its otherworldly glow; but this was a billion times lovelier – and more dangerous.

'Alison? Are you still with me?'

'The rift,' I whispered. 'I can see it.'

'Excellent. I'm going to increase the magnification,'

said Faraday. 'Let me know if it gets too much.'

And with that I found myself drifting closer to the rift, until my whole vision filled with its rippling magnificence. Dreamily I lifted my hand to touch it, and only when my fingers bumped the lid of the crate did I remember that I wasn't actually floating in space.

'Tori,' I heard Faraday say, 'is the impulse generator ready?'

'Ready,' she replied.

'All right, Alison. Here we go.'

Until he said that, I'd thought I was prepared. But now I felt as though someone was scooping out my insides with a melon baller. I grabbed at the helmet, about to yell at Faraday to stop—

But it was already too late.

A needle of purple light streaked across my vision and pierced the delicate fabric of the rift. Darkness bloomed before my eyes, licking through the rainbow veil to expose a glimpse of unknown space beyond. Then the shockwave hit, and a roaring flood of synesthesia swept over me.

Ice-hot stabbing eighty-seven sour crimson slashes suffocating wet ochre thickness pounding dizzy hideous triangles fifty pulsating opaque acrid zigzags crushing white fire hurthurthurthurthurt—

My self-control shredded like tissue paper, flaying my emotions bare. I screamed and bolted upright, throwing the lid open.

'Whoa!' Tori grabbed the helmet out of my hands before I could hurl it to the floor. I collapsed back into the box, one forearm thrown over my burning eyes.

'I'm sorry,' I sobbed. 'I can't do this. I can't.'

'Alison.' Faraday knelt beside me, his face drawn with concern. 'What happened?'

'The wormhole – close it – please—'

Faraday got up quickly and touched something on the console. Within seconds the terror receded, and I could breathe again.

'So what's going on?' Tori demanded. 'What's wrong with her?'

'It seems to be something to do with the impulse generator,' Faraday replied. 'As soon as we fired the beam to open the wormhole, her synesthesia became unbearably intense, and as soon as we shut it down she felt better again. But what about the generator could possibly be affecting...' He stopped, his violet eyes widening. 'Exotic matter.'

Tori frowned. 'What?'

'That's what your scientists call it. The matter we use to keep the wormhole stable once it's open has properties unlike any other kind of matter in the universe, and there's a great deal about it that we don't understand. I'm wondering if somehow, between her synesthesia and her tetrachromacy, Alison is sensitive to exotic matter – and the more of it she's exposed to, the stronger her abilities become.'

'I can't do it,' I mumbled again, resting my head against the side of the box. 'It's too much.'

'But you hardly even *tried*,' Tori said. 'We'd only just started, and you…' She threw up her hands and stalked a few paces before whirling back to me. 'You're fine now, aren't you? So take a break and get your strength back, and then try again.'

'Tori,' said Faraday.

She pushed her hands impatiently through her tangled hair. 'You want me to say please? To beg? I'll do all of that. But don't ask me to apologise. You think I don't know what's going to happen to me – and to her – if Mathis and those other scientists get hold of us?' She crouched down and gripped my wrist. 'Please, Alison. I'm begging you. Don't give up.'

Anger sparked inside me, white-hot and blinding. I wrenched my arm away. 'I will go crazy!' I shouted at her. 'My mind will snap, and I'll fall apart, and never be the same person again! Is that what you want? You think I wouldn't rather stay here and risk the chance of dying, than spend the rest of my life locked up in a place like Pine Hills – or worse?'

Tori's face turned white. She leaped to her feet and walked out, leaving Faraday and me alone.

I slumped, exhausted by the force of my own emotion. 'I'm sorry,' I said to Faraday.

He slipped a hand beneath my chin and lifted it up again. 'Every time you show your feelings, you apologise. Have you ever had an emotion in your life that you weren't ashamed of?'

I couldn't answer. All I could do was blink at him, as his features blurred and my lashes clumped together with tears.

'I've seen your medical records,' he said. 'Migraines. Stomach cramps. You've held back so much, Alison, for so long, that you're making yourself sick. What would happen if you stopped fighting, and gave yourself permission to feel? Not just the good things, but everything?'

'I'd lose my mind,' I whispered.

'I don't think so. Do you know something about antipsychotic drugs, Alison? If you aren't psychotic when you start taking them, you soon will be. Hearing voices, hallucinating, experiencing all kinds of delusions and paranoid thoughts. When I first came to Pine Hills to meet you, that was the state I expected to find you in. But instead, I discovered a young woman who was confused and hurting, but also fully aware of who she was, where she was, and what was and wasn't real. After all you'd been through, you had every reason to be insane – but you weren't.' His voice lowered. 'You're not.'

He'd never stopped believing in me, even when the evidence against my sanity seemed overwhelming. I only wished I had half as much faith in myself as he did. I leaned my cheek against his palm, and closed my eyes.

'All I ask,' Faraday went on, his thumb stroking my face, 'is that you try one more time. I will shut the wormhole down, I promise you, the instant you tell me it's too much. But you're stronger than you give yourself credit for, Alison.'

I wasn't sure about that. But I knew that if I gave up now, I'd regret it for the rest of my life. I sat back, rubbing my eyes until patterns exploded behind the lids. 'All right,' I said. 'I'll try again.'

I whirled through a sandstorm of cosmic dust, floundered in a sucking bog of dark matter. Neutrinos riddled my body, and the beams of a trillion stars lasered through my skin. I opened my mouth to scream, but nothing came out—

'Alison.' Faraday's voice washed over me, soothing as aloe. 'Talk to me. Tell me what you're seeing.'

I wasn't seeing anything, because my eyes were squeezed shut. I was lying face-first on the pavement outside Champlain Secondary, my hands sticky with Tori's blood. I was strapped to a bed in an isolation room, writhing and sobbing. I was huddled in my lonely cell in Red Ward, staring into space.

'I need you to look, Alison. I need you to tell me if you sense anything on the other side of that wormhole that's familiar. Anything that feels like home.'

I was struggling to get away as Kirk's hands wandered over my body. I was listening to my mother weep as she told me my grandmother had been mentally ill. I was sitting in Dr Minta's office while he told me the man I had known as Dr Sebastian Faraday was nothing more than a dream.

'She can't do it.' That was Tori, a flat line of despair. 'Just forget it. Let her out.'

'Is that what you want, Alison?'

'Wait,' I said.

And then I opened my eyes, and looked straight into the wormhole.

It was black, but it wasn't empty. It was full of wonders visible and invisible, a teeming pool of energy and cold heat. I tasted icy comets shooting through the void, cringed away from the blaze of a supernova—

'No,' I gasped, surfacing. 'It's not home.'

'Well done.' Faraday's words stroked my aching back, as the wormhole's dark iris snapped shut and disappeared. 'How do you feel?'

I relaxed into my bed of foam. 'Better. Now.'

'Take a couple of minutes,' said Faraday. 'And then, if you're ready, we'll try again.'

By the time we'd opened and closed six more wormholes, I was exhausted. The effort of holding myself together was so enormous that I felt ready to shatter.

'There has to be another way,' I panted to Faraday.

'If I could give you one, I would.' He spoke levelly, but even through the walls of the box I could smell his worry, his guilt. 'Tell me to stop, Alison. That's all you have to do.'

'You are doing *amazing*, Ali,' Tori told me, her voice clogged with tears. 'I know you can do this.

Just – hang on a little longer. Please.'

I didn't answer. I just lay there, staring at the inside of the helmet, as the beam streaked purple across the blackness and tore open the rift again.

This time I didn't even brace myself. I was too weak for that. I was a dry reed, a spent candle, insubstantial as a breath. My life was meaningless, my thoughts futile. If the universe wanted to erase me, in all its eternal and infinite might, who was I to resist?

In my mind's eye I saw Faraday leaning heavily on the console, his eyes shut in anguish and his unruly hair tumbling over his forehead. I saw Tori slumped against the side of my crate, one arm slung across the lid as though she could hug me through its metal surface, and give me comfort. And I saw Mathis, dishevelled and furious, smashing a chair into the door of his room again and again until it buckled, and began to give way—

Sensations poured over me, into me, filling me up and spilling over. I could feel my shell of sanity cracking, my worst fears and darkest memories trying to break through, but I had no energy left to try and hold myself together. My only thought now was for Tori and Faraday – and what would happen to them if I failed.

So instead of fighting, I surrendered. I abandoned all dignity, every pretence of shame or self-control, and threw myself wide open to it all.

The emotions poured out of me, a torrent of sobs and tears and rage, a babble of all the words I'd never spoken, all the thoughts I'd never dared voice. I loved my mother, even though her fears had haunted my childhood and left me afraid to get close to anyone. I hated my father for teaching me to avoid confrontation, and hide from the truth instead of facing it. I missed Mel, the closest friend and worst betrayer I'd ever had. I envied Tori her popularity and her self-confidence and her loving family, even though it wasn't her fault she had all those things and I didn't. And I was terrified of losing Faraday, a soulmate so perfectly made for me that even now I was half afraid I'd invented him.

As the past few weeks of my life raced through my memory, I saw with painful clarity how ignorant I'd been, how many foolish mistakes I'd made. I'd resented Dr Minta for misdiagnosing my problems and forcing medication on me against my will. I'd pitied Sanjay for living in a fantasy world, and I'd avoided Micheline because her angry cynicism and lapses into self-injury made her the last kind of person I wanted to be. But the truth was that I had no right to judge any of them, not even Kirk. Because even if I hadn't inherited my grandmother's schizophrenia, I was still full of ignorance and delusion and buried rage, and I needed help.

I had no idea if I was only saying these things in my mind, or right out loud for Faraday and Tori to hear. But it didn't matter, because I'd finally reached the end of myself, all my self-reliance and denial and pride unravelling into nothingness, leaving only a blank Alison-shaped space behind. It was finished. I was done.

But just as I felt myself dissolving on the tide of my own self-condemnation, the dark waves receded, and I floated into a celestial calm.

I saw the whole universe laid out before me, a vast shining machine of indescribable beauty and complexity. Its design was too intricate for me to understand, and I knew I could never begin to grasp more than the smallest idea of its purpose. But I sensed that every part of it, from quark to quasar, was unique and – in some mysterious way – significant.

I heard the universe as an oratorio sung by a master choir of stars, accompanied by the orchestra of the planets and the percussion of satellites and moons. The aria they performed was a song to break the heart, full of tragic dissonance and deferred hope, and yet somewhere beneath it all was a piercing refrain of *glory, glory, glory*. And I sensed that not only the grand movements of the cosmos, but everything that had happened in my life, was a part of that song. Even the hurts that seemed most senseless, the mistakes I would have done anything to erase – nothing could make those things good, but good could still come out of them all the same, and in the end the oratorio would be no less beautiful for it.

I realised then that even though I was a tiny speck in an infinite cosmos, a blip on the timeline of eternity, I was not without purpose. And as long as I had a part in the music of the spheres, even if it was only a single grace note, I was not worthless. Nor was I alone.

God help me, I prayed as I gathered up my raw and weary senses, flung them into the wormhole—

And at last, found what I'd been looking for.

There was no way I should have been able to recognise Earth from such a distance, when it was nothing but a bluish-white dot among the stars. But I heard the cosmic orchestra change its tune, caught the barely perceptible buzz of the signal I would always think of as Tori's Noise, and I knew.

'That's it!' I yelled.

Faraday bolted upright and slapped his hand down on the console. Another pulse of light streaked past me into the wormhole, frilling its edges with a thousand unnameable hues, as the signal from the two relays connected. Tearing off my helmet, I flung myself out of the box into Faraday's arms, and Tori grabbed both of us simultaneously in an exuberant group hug.

'You have to stop him,' I panted at them both. 'Mathis – he's almost got the door open – he'll be here any minute—'

'There's no time for that,' said Faraday. 'The wormhole won't stay stable for much longer. It's already in a state of temporal flux, and it's only going to get worse. You and Tori have to go.'

Tori's face sobered. She pulled the relay out of her tool-bag and set it down carefully on the floor, then backed up a step, shaking out her hands and arms as though warming up for a marathon. 'OK,' she breathed. 'This is going to hurt, but it's going to get us home. I can do this.'

Faraday moved towards the console again, but I caught his hand. 'Don't stay here. Come with us.'

'I can't.' His voice was square with resolve. 'The impulse generator we rigged up isn't stable enough.

Someone has to stay on this end and keep the readings constant, to make sure you get through safely.'

I began to protest, but he stopped my lips with a finger. 'You're still young, Alison. Too young, for all that I allowed myself to forget that for a while. You need time to decide who you are and where you want to be, and I'd only get in your way.'

Hot tears welled up in my eyes. I wanted to deny it, to tell him we could work things out, but there was no point. When he'd told me I was too young, he'd meant it.

'But…what's going to happen to you?' I asked. 'When Mathis finds out what you've done—'

'Don't worry about that. I'll be all right.' He took my face in his hands and brushed his lips against mine in a final, achingly brief kiss. 'Goodbye, Alison.'

Then he let go of my hand and stepped back. Away from me. Forever.

Tori stood by the relay, waiting. With leaden feet, I walked to stand beside her as Faraday reached towards the console, ready to send us both home. Grief surged inside me, filling my mouth with the bitterness of unsaid words, and I almost swallowed before I remembered that I didn't want to do that any more.

'I love you,' I blurted at Faraday.

His violet eyes met mine, deep and serene as ever.
'I don't love you.'

'Liar,' I said with a tear-stained laugh, and then
his hand came down and the world splintered into
a trillion pieces as the relay tore us apart.

NINETEEN (IS COMFORTED)

When I came back to consciousness I felt rock beneath me, a slab of porous black. Lichen scratched my cheek, and a potpourri of wet soil, fallen leaves and dry pine needles filled the air. Between that and the faint taste of sulphur in my mouth, I didn't even have to open my eyes to know where I was. Faraday had kept his word, and brought us home.

'We did it!' exclaimed Tori, and panic knifed through me as all my senses protested at once. But I made myself lie still, reminding myself to accept the feeling and give it a chance to pass. If nothing else, I'd had plenty of practice.

'Sorry.' Tori dropped her voice to a whisper. 'Forgot about the synesthesia thing.' She got up stiffly, rubbing her arms, and looked around. 'Hey, we're at the top of Adanac!'

'The ski hill?' I said weakly. 'How did that happen?'

'I don't know,' she said. 'Maybe Faraday told the relay to move here or something, right before he sent us through. But,' – she rubbed her arms – 'it's not exactly summer any more, is it?'

Late September, judging by the colour in my mind. We'd lost six weeks on the journey – that was what Faraday must have been warning us about when he said the wormhole was in a state of temporal flux.

'Come on,' Tori said. 'Let's get out of here.'

I could hold myself together for the moment, if I lay still and kept my eyes mostly shut. But my senses were still raw and my nerves fragile, and I didn't dare move. 'You go,' I said. 'Get help.'

'And leave you alone? No way.'

'Go,' I repeated. 'I can't. Until the wormhole closes…it's just too much.'

Tori hesitated, then pulled off her lacy sweater and draped it over my shoulders. 'Don't be scared, OK? I'll be back as soon as I can. And even if you have to go to hospital, I won't forget about you. I'll talk to the police and your psychiatrist and everybody. Whatever it takes to get you home.'

Even with the bruises on her face and the slight crook in her nose, she was beautiful. But I no longer resented her for that. This forthright, no-nonsense Tori with her obvious quirks and flaws, the one who loved to fix things and threaten people with blunt instruments, was totally unlike the pampered princess

I'd always imagined her to be. And after what we'd just been through together, I was pretty sure that not even her closest friends had ever seen as much of the real Tori as I had. Just as nobody on this planet but Tori had ever seen so much of the real me.

'I know you will,' I said softly. 'I trust you.'

By the time the rescuers found me I was shivering all over, but Tori was true to her word. She stayed with me as they lifted me onto a stretcher and carried me down the ski hill, insisting in fierce whispers that they walk carefully and make as little noise as possible. She refused to even give her name until they were bundling me into the back of an ambulance, and I could hear her passionately defending me to the police officers as we drove away.

Her return caused a huge sensation, of course; it was all over the news for days. Parents weeping with relief, friends and neighbours declaring that they'd always known she was alive, reporters with cameras and microphones following her everywhere she went. Everyone wanted to hear her story, but she refused to give any details. All she would say was that she was glad to be home.

My family were relieved to see me, too, but they

were also worried, and I couldn't blame them. I'd run away without my medication while I was still legally in psychiatric care, and then come back six weeks later in a state almost as vulnerable and hypersensitive as the one that had landed me in hospital in the first place. What could they do but send me back to Pine Hills?

It was two days before I was well enough to come out of my room in Red Ward, and another before Dr Minta felt I was stable enough to move back to Yellow. It was a very different atmosphere than when I'd left, more crowded than it had been in the summer and full of strange faces and unknown names. Kirk wasn't there any more, or at least not at the moment, and Roberto had been discharged a month ago. Even Micheline had finished her course of treatment and gone home. The only one I recognised was Sanjay, and he was shy and evasive. He was on a different medication now, he said, and didn't think much about aliens any more.

But Tori had been calling the hospital every day to see how I was doing, and as soon as I was back on my feet again, she set up a meeting with me and Dr Minta in his office.

'I know this story is going to sound crazy,' she told him, as we all sat down. She'd covered up the bruises beneath her eyes and the scratch across her cheek with makeup, and everything about her radiated health and vitality. She might as well have come in wearing a name tag reading HELLO, I'M SANE. 'I mean, if it hadn't happened to me, and if I didn't have Alison to back me up on it, I'm not sure I'd believe any of it either. That's why I haven't told this story to anyone but the police, my parents…and now you. Because I think you have a right to know.'

And just like that, she had him. I could see Dr Minta leaning forward with hands clasped in anticipation, like a little boy waiting for his bedtime story, and I wondered what on earth Tori was going to tell him. Not the truth, surely? And yet what other explanation could she give for everything that had happened to us?

I needn't have worried. The tale Tori spun for Dr Minta was dramatic, bizarre and in parts completely preposterous, but I'd forgotten what a brilliant actress she was. When she told him that the two of us had been assaulted just outside the school by three men in stocking masks, one of whom had thrown me to the ground and stuck a needle in my arm while the others dragged Tori into their unmarked van, the tremor in her voice was so convincing that I almost believed her myself.

As the van drove away Tori had struggled with her assailants, but they'd injected her with a sedative and she lost consciousness. She'd woken several hours later to find herself strapped to a table in a stark, windowless room, where a team of doctors in surgical masks had done tests on her. They'd inserted a chip in her arm and pumped her full of experimental drugs that had changed her biochemistry – her family doctor could confirm both those things, she said, if Dr Minta didn't believe it. And when she'd tried to escape, they'd beaten her.

As the weeks passed and the experiments went on, Tori had lost hope of ever getting away. But then I showed up unexpectedly one night with Faraday. He'd been hired by her captors to keep tabs on the local investigation into Tori's disappearance, and also to make sure I didn't remember what had really happened. But he'd been horrified when he realised the kind of research his employers were doing, and how much she and I had suffered because of it. He and I had sneaked Tori out of the facility and then Faraday had flown us both back to Sudbury by helicopter, where he'd dropped us off on the top of the ski hill and then flown away.

'I don't know where he is now,' she finished. 'But

Alison was the one who talked him into helping me, and without her, I'd still be back in that place. She risked everything for me, and it wasn't her fault they gave her that weird drug that messed her up so badly. Can't you let her go?'

Even after the space station, Tori's resourcefulness amazed me. She'd concocted a story that served *both* our needs, and she'd used every ounce of her undeniable sanity to sell it. And whether he believed it or not, Dr Minta was clearly powerless against her. He stammered out something about sympathising with her sense of injustice, but my situation was complicated, and he had reason to believe I was still in need of psychiatric care. Not that he wanted to keep me at Pine Hills any longer than necessary, of course, but...

'It's OK, Tori,' I said hastily, noticing the belligerent angle of her jaw and the way her turquoise eyes had hardened. 'Dr Minta's only doing his job. If he thinks I need to stay here for a few more days, then I'm willing to go along with it. Just to make sure I'm really better.'

Dr Minta's thick eyebrows rose, and I could tell I'd made an impression on him. He thanked Tori for coming, shook her hand, and ushered her to the door.

I walked out to the corridor with her.

'Thanks for trying,' I said. 'That was quite the story. I had no idea you were so creative.'

Her blank look was unnervingly convincing. 'Creative? What do you mean? All I did was tell him what happened. Just like I told the police.'

I was pretty sure she hadn't told the police *that* story, but I could play along. I forced a laugh. 'Well, I suppose it's a little more believable than wormholes and aliens…but not by much.'

For the first time since I'd known her, Tori looked uncomfortable. 'Ali…I think you might not want to talk about that alien stuff again. Even to me. Just let it go, OK? I really think you'll be happier if you do.' She gave me an apologetic smile, and walked away.

I watched her go, then turned back to Dr Minta's office. He motioned me to a seat and sat down across from me, still looking flustered. 'Well, that was an interesting visit,' he said. 'I'm not sure what the police investigation will turn up, but it does seem clear that she considers you to be innocent. Tell me, Alison – how do you feel about all this?'

I laced my fingers together and gazed down at them. 'I'm glad Tori's home,' I said. 'I'm glad I could help her, and I'm glad she was grateful enough to try

and help me. I think we're going to be friends. But…
I miss Faraday. I don't think I'll ever forget him.'

Dr Minta was silent. Then he said, 'I've thought
some more about your case, Alison, and I believe
Ms Beaugrand has a point. You seem to have got
through your most recent crisis without any incidents
of violence or self-harm, and while I can see you're
somewhat depressed at the moment, that depression
doesn't appear to be of a suicidal nature. Your mother
has expressed her desire to bring you home as soon as
possible, so you have good family support. And you
seem to be doing well on even a reduced dose of your
medication, so I don't see any compelling reason to
keep you here.'

I was startled. 'Are you saying you're going to
discharge me?'

'I can't keep you any longer as an involuntary
patient,' he said. 'If you wish to leave, that's your
decision.'

I let out my breath. 'Thank you. Yes, I do.'

Dr Minta took off his glasses, cleaned them and put
them on again, not looking at me. 'However, I do have
a professional recommendation. Given the trauma
you've been through and the need to wean yourself off
your medication gradually, I think it would be a good

idea for you to continue seeing a psychiatrist on an outpatient basis for a while.'

I looked out the window at the pine trees gilded by afternoon sunlight, the blue dazzle of water in the distance, the red-gold leaves drifting slowly down. Then I turned back to Dr Minta.

'OK,' I said. 'I will.'

I'd only been home a couple of days when Constable Deckard rang the front doorbell and handed me back my grandmother's ring, which I supposed was the closest thing I could expect to an apology. 'Stay safe,' he said, but there was an edge in his voice that chilled me. *I'll be keeping my eye on you*, it said. *This isn't over yet.*

He'd only just driven away when Mel called and asked me to come over. I told her I wasn't talking to the press right now, and hung up.

That same week, the Beaugrands put their house up for sale and went on vacation to somewhere hot and sunny. By the time they got back, the house had sold. And an improbably short time after that, their wine-coloured Mercedes sat idling at the end of our driveway while Tori and I hugged each other in the front hall, saying goodbye.

She hadn't told me where she and her parents were moving. Not because she didn't trust me, she said, but because it would be safer for all of us if I didn't know. After what she'd been through, she couldn't take the risk of anyone finding her again. With a catch in her voice, she wished me good luck—

And just like that, Tori Beaugrand was gone.

Almost as though she'd never come back at all.

INFINITY (IS EVERY COLOUR THERE IS)

You may not believe any of what I've just told you. Or you may think only part of it is true. For all I know, you might decide that the explanation Tori gave Dr Minta is what really happened, and that the parts about the space station and the wormhole were all in my crazed imagination.

Or maybe it's easier for you to believe that Tori was never found, and Faraday never existed, and I'm still locked up somewhere in Red Ward beating my head against the wall. Maybe you even think you can prove it.

But you'll be wrong. Because I know what happened, and I know what's real. No matter what you or anyone else says.

Once upon a time there was a girl who was extraordinary. She could hear colours, and see sounds, and taste the difference between truth and lies. But hardly anybody knew that, and she preferred to keep it that way.

People thought she'd killed someone, but she hadn't. They didn't believe her – some still don't – but that doesn't bother her much any more. Because she has her family and her music and her freedom, and somewhere in the universe is a man with violet eyes who loves her.

And deep down, part of her still believes that one day she'll see him again.

This is my story.

AUTHOR'S NOTE

Pine Hills, like St Luke's, is not a real hospital. It is a compilation of numerous psychiatric institutions for young people in Canada and elsewhere, based on my own research and personal interviews with a number of former psychiatric patients and their families. However, every psychiatric institution is different, even if they operate by similar policies; and every individual's experience of psychiatric care also varies widely according to their circumstances, personality and diagnosis. Alison's story is not meant to represent a normative experience of psychiatric care, and I hope readers will not take it as such. If you are experiencing depression or other symptoms that you fear may indicate mental illness, please talk to your doctor or local mental health organization.

Synesthesia is, as Faraday tells Alison, not a mental illness. It is a testable and well-documented neurological phenomenon, which is being studied by researchers around the world. Many synesthetes are unaware that their perceptions are unusual; others are aware of the difference but have no name for it. If you think you or someone you know may be a synesthete, you may find it interesting to go online and check out some of the free tests at The Synesthesia Battery (synesthete.org); or visit the information pages and discussion board at Mixed Signals (www.mixsig.net).

ACKNOWLEDGMENTS

Thanks to Sarah Lilly at Orchard Books and Andrew Karre at Carolrhoda Lab, whose sage editorial advice helped me work out many a narrative tangle; and to Josh Adams and Caroline Walsh, my fantastic US and UK agents.

I am also hugely indebted to a number of friends and family whose warm hospitality and encouragement, perceptive critical observations, candid testimonials and/or professional insights into synesthesia, psychiatric care, mental health law, police procedure, and astrophysics helped me greatly as I was researching and writing this book. These include Mark and Lisa Anderson, Pete Anderson, Liz Barr, Nicholas Bohner, Erin Brown, Tad DiBiase, Deva Fagan, Anthony Freeman, Holly Hammershoy LMHC, Brittany Harrison, Edward M. Hubbard PhD, Jonathan K. and the K. family, Doug McNeil, Saundra Mitchell, Hallie and Becca O'Donovan, and Andrew Slater. Thank you all.

Questions and Answers with R.J. Anderson

Where did the idea for *Ultraviolet* come from? And what inspired you to give Alison synesthesia?

The first time I heard of "synesthesia" was while flipping through a dictionary of literary terms. I found it described as a kind of poetic metaphor, where the effects of one sense are substituted for another (as in Robert Graves's "How hot the scent is of the summer rose!"). The book also briefly mentioned that the novelist Vladimir Nabokov considered himself to have synesthesia and described the sounds of the alphabet in terms of shape and colour. And immediately I thought, "Wouldn't it be amazing if someone actually did perceive the world that way? What would life be like for someone who could see sounds and taste words?"

My first conclusion was that other people might think - wrongly of course - that the person with synesthesia was crazy. My second was that it would be kind of like having superpowers. It didn't take me long after that to write the first version of the short story that eventually became *Ultraviolet*.

Later, I discovered that synesthesia is an actual neurological condition and not just a form of metaphor after all. That's when I started really studying the phenomenon and trying to figure out how to make Alison's experiences more realistic and at the same time even more extraordinary.

This book is very different to your previous novels; did you enjoy the change in writing style?

Writing a story in the first person was a definite change from my earlier books. It was also a challenge to describe the unique way that Alison's synesthesia causes her to perceive and interpret the world around her. But I enjoyed it and am pleased with the way it turned out.

What music were you listening to as you wrote this book?
I put together a large collection of songs that related in some way to the book's mood and themes - songs dealing with isolation, with mental illness, love and loss, and/or which reflected unusual ways of seeing the world. I started off with the title track from Peter Himmelman's 1989 pop-rock album "Synesthesia", as well as the haunting ballad "Name"; added in a lot of ambient and alternative music by artists like David Sylvian and Talk Talk, and finished off with more recent tracks like "Another Little Hole" and "Sundowning" by Aqualung.

How does it feel when you see your books in a bookstore?
It never gets old. Whenever I browse the children's and teen sections of a new bookstore I get a little thrill of anticipation - will my books be there? Or not? Will there be one copy or two, or - could it be, perhaps even more? - and I'm always happy when I find them and a little sad when I don't. And in North America, it's actually quite common that I don't find them, even in my own hometown! So I'm grateful for every bookseller who supports my books and every reader who buys them, and I'm especially thrilled that my books are doing well in the UK.

Where is your favourite place to write?
I wish I could say it was some gloriously poetic or inspiring place, but actually I write sitting on an office chair in my bedroom, with nothing but a tiny little wooden table to hold my manuscript or notes while I'm working. We have an office, but my kids are usually in it playing on the computer, so I take my laptop wherever I can get some peace and quiet!

What's your next project?
I'm currently working on *Swift*, the next book in my faery series. After that I'm thinking about writing a companion novel to *Ultraviolet* - but we'll see!

JESSICA SHIRVINGTON

Embrace

ANGELS WILL FALL...

Violet Eden has only ever wanted to
be with Lincoln. But when he reveals
a secret so powerful it could tear
them apart, her world spins out of
control. Then she meets Phoenix.
Intense and beautiful, Violet is
helplessly drawn to him...

Caught up in a battle between
light and dark - where angels seek
vengence and humans are warriors -
Violet must decide how much she's
willing to sacrifice.
And who she can love...

978 1 40831 481 4 £6.99 Pbk
Oct 2011

ORCHARD BOOKS
www.orchardbooks.co.uk